Trained as an oral surgeon, Stephen practised in an NHS maxilla-facial unit for nearly 20 years. Alongside his clinical work, he pursued his love of music, gaining a diploma in performance studies at the Birmingham Conservatoire. He went on to sing principal roles for Mid-Wales Opera, Scottish Opera and English National Opera.

Now retired from clinical practice, he is able to pursue a lifelong love of the written word, this being his debut novel.

He lives in Bollington with his sculptor wife, Jane, and now enjoys an extended family with two children of his own, two stepchildren, and three grandchildren.
A keen rock climber and mountaineer in his youth, Stephen still enjoys forays into the fells and moors surrounding their home on the western edge of the Peak District.

For my wife Jane; Alistair, Kirsten, Bill and Katie.
"In memory of my son James (Jim) Alexander Raven Garner 1983–2004"

Stephen J. Garner

TRAUMA AND REDEMPTION

AUSTIN MACAULEY PUBLISHERS™

LONDON • CAMBRIDGE • NEW YORK • SHARJAH

A CIP catalogue record for this title is available from the British Library.

ISBN 9781035807116 (Paperback)
ISBN 9781035807123 (ePub e-book)

www.austinmacauley.com

First Published 2023
Austin Macauley Publishers Ltd®
1 Canada Square
Canary Wharf
London
E14 5AA

I have been fortunate to work alongside and taught by some brilliant surgeons, including Gordon Fordyce at Mt Vernon Hospital, Rickmansworth, and Peter Leopard and Geoff Manning at Stoke. Much of what I learned from them informs the clinical text.

I must also thank my long-suffering wife, Jane who has managed the many ups and downs in my transition from a clinician to a novice writer.

My son Alistair for proofreading my first three chapters and encouraging me to carry on.

My daughter Kirsten, a brilliant doctor of cell biology for the invaluable molecular research bits and my stepchildren, Bill and Kate for their constant ability to let me believe.

Also, my brother-in-law, Robert (Bob) Daws himself an established author, for his help and guidance through the minefield of publishing for the first-time novelist.

I must not forget my life-long friend Scott Evans for reading the finished novel and hauling me up various rock climbs and mountains.

And last but not least, my lovely sister, Gilly, once lost, now found.

Part 1

Chapter 1

The increasing rhythmic slap-slap of the wipers betrayed the hard work of clearing the windscreen of the BMW 5 series as it breasted the crest of the A5 before descending into the Severn valley, east of Shrewsbury. The rain, biblical in intensity, rendered them useless. The couple, however, seemed blissfully unaware. They felt cocooned in the apparently safe, warm and luxurious interior.

They had enjoyed lunch in Birmingham and an evening of passion beckoned. Perhaps the light touch of her hand against his thigh led to the brief delay in braking. He glimpsed her silver bracelet as the deer leapt in front of the vehicle. When he did brake, he pressed too hard and too late; the car lurching to the left as it aquaplaned across the carriageway, tipping onto its side and rolling as it hit the verge. The gleaming aquamarine exemplar of modern technology lay wrecked. Only the steady patter of raindrops now disturbed the silence.

******

'Christ!' Andy muttered. An hour before he had been enjoying an excellent glass of Cote-du-Rhone with his brother-in-law, Ben, with whom he enjoyed an abiding friendship. The family had finished a late Sunday lunch, life's vicissitudes discussed. Now he found himself up to his wrists in arterial blood.

Mr Andrew Saunders enjoyed his position as Consultant Oral and Maxillofacial surgeon in the department of head and neck trauma at Shropshire University Hospital Trust, recently established following the implementation of the Griffiths report. Although on-call he had settled into the routine of Sunday afternoon, having discharged his weekend duties, fully expecting not to be disturbed. After all, he had full trust in the capabilities of his senior registrar, his immediate junior, who had already proved himself perfectly capable of dealing with any incoming emergencies.

However, instead of enjoying a post-prandial glass or two, he was attempting to control a bleed from the facial artery of what appeared to be a youngish female injured in an RTA on the A5. His S.R. had also been called into duty, now operating on the other casualty from the same incident. Thus, it was that Andy was now head-down, intent on sorting out the mess that once resembled this patient's face.

She had suffered a severe injury of the lower jaw and now intubated and anaesthetised, Andy could assess the full extent of the injury. His assistant, Bernadine, a rather green S.H.O. insisted on dipping her sucker tube into the welling red tide, rather in the manner of a woodpecker. Lifting the soft tissue facial flap, Andy had found the lower jaw fragmented as a result of the impact, and shards of bone had become embedded in the tissues of the neck and had apparently torn the facial artery.

Normally, such an arterial bleed would close itself down spontaneously as the muscles in the arterial wall constricted, but in this case, the vessel had ripped, only half severing the artery thus preventing this natural self-defence mechanism. Andy had to find it, surgically divide it and tie off the ends, before he could even think about sorting out the hard and soft tissue injuries.

'Give me the sucker,' he muttered again, this time to the poor SHO who, after all, had only recently qualified as a dentist. The closest she had been to blood until now was during a difficult wisdom tooth extraction. Andy now regretted that third glass of wine as he struggled to concentrate.

However, his fingers soon found their natural rhythm and he could 'feel' the pulsing artery within the mess and could direct the suction at the source of the bleeding. Using gauze, he mopped and bluntly dissected the tissues apart until he could see the offending vessel. Calling for clamps, he expertly placed these on either side of the bleed and, 'thank God', the bleeding stopped.

Tying off the ends enabled him to draw breath and assess the situation more calmly. Turning to his left to retrieve a retractor, he caught the glint of the young lady's bracelet and not for the first time found himself appalled at the fragility of the human body in the face of high-velocity carbon fibre and aluminium.

It was at this point that the theatre sister leaned across the casualty and remarked on the smell of alcohol lingering over the operating area.

'Ah, yes, fair point. Pretty sure this is a drink-drive incident.'

Andy hurriedly decided not to exhale so forcefully again. Calmer now, he began the lengthy task of separating out the bony fragments and assessing which could be fixed using bone-plates. He informed his junior assistant of the surgical rule that stated that one had to get the bony skeleton fixed before even thinking about closing the soft tissues. Each viable fragment (i.e. that still attached to muscle) had to be re-attached to its neighbour-jigsaw style-using tiny titanium plates which could be bent to shape and fixed using tiny screws.

In this manner, the bow-shaped structure of the lower jaw took shape. Fragments of teeth now had to be sorted with those not saveable removed, complete with their roots from what remained of the jaw. Andy used surgical wire to splint teeth loosened in the impact. The tongue, again, thank God, appeared to be intact.

After three hours of meticulous work and concentration, he, at last, could bring the soft tissue flap to cover the exposed bone and begin the laborious task of closing in layers. The inner mucosa first, then the muscle layers and finally the skin. The injury had divided the lower lip and Andy took care to align the crucial red margin before he fanned out and closed the extensive laceration. Thankfully, it seemed the force of impact had created an almost surgical flap rather than crushing the flesh, the major force being absorbed by the jaw. He then assessed that the scar might not be as bad as he had initially feared.

The operation had taken five hours and Andy returned to the surgeon's common room to write up the notes, leaving the anaesthetist to wake the patient up. Going to sit down, he noticed his operating scrubs, soaked in the patient's blood and sticking to his body, so he elected to get changed first.

Removing his white wellington boots, he heard a sucking noise as his foot pulled out of a boot full of congealed, foul-smelling blood, his socks ruined. Stripping off, he muttered 'Christ' for the second time that evening as he saw his briefs also soaked through. With a wry smile, he thought back to his lunch six hours before and not for the first time, wondered why on earth he was doing this bloody job!

Andy returned to the restroom, having divested himself of his soiled underwear and was now forced to go commando in slacks and a pink linen shirt. It surprised him to see the theatre sister, sitting with a coffee.

'Well done in there, Andy,' she began, 'got off to a tricky start though—everything OK?' she wanted to know.

'Yeah, thanks, I'm fine. Just not geared up for a major procedure tonight, that's all.' Perhaps not quite satisfied, Julie pressed on.

'The alcohol thing, you're sure that was the patient? You know we have to keep tabs on these things—audit and all that?'

'Bloody audit—don't get me started on that rigmarole—we're here to do a tough job. Pseudo-managers, administrators or whatever they're called, can keep their noses out of my business.' Andy wasn't a fan of the alternative management systems being introduced by the NHS! He continued, 'Look, Julie, they contacted me after enjoying a glass of wine over lunch—no big deal.'

'One glass?' Julie looked at him quizzically.

'Oh, come on, we've known each other for years, you know how it is.'

'Yes, I know, but all I'm saying is, if I notice these things, then others will too—and yes, five hours, Andy. That case occupied the major trauma theatre for five hours. I've now got to explain to the general surgeons why they have had to queue to deal with a bowel torsion behind the dentists again.'

'Well, let's see if those clumsy idiots could put a face back together in less than five hours.' And with that Andy stood and left the theatre suite for the lonely half-hour drive back home along the quiet darkness of the A49 and back towards the Shropshire Hills.

Chapter 2

The powerful beams from his SUV illuminated the darkness as Andy headed home. As always, he mulled over the events of the evening; evaluating his performance. Could he have done anything different or better? Overall, he knew that his work had been largely unaffected by the circumstances around the call-out and he could be confident that the young patient would recover function with less than devastating scarring.

Dental implants would replace the missing teeth and he knew that plastic scar revision increasingly produced excellent results these days. He pressed the play button and a Bach cantata flooded the car and helped him settle. The plangent tones of oboe set against the haunting flute of the counter-tenor always managed to soothe this man's often complex thinking.

The comments regarding his surgical colleagues concerned him, but he was well used to these barbs by now. In fact, he was probably the most garlanded of all the surgeons in the hospital, having two degrees; dentistry and medicine. And two post-graduate surgical fellowships. He knew also that he enjoyed the full confidence of his ENT and plastic surgeon colleagues, although it still galled him that one of the general surgeons would occasionally come to his clinic asking for a 'check-up'.

As for the red wine, he knew he had let his guard down and accordingly resolved to do better in the future, but as for audit and performance assessment, he had no truck with these new-fangled ideas and fully intended to let management know his thoughts on the matter when the opportunity presented itself.

In this way, it didn't take too long before he turned into the drive leading to his lovely Georgian manor house, the study light bearing witness to the fact that his wife, Isabel, was still awake. That was nice. He would enjoy a stiff whiskey with her before he turned in, aware however that he needed to be up at 6 o'clock in the morning in order to lead the hand-over ward round at seven before the routine work of the week ahead began. He also, of course, wanted to assess his patient's progress.

Isabel was indeed awake and apparently working, as he noticed the cold blue glow of the computer screen reflected in her lovely face as he walked in.

'Tough one?' she asked as she noted his drawn features, jumping up to greet him with a hug and kiss. It had always attracted her to this side of her husband, his devotion to his patients, his apparent energy in the face of the ever-increasing demands of his work; the teaching and of course the hospital politics.

'Did they get off OK?' Andy wanted to know.

'Yeah, it disappointed them to see you go; I think Ben had his heart set on another bottle of your burgundy!' Isabel remarked. She had waved her sister Alice off shortly after Andy had left and had cleared away the aftermath of their lunch. Alice and Ben had a long drive back down to Gloucestershire and Alice, in particular, having not imbibed, wanted to hit the road.

'How come you're still up?' Andy asked as he poured himself a glass of Laphroaig.

'Well, I'm still trying to get to grips with this new cell line we keep losing. They are not growing as they should and it's holding up the whole programme.'

'Still,' Andy answered, 'no point us both starting the week knackered. Let's get to bed—I need a cuddle!'

'You'll be lucky!' Isabel smiled at her husband as they made their way upstairs.

******

'Morning all!' Andy greeted his colleagues gathered outside ICU, refreshed after a decent six-hour kip and accepted the pile of clinical notes handed to him by his SHO, who, incidentally, had not enjoyed the luxury of a night's sleep. Instead, Bernadine had attended to the patient post-resuscitation and escorted her on the transfer to the unit where she had to complete the drugs chart and set up the infusion rates for the antibiotic drip.

The 'hand-over' ward round ensured continuity of care for the patient as the team on-call for the following week became acquainted with any admitted patient's history and treatment plans. It usually relieved Andy to have this responsibility transferred on to his colleagues, allowing him to concentrate on other matters, but on this occasion, he was very keen to monitor the progress of last night's case.

This morning, extubated, her breathing appeared unimpeded, her airways now cleared of old blood and debris. However, her face, not unexpectedly, had swollen, her lips now grotesque with a vivid scar apparent around the edges of her dressings, all of which combined to create an alarming effect. Various lines fanned out from her wrists and arms and communication was a no-go.

The SHO gave a fairly coherent summary of the damage and repair procedure, whilst Andy's immediate colleague, Stuart, asked some pertinent questions. 'How many units of blood did she require?'

Bernadine hesitated.

'Why no IMF?' he continued, referring to the fact that Andy had elected not to fix the lower teeth to the upper, thus immobilising the fracture. The clearly bemused SHO stammered again so Andy jumped in to her rescue and explained that he felt the plating had secured a stable reduction and that the patient would need teeth replacing in the future.

His primary concern, together with the anaesthetist, had been the integrity of the airway as he predicted the soft tissue swelling would be severe and possibly enough to occlude the patient's throat. They had therefore left the mouth free to open as required for access and suction. Andy looked across at his SHO and felt a pang of sympathy as he realised just how far out of her comfort zone she was.

Not only might she be struggling slightly with language, but this complexity of clinical care was unsurprisingly beyond her. He resolved to sit with her over lunch and have a chat. Next, they examined the severe bruising around the patient's shoulder and chest, testimony to the life-saving effect of the safety belt. Having reassured themselves and after checking the CXR that there were no severe injuries to the torso, the team dispersed to their various duties.

For his part, Andy could get back to the daily routine of clinics: reviewing old treatments and assessing any new patients for diagnosis and treatment planning.

His clinic started at 9 AM and he bolted down a bacon sarnie before entering the out-patients department. He loved this part of the job, the bread and butter as he saw it. He enjoyed the company of his staff and the banter between the nurses and the clinical staff. Always happy to sit at the top of the hierarchy he exercised his authority with compassion and wit. He was an excellent teacher and a good listener and clinicians from all over the country considered themselves fortunate to achieve a training post at the unit.

This morning was a teaching clinic and Andy had his registrar shadowing him. He had let Bernadine off to go back to bed. Andy would ask his junior to see new patients in one clinic, assess their problem and come up with a coherent treatment plan before coming next door to Andy and presenting the case for discussion.

Patients, if not too unwell, seemed to enjoy the to and fro of questions and answers pertaining to their condition; it made them feel special, part of the system. Andy loved this. He enjoyed speaking to concerned patients, enjoyed reassuring them. Also, if truth be told, he enjoyed exhibiting his extensive knowledge, gleaned over nearly 20 years of training. He knew his staff and patients looked up to him and, for a time at least, his inner rat stopped its gnawing.

He had always been an achiever, had climbed in the Alps as a young man, played rugby and enjoyed music. He had been a choral scholar and though years of sport and training had prevented him from pursuing his love of singing, he still deployed his considerable bass-baritone whenever he could. He had joined various choirs but had quickly realised that on-call duties didn't allow for regular rehearsal and performance schedules. No, his inner rat had more to do with the loss of his son years earlier.

As a young clinician, in training, he had met a lovely orthopaedic nurse and, within the confines of the residential hospital in which they had both trained, they had enjoyed an intense love affair. Pregnancy ensued and Andy, feeling he was doing the right thing, married his girlfriend and enjoyed being a father to their son, Sebastian.

Whilst on holiday, the family visited a beach in the south of Spain in Tarifa. After an excellent lunch, the three of them had gone for a swim, Seb leaping into the short, choppy waves without a care in the world. Although only 14, he was an accomplished swimmer and Andy and Maggie had relaxed back in the tropical sun.

Hearing the shout, Andy looked up and noticed that Seb was beyond the waves and struggling to get back to shore. Andy had leapt to his aid and on entering the surf had noted a severe undertow below the breaking waves, rendering it almost impossible to push his way through to the calmer water beyond. By now, Seb had drifted further out to sea, now clearly in distress. By sheer force of will, Andy plunged through the waves and swam towards his son, now disappearing from view before reappearing, gasping for breath.

Andy had reached him and grabbing him, found he couldn't swim as he struggled to control his son. He himself, now taking on water, became desperate. Grasping one of Seb's outstretched arms and clinging on, he turned for shore before realising that he too was actually drifting-pulled-further out to sea. Aroused from her sunbathing and sensing something amiss, Maggie now saw what was happening but realised that there was no one around to help. No coastguards! How stupid could they have been?

Despairing, Andy had let slip Seb's arm and he disappeared beneath the surface. Andy dived, couldn't breathe, was panicking. Oh, God! What to do? He dived again. Seb had gone! He realised he had to save himself but, exhausted, had flipped over onto his back, fully expecting to join his son. Instead, he drifted west and toward a peninsula of sand which jutted out into the sea. Allowing himself to go (in fact he had no option as now too exhausted to move) he beached on the spur of sand and lay there, unable to understand what had just happened. His son had gone. His life was over!

Guilt, self-blame, followed this appalling episode and his wife never really forgave Andy, even though he had almost sacrificed his own life in his attempt to save Seb's. But, according to Maggie, it had been Andy's decision to come to this deserted beach and his decision to let Seb swim alone and Andy who had taken his eye off the ball. This nagging resentment ended in divorce eventually, while Andy's escape mechanism caused him to immerse himself in his studies and career.

Years on, Andy learned to quell his guilt, his remorse, his 'rat,' by drinking just that little too much, balancing this with escapes into the hills whenever time allowed. The lovely Shropshire hills formed the backdrop to his home and he would walk on fine days and occasionally foul, exploring the hidden valleys and cascades of these 'Blue remembered Hills,' immortalised by Housman. Striding along the ridge crests, the wind and sun in his face, the scent of peat in his lungs, he found some solace.

Occasionally, almost as an afterthought, he would also find solutions to clinical conundrums. Answers would seem to form in his mind as he strode along. Music also helped to quieten the inner cacophony and in the majesty of the great romantic composers; Beethoven, Mozart, Brahms, Mahler and Bach he found balm for his troubled soul, perhaps the beauty of the music taking him closer to Seb's last resting place.

Not allowing his ambition to be dampened by this tragedy, it had spurred him on to achieve his dream of becoming a consultant in his chosen speciality. Trained initially as a dentist, he had found the work repetitive and insufficiently challenging and had embraced the challenges of surgery and study presented by his decision to train on in medicine. Away on a weekend course in Birmingham, he had met up with a group of students from another conference at the centre and had asked Isabel out for a drink.

He knew of a little old-fashioned French brasserie just off the main drag, where bench tables, draped in red-checked tablecloths gave the impression of a French café, this impression completed by faux French-speaking servers, holding little pans of potatoes gratin aloft in the grand manner—piping hot and bubbling. Over a bottle or two of red, they had agreed to miss the afternoon lectures and Andy had unburdened himself of his lingering guilt and found an apparent soulmate in Isabel.

She was a proper doctor, having a PhD in cell biology. She told him proudly of her involvement in post-graduate research, working towards finding the cure-all, if such existed, for the continuing curse that was cancer. Their two minds, embracing the toil of study, had gelled and they married shortly after.

Once Andy had landed his Consultancy, they bought the beautiful Georgian mansion just south of Shrewsbury, helped by a considerable legacy from Isabel's grandmother. There they settled into married life, bringing up their two daughters whilst Isabel pursued her career at Birmingham University. Both sociable people, they had settled happily into the round of dinner parties consequent upon hospital life, whilst the grand house, in the shadow of the hills, became a well-used destination for weekends with relatives.

All this activity provided a ready backdrop, perhaps even a screen, whilst a well-stocked cellar quenched the universal thirst. In this, of course, he needed little encouragement and his medical colleagues all seemed to share in a love of the grape, whilst pre-prandial trips to the Ragleth Arms in Little Stretton became a well-proven male bonding exercise.

Andy's clinical background as a dentist had however informed his rehab work and he had set up an implant training unit at the hospital. Constantly fighting administrators for funding, he had secured enough to set up a dental rehab provision whereby victims of trauma or of post-cancer ablation surgery could have their function and aesthetics improved by the insertion of tiny titanium screws, (or root replacement implants) to allow for the reconstruction of the dental arches.

Normally such implants were only available out-with hospital practice and under private contract, but Andy had convinced the powers that be that replacing teeth to enable normal life was as important as any other branch of healing. He had then attracted junior clinicians who wanted to train in this new technology but who didn't want to become Maxfac surgeons. He also knew he could attract research funds from the big operators in the new field, which went some way to appease the hospital accountants.

His new SHO then represented this new tranche of trainees but, perhaps unsurprisingly, Andy had observed her struggling with the surgical side of things. These concerns formed the backdrop to his meeting over lunch.

'Did you get some kip?' Andy asked his SHO.

'Yah, Danke, thank you, yes, a few hours. Please allow me to apologise about last night by the way,' Bernadine answered.

'Look, that was an emergency-even I found myself struggling for a while,' Andy laughed.

Bernadine explained that whilst she wanted to expand her surgical skills in order to place bone-grafts for dental implants in private practice, she hadn't reckoned on the full-on theatre exposure she had experienced recently. The technical demands of the job: the prescribing of drugs, the setting-up of drips and the 'clerking in' of new patients had all taken their toll.

She confessed that Stuart's cross-examination hadn't helped. She welled up and Andy instinctively reached out his hand and placed it on hers; after all, he well understood the stresses of being plunged in at the deep-end. In the NHS, there still prevailed the tenets of 'see one-do one-teach one', and future exponents of the surgical arts understood the need to learn on the job.

'What you need is a good night's sleep. You've got the next few days off-call, so why don't you take a few days off instead,—-get some rest?'

'That's lovely of you—but I know we are understaffed at the moment—' Bernadine replied.

'No worries, I'll get the registrars to step up and do a few clinics. Go on— Get away from here for a few days—enjoy yourself!'

'Ah, Danke. Forgive me, thank you. I've been wanting to explore the Shropshire Hills ever since I got here!' And with that, she finished her sandwich and left, leaving Andy only half-raising an eyebrow as he watched her shimmy from the canteen.

Chapter 3

Andy arrived back from his day's work apparently buoyant. Isabel had learned to read his mood as he entered the kitchen and on this occasion, she smiled as she heard his approaching whistle. On good days he had even been heard to sing an Aria as he entered the house. His first action, after the usual peck on the cheek, was a visit to the drinks cabinet where he prepared himself a generous G and T.

Apparently forgetting his slightly awkward chat with his friend and theatre sister the day before, Andy was keen to enjoy supper and the accompanying bottle (or two) of red wine. Isabel usually joined him once she had seen to the rituals of child care; the homework, the baths and stories in bed. She occasionally thought it would be nice if her husband could be bothered to join her in these activities, but she had become well used to her husband's ways after all this time.

And, she thought to herself, he had spent most of last night in the operating theatre. He had though, she remembered with a smile, at least had the good manners to flirt with her. They ate supper on their laps watching, with little enthusiasm, a drama on the TV, Andy helping himself to a whiskey before retiring to bed.

After Andy had fallen asleep, Isabel laid quiet, thoughts tumbling through her mind, unable to reach the sanctity of sleep. Andy's work consumed him and if he wasn't working or planning meetings, he was off walking in the hills or planning early doors drinks in the Ragleth-Lucy and Imogen didn't get a look in. She could not recall the last parent's evening or sports day they had attended together as parents. Instead it was she, Isabel left to do all the to-ing and fro-ing, that made up young people's lives in this era. It was she, Isabel, who sorted out all the practicalities of homework, sleepovers and the consequent laundry.

On top of it all, she had her own career to think about. This last thought led on to concerns about recent developments at the University. On her initiative, the idea of preserving the cell lines so essential to cancer research had begun to take shape. Her ideas had even led to an approach by a German pharmaceutical company, apparently also challenged by the same issue.

More unbidden thoughts marched round and round until she returned to the subject of her husband, currently snoring away without a care in the world. She, of course, knew that this was a false impression; she knew and understood Andy's turmoil, but just wished he didn't always have to resort to the drinks cabinet in order to bring peace.

After Andy had gone up to bed, she had cleared up the whiskey glass and noted yet another green bottle of malt whiskey, nearly empty. Apart from anything else, they hadn't made love in ages. Andy's playful invitation from last evening had quickly dwindled as fatigue and booze hit their mark.

Eventually, Isabel drifted off but woke the next morning anxious and in no mood to get the girls off to school. Despite Andy's objections and her old-fashioned views on parenting, perhaps now was the time to think about engaging a nanny. Something had to give. So when Andy returned from work, again on time and whistling and as he made straight for the drinks cabinet, she asked.

'How was your day?'

'Mostly routine, really, but glad to say my patient from the weekend has improved and has been discharged to the wards from ICU.' Andy filled his glass.

'Why don't we have dinner after the girls have gone to bed? There's something I'd like to discuss. I'll cook your favourite. How about it?' Isabel watched Andy drain his glass.

'What about?' he asked. 'Let's leave it till later, OK?' And with that, he walked out, clearly intent on enjoying his second glass. Isabel found herself, not for the first time, feeling helpless.

She tried hard to ration the girls' time on their various pieces of electronic devices, but tonight, tired and worried, she let this pass. She had spent most of the day on her computer, dialling into the lab from home. Encouraged by the survival of her new cell lines (the longest spell in her experience), she was nonetheless troubled by the intervention by the German Pharmaceutical giant. Why were they poking their noses in? So, tonight, she let Imogen and Lucy take their laptops to their rooms and finally got Andy sat down in the kitchen, who by now, somewhat predictably, was opening a bottle of red.

'So, what's all this about?' Andy started off the conversation, unable to escape on this occasion.

'Well, Andy, I know how difficult your work is, how time-consuming, but I have a career as well and yet I'm expected to run the household, see to the kids, on top of my work. It doesn't seem fair really—' Isabel petered out. Then after a moment's thought, added '—And yes, the girls, they hardly ever see you. You don't seem to get involved in their lives at all.'

'Well, darling,' (he always called her 'darling' when caught on the back foot) 'what do you want me to do about it?' All he really wanted to do was watch the rugby highlights from the weekend and enjoy his wine-he'd answered enough hard questions at the bloody hospital after all. Still, he recognised the truth in what his wife was saying and so there was, at least, some sincerity in his question.

'Well,' Isabel said, encouraged, 'I think it's about time we employed a nanny-someone to help me with the household jobs and who can run the girls to school and stuff.'

'I thought you were keen on doing all that yourself; hands-on parenting you said.'

'Yes, but, I need to get to the lab predictably and on time for once. It's not fair to my colleagues—I'm making excuses all the time. And my research is showing some very exciting results—I need to be there.'

By now Isabel had joined her husband in a glass of wine and was more animated now that she had stated her case. She went on, '—and, who knows? If I'm not up to my eyeballs all the time, juggling everything around then perhaps—' She paused as she looked across the table at Andy and smiled, 'well, you know—you and I—who knows we might even get together a little more.' She blushed.

Andy drained his glass.

'Ah, I see, bribery now is it?'

'Look, Andy, I'm serious about this. We need to get our lives sorted out—we can't carry on like this.'

'Like what?' Andy was disingenuous, knew what was coming.

'You know, all the booze. You're never fit for anything after a day's work and drowning your sorrows.'

'I am not, Izzy, 'drowning my sorrows'.' Andy replied. 'But sometimes it's the only way I can be rid of all that goes on at the hospital-politics-the nonsense of admin. I need to relax as well.'

Isabel realised that now was not the time to bring up Seb's upcoming anniversary, but still, she could see the lingering sadness in her husband's eyes as he drained his glass.

'Look, let's think about the nanny thing—please?' She got up and started the supper, while Andy, deep in his own thoughts, drifted off to watch the TV.

Chapter 4

Having been on call since Friday, Andy, as usual, took Wednesday morning off and now went for a walk along the Long Mynd Ridge. Perhaps a little disarmed by last evening's conversation, he had risen early and taken the girls to school. Isabel had left to go to her lab and Andy, for once, was free. He strode up the familiar Cardington Mill path and up onto the plateau of the complex group of hills known as the long Mynd.

These undulating uplands effectively consisted of a flat-topped peat and heather moor from which fell a series of valleys, each running its own clear cascades. The plateau fell away on its western flank to reveal glorious views across to the Welsh hills. Snowdon was even visible on clear, crisp days such as this. Gliders, also enjoying the weather, soared on the early summer thermals, taking off from the southern end of the plateau from the little airfield on its summit.

Up here Andy could feel his brain clear, the problems dissolve into the thin, clear air. He strode along with glad abandon, wind in his hair. Enjoying the solitude, it therefore surprised him to see a familiar figure walking towards him, clearly descending from the summit trig point. Her long, blonde pigtail gave testimony to her identity.

'Hi!' he called out as his SHO, Bernadine, approached him.

'Ah, Mr Saunders.' his junior replied, grinning.

'Please, Andy—call me Andy away from the hospital,' he told her.

'What are you doing up here?' A rhetorical question as she remembered her informing her boss of her intentions at the end of their lunchtime meeting on Monday. 'Surely, Mr Saunders wouldn't stalk her?' she thought, smiling inwardly at the silly idea.

'I'm always up here whenever I get the chance. I—we—live just down there—in Church Stretton,' Andy pointed to the village spread out in the valley below. 'Look, I'm planning on a cup of tea and a sandwich down in the town on the way back. Fancy joining me?'

And so it was that Andy and Bernadine enjoyed a second lunch together in quick succession.

Sitting chatting with her reminded Andy of why he had selected her from the interview. He found her to be charming, confident and aware of her goals in life. Initially, the panel had wanted a career appointment in Maxfac, but Andy's interest in developing the dental implant-based rehab. unit swung the day in this young lady's favour who made no bones about the fact that she wanted to pursue a career based on Dental implantology. Once again, regretting his rather boorish behaviour at the weekend, he resolved to take Bernadine's training under his wing.

In this way, an hour passed quickly and Andy realised he would be late for his afternoon clinic. Before leaving the tearooms, he paused to explain that he picked up the girls from school today, promising to continue this conversation when Bernadine returned to work.

'I'd have thought you would have a nanny to do all that stuff?' She suggested.

Ignoring the fact that this comment was perhaps rather personal, he replied, 'Strange you mentioned that. Isabel—my wife—and I discussed that exact subject last evening. Why do you ask?'

Bernadine appeared to pause before replying, 'Well, it's just that my sister has finished her training as a nanny back home and was asking me only last week if I thought it might be a good idea to join me in the UK and look for a job here.'

Andy paused at the door, scratching his chin before replying.

'Well, why not? Isabel and I would be happy to meet her if she comes over-let her know. Thanks for that.'

And with that, he hurried away to his car, unaware of the lingering smile on his junior's lips as he left.

Chapter 5

Isabel settled in her office, ready for the morning, relieved for once to be away from the demands of domestic life and looking forward to the relative peace and order of the day in the laboratory. Although the trip from Shropshire to Birmingham took usually about an hour, she found that with music playing (BBC4) she could emerge from the chrysalis of motherhood, wife and housekeeper and become the butterfly she had envisaged, once in her science kingdom.

10:00 am starts, usually three times a week suited her just fine. 10:15 am saw her meeting her colleagues at the researcher group meeting in the University common room, coffees all round. The buzz that day centred around Isabel's breakthrough with her cell lines and her discovery that an enzyme could keep these precious research tools alive indefinitely.

Previously, these HeLa cell lines had a limited life and new lines had to be developed—a time-consuming business—and cultured in order to keep a thread of research continuing. Isabel was itching to get to work on a recently cultured set of cells to put her theory to the test and 11:30 am saw her ensconced in front of her tissue-culture hood, only her blue gloved hands, robot-like, protruding into the sterile racks of tubes and pipettes.

What she hadn't shared with her colleagues remained as a still-unformed thought developing in her subconscious mind. She anticipated using this enzyme to enhance stem cell cultures' longevity in order to allow her time to observe the genetic profile of these pluripotential cells. She then hoped she could engineer these cells in such a way as to trigger an immune response targeting human cancer cells.

These altered cells, combined with a viral vector, almost represented a vaccine against cancer. Literally the 'magic bullet' of cancer research. She intended to use that morning to create a workable tissue culture before lunch, (which she would enjoy again with her colleagues) and there perhaps talk about more mundane matters such as childcare and mortgages. She fully intended to keep her powder dry on the science for the time being.

Returning to her desk Isabel spent the afternoon realising that using HeLa cell lines to advance her research was one thing but getting permission to try the technique on human stem cell lines was quite another. Medical politics stood in her way. However, she arrived back home, elated by the progress so far and happy for once to see Andy doing his best to entertain the girls. He had contrived a supper of egg and beans on toast and was now enjoying a daft film on television.

'Have they done their homework?' Isabel asked.

'Yes, dear, I'm very well!' came the faintly sarcastic riposte. Ignoring this, Isabel crossed the living room and kissed the top of her husband's head. 'Yes,' he continued, 'they have done their homework and are almost ready for bed. Aren't you, ladies?' This is directed at his giggling daughters. They seemed happy to have both parents at home together for once.

With the girls happily tucked up, Isabel accepted Andy's proffered glass of wine and they sat and talked about their respective days.

'Patient from Sunday,' Andy began, 'is doing well, but there is some numbness of the trigeminal nerve which is not surprising really given the injury.'

'Tur-trigeminal?'

'Yes, it's a sensory nerve, provides sensation to the head and neck. In this case, it's the branch of the nerve supplying her lower lip. Because the jaw was so badly injured in the accident the branch which passes through it ruptured. Occasionally the nerve will repair itself, but I doubt that will be the case here.'

'Is that bad?'

'Well, for such a young girl, it is quite a deficit. She will have problems with eating, controlling saliva—that sort of thing. To a certain extent, nerves will cross the midline—from the other side of the face—to compensate, but only up to a point. The miracle is, though, that the facial nerve was spared.'

Andy then used his fingers to show how the five branches of this nerve (which supplied function, not sensation, to the muscles of the face) fanned out through the cheek. That given the flap nature of the injury, he had repositioned the whole cheek and soft tissue of the face such that these crucial branches had remained intact. This meant, he went on, that his patient could smile, blink and screw their eyes up. It was for this reason that this nerve supplied what was referred to as the muscles of facial expression.

'The thing that drives me nuts though,' he went on, 'is that management wants to audit the results of our trauma service and are using this case as a presentation for a meeting: one question they will ask is why I didn't bring in the plastic surgeons in order to attempt a fusion of the nerve endings in the jaw.'

Isabel wanted to know if this was normal practice.

'Absolutely not!' Andy said, taking a large gulp of his red wine. 'It's a bloody witch hunt. The general surgeons and the orthopods are already up in arms because of the time we spend on emergency facial trauma and now the bloody administrators are asking me why we are not spending more time pursuing hopeless causes. They never chase the plastics and ENT guys. I'm literally between a rock and a hard place. As if the bloody job isn't difficult enough as it is.'

Andy used this mini rant as an excuse to open another bottle of wine.

'Still, enough about me—how was your day?'

Isabel thought for a few seconds and decided that now was not perhaps the best time to discuss cell biology. Instead, she asked, 'Have you given any more thought to the idea of a nanny?'

'Strange you should ask that—' Andy took a long swig '—You know the new SHO—well, it just so happens that she has a sister, recently qualified as a nanny.'

Andy explained how his German SHO had a sister, eager to start work in the UK. Isabel looked dubious.

'Do you not think we need to research this? Go through normal channels? Perhaps—' she paused, 'closer to home?'

Andy laughed, 'you little Anglophile, you. There's no harm in giving her an interview, is there?'

Isabel pondered this.

'Yeah, OK. Let's meet her and see what we think.'

For the moment, her mind was more occupied by her new cell culture, even now dividing away in Birmingham. No more was said on the subject.

'How about an early night?' Isabel offered instead, eyeing up her husband and trying to assess whether sex was entirely out of the question. 'I fancy a bath—Why don't you come and join me in a few minutes?'

As his wife disappeared upstairs, Andy gave this rare invitation a few moments' consideration, took another gulp of wine and, albeit unsteadily, made his way after her. The inviting smells of patchouli bath oil permeated the atmosphere. Stripping off, he made his way into the bathroom, where, through the steam, he saw his wife's thigh, invitingly exposed above the froth, just revealing the electric blue and red butterfly tattoo, the only remaining evidence of a hedonistic weekend in Barcelona, inviting him in.

******

Andy stood, allowing the rush of water to wash away the customary morning fuzziness. Something else occupied him this morning; a nice comforting warm sensation following last evening's lovemaking. The feel, unaccustomed of late, of family closeness. He realised he loved his wife and his two children; it was just the sheer business of modern life, his work, Isabel's work and that nagging stab of guilt every time his heart opened fully to embrace his daughters and their uncomplicated love.

He knew Seb was gone and, in reality, there had been nothing he could have done to save him—but still—the guilt lingered and cast its shadow on everything. He also realised he loved his work, he loved the feeling and calling of being a healer, of being there for people afflicted by sickness or injury—but, then—always the counterbalance; the politics of hospital life. He had received an email summoning him and his colleague, Stuart, to a meeting to discuss trauma provision; audit again. What the hell did they know about the management of injured people?

With these conflicting emotions swirling, he got dressed, kissed his still sleeping wife and jumped into his car to drive to the early morning team meeting. Thursday afternoon's operating list represented his favourite routine surgery; elective as opposed to emergency and he wanted to make sure someone properly clerked the patients in. Also, he wanted a chat with Bernadine about the implant rehabilitation of the weekend patient. Oh yes, he might even mention the nanny issue.

Whilst the speciality of Max-fac had moved further away from its dental origins, Andy still enjoyed the business of providing a service for the local dentists: keeping that oral surgery referral channel open. This afternoon, for example, he had an excision biopsy of a suspect lesion on the side of the tongue, removal of a chronically infected submandibular salivary gland and a scar revision for a patient who had the misfortune to have a botched removal of a haemangioma on the lip.

Following a phone-call from a dental practitioner, he had also squeezed in a closure of an oro-antral fistula. The dentist, who he knew well, had been over-enthusiastic in the removal of an upper right first molar tooth and inexpertly had removed the three-rooted tooth with the bone forming the floor of the sinus, still attached to the tooth. The patient had subsequently suffered the embarrassment of his cup of tea escaping through his nose and he intended to teach his registrar, Sandeep, how to raise a soft tissue flap from the palate and rotate it in such a way as to seal off the opening.

San also had a research interest in dental implantology and was fully expecting to get involved in the rehabilitation of last weekend's case. Aware that he had given Bernadine a hard time during this procedure, Andy had, however, changed his mind. He had decided to hand over responsibility for the implant placements to her instead.

'Look, San, I'll take you through the OAF closure and assist you to dissect out the salivary gland, but on this occasion, I want to get Bernadine to help with the dental rehab.'

'But, Sir?' protested San.

'Don't worry—I'm on it—I have a case for a facial obturator coming up which will need implants to support a prosthesis. You can help me with that.'

They had then gathered around the bed of the trauma patient, who seemed a little better and now sitting up and taking fluids. Andy noted that her facial muscles responded as expected, but that the lip and chin, on testing and perhaps inevitably, did not react to sharp stimulus and were clinically numb.

The young girl had lost all the teeth in the lower left quadrant beyond the canine tooth and Andy explained how he planned to replace the missing bone with grafts and implant these with tooth replacement implants to restore her bite. This would take place in about 4 to 6 months and he asked Bernadine to work the case up. San had to leave to attend an out-patient clinic, leaving the SHO and Andy once again sharing coffee together.

'I had a chat with my wife last evening and she is more than happy to meet up with your sister whenever you can arrange it.'

Bernadine appeared pleased by this proposition and Andy left her to sort out the arrangements.

******

Isabel had woken, also feeling affection towards her husband and lay for a while, enjoying the sensation. After a while she went downstairs and before waking the girls, posted an email requesting permission from the University to transfer her research findings to human cell lines. A big step, crucial to her research progression. Next, she spoke with her old friend and colleague in Frankfurt. Isabel, concerned about the approaches from the German biotech firm, wanted to know if Lisbeth knew anything about it.

After all, Isabel's research, combined with Lisbeth's, whose work was focusing purely on human stem-cells, would have major interest to any big Pharma company the globe over. These duties dispensed with, she could concentrate on domestic matters and dispatch the girls to school. She then drove down to Birmingham, having arranged for the children to go to friends for a sleepover. At least, she would have a clear run now at her bench for the rest of the day.

Chapter 6

Bernadine had contacted her sister, Heidi and arranged for her to come over to the UK to meet Mr and Mrs Saunders over the weekend. Heidi had been pressing for this opportunity ever since Bernie had landed the job as Mr Saunders's Jr. Things were going better than she could ever have imagined. So it was that the following Saturday saw Heidi and Bernadine present themselves at the Church Stretton home and Bernie made herself scarce whilst the interview took place.

Bernadine's sister had arrived in the UK fully prepared with work visas, certificates and excellent references from the private course for das Kindermädchen as provided in her home country. Her English was excellent. Lucy and Imogen presented themselves for inspection and seemed to get on very well with the prospective carer.

Andy and Isabel had agreed to let Heidi stay in the converted barn next to the main house, where she would enjoy independence, but also be on hand whenever her services were required. This arrangement seemed to suit everyone ideally and Heidi was duly engaged for one month, on trial.

Afterwards, Andy and Isabel congratulated themselves on the appointment and enjoyed a celebratory glass of fizz. Andy was not on call and they went out for supper. Privately, Isabel relished the prospect of furthering her research, with at least some of her responsibilities now transferred.

Yesterday, she had enjoyed a long chat with her colleague, Lisbeth, who had expressed some concern over the idea that Isabel's research had come to the attention of CellProcure, which company she described as a pretty aggressive player in stem cell research. She warned Isabel that she should check her online security when discussing her results, suggesting that cyber-attacks were not uncommon. She had also taken care to congratulate Isabel on the apparent advances in her recent work and agreed to collaborate in any way she could.

******

Back at work after the weekend, Andy met with Stuart, agreeing to defend their speciality robustly. The two surgeons accordingly found themselves being interrogated by the admin and audit team. Hospitals were now increasingly run by administrators rather than doctors, but they both accepted the need to present their cases if they expected to receive funding in order to achieve their clinical goals.

Andy had convinced them that Dental Implantology now formed a vital part of reparative treatment for patients undergoing surgery to correct facial deformity, post-trauma and for those patients who had received post-ablative surgery to eradicate cancer of the face and jaws.

To his delight, he had secured funding for this and gained permission for Sandeep to continue his implant superstructure research. The two colleagues had also convinced the administrators that micro-surgery had no part to play in primary trauma surgery. They also argued for another theatre to be made available to them at weekends: after all, they were supposed to be a regional centre for head and neck trauma. Andy also discussed the vacancy for a new senior registrar, as his current appointee had left on sabbatical.

Encouraged following the meeting, Andy had sought out Bernadine ('please call me Bernie,') and talked about last weekend's patient and gone to the ward to check on her progress. They were delighted to see her up and about, able to take fluids and solids and attend to her ablutions. With any luck, she would be able to go home soon equipped with appointments to return to outpatients and instructions to use daily exercise to improve her jaw movement.

At the end of the weekend, all seemed to be rosy for once in the Saunders's household. Heidi had agreed to move her few belongings into her new quarters by the end of the week when the trial period would begin. One blot on Andy's horizon was an awkward conversation he had had before he left the hospital last evening with the theatre sister.

Julie had explained that she knew the circumstances of the admission of last weekend's patient and had realised that it had not been a 'drink-drive' incident. She warned Andy, off the record, that she had a duty to report her suspicions pertaining to Andy's drinking. That this knowledge placed her in a difficult situation. She liked and respected Andy but had given him a friendly shot across the bows. He had been warned.

******

Marriage had stilted Isabel's development as a scientist—she realised that. Much as she loved her family, her proper sense of self-worth was inextricably linked to scientific achievement. She relished the idea that employing Heidi would give her more time at her beloved bench. This afternoon she arrived at the lab, delighted to see her cells not only alive but behaving as expected, having received a tiny dose of the enzyme.

She now had to 'engineer' the cell RNA to enable her to create a culture of cells which she knew could be replaced by stem cells in the future. If this experiment worked, it would enable her to develop the science so that she could take a sample of a cancer patient's stem cells and manipulate their RNA so that when injected back into the patient these cells would initiate an immune response which would target the rogue cells and destroy them. She would use a viral vector in much the same way as a vaccine. She knew this would revolutionise the treatment of terminal disease. She set to work.

Chapter 7

Every year, the promise of spring would bring joy to Andy's heart. This year felt no different, in spite of the daily challenges informing his life. On this occasion, he used this Wednesday morning off to walk in the bluebell woods across the road from his home.

He loved the dappled light dancing on the carpet of blue, the white celandines glimpsed through the gently nodding bells. The scent overwhelmed him with its sweet promise of summer to come. In the adjacent fields, lambs danced, pranced and chased each other and he allowed memories of Seb to flood into his briefly empty mind. He imagined the man Seb would be now and a tear flowed down his cheek as he gazed upon this elemental beauty.

He had considered Julie's warning and determined that he would not drink at all in future whilst on call. What happened in the rest of his life: well, that was no business of theirs, so far as he was concerned. Feeling better after his stroll through the woods, he grabbed a quick coffee before heading off to the hospital for a meeting with an ENT colleague. He planned to ask him for his help in dealing with his patient's inferior alveolar nerve. He met his team first only missing his S.R.

'OK, here is what I have in mind for this rehab. We'll open up the mandible, remove some of the bone plates and access the nerve just before it dips into the jaw. My colleague will then attempt a microsurgery repair on the nerve sheath which I will protect with a rib graft to reinforce the whole lingual aspect of the jaw. This will create a 'sandwich' which I intend to fill with artificial bone particles packed around three implants. San, I would like you to contact OsseoTech's Head Office in Gothenburg and get the lowdown on the new bio-active implants. With any luck, using these, we can get the whole shebang done in one go.'

San's approach to OsseoTech had evidently gone down well and Andy was thrilled to receive a phone call from their head office inviting him and a colleague over to Gothenburg for a weekend, in order to view the new implant facility and to be entertained in the Swedish manner.

The company had apparently expressed their keen interest in establishing a foothold in the hospital provision of dental implants. Bernadine had found Andy in his office arranging a suitable date for the trip and checking on the on-call rotas. It was only afterwards that he realised how profound her presence at this precise moment would turn out to be. On a whim and with her future training in mind, he invited her on the trip. San once again vented his displeasure. After all, it was he who had contacted Osseo Tech in the first place.

'Surely as research registrar I should get to go on the trip?'

'Yes, but I'm afraid you're on-call that weekend and I've already asked Bernie,' Andy replied.

'But I only swapped the weekend with Bernie a few days ago.'

'San, she couldn't possibly have known about the Swedish trip and if this goes well, there will be plenty of opportunities in the future. How about you take the rib for the graft in next month's op? And I promise you will be next on the list for a trip to Sweden.'

San, of course, had heard this before but realised there was little point in arguing. He was beginning to resent Bernadine and her influence on his boss.

******

Isabel, meanwhile, was making up for lost time. In the lab, she had manipulated her cell's genetic material in such a way that it's RNA would stimulate the required immune response once introduced into the body, theoretically at least. She had gotten together with her colleagues involved in vaccine research and had learned how to transfer these cells onto a primate adenovirus which would act as the vector to allow injection as a vaccine.

So far, this represented known science but her next challenge would be to identify a diseased patient's cancer cell genotype and copy this into a cell line derived from the patients' own stem cells. Being pluripotential, these cells would mimic the diseased cells so that when injected back into the patient, they would stimulate the immune system to target the tumour. A real 'magic bullet.'

She had confided some of this with her German colleague but had been sure to correspond on the secure university computers. What she hoped to do next involved the eventual transfer of this research to clinical trials. Years of hard work appeared to be coming to fruition.

She decided to celebrate and, sending a text to Andy, she left her lab early in order to get home, spend some time with the girls, before going out for supper. Since their last coming together, she and Andy had not been intimate again and she aimed to put that right. The experiment with Heidi appeared to be going well, the girls seemed happy and Heidi worked very hard, anticipating the girls' activities and sorting out laundry and homework.

Not for the first time, Isabel wondered how on earth she had managed before. In good spirits, she let herself into the house via the side door and paused in the kitchen as she heard muttering from her study. She paused. Then, peering round the living room door, saw Lucy and Imogen ensconced happily in front of the TV. She then moved towards her study door, partly open. She stood and listened. Heidi was talking to someone in German. What the hell?

She knocked on the door, walked in and was surprised to see her nanny on the phone. Immediately, she jumped and put the receiver down on the hook. Later, she mentioned this to Andy, who didn't seem particularly surprised.

'Perhaps she was talking to her sister. What did Heidi say?'

'She said nothing. She just looked startled. Surely if she had been talking to, what's her name?'

'Bernadine.'

'Surely, she would have told me. Apart from anything else, that's my study—strictly out of bounds.'

'Don't worry, Izzy. I'll have a word with her-OK? How was your day?'

Isabel told him how well her research was going, encouraging Andy to toast his wife's success with a healthy gulp of best malt. Still mulling over the events of the day, Isabel made her way upstairs, leaving her husband free to enjoy his drink. She wanted to dress nicely for once, apply some make-up, not that she really needed it.

Privately she also hoped that they would discuss her career for once, rather than his. She would be disappointed, however, to realise that right now Andy's mind was preoccupied and not for the first time, by his SHO and how she seemed to infiltrate his life. Popping up when least expected. Strangely familiar with him. He had to admit to himself that he found her very attractive, alluring almost and completely different to her darker, more severe sister. These thoughts continued to occupy him as he helped himself to another whiskey.

Chapter 8

Andy settled back into his seat as the plane took off. God, it felt good to get away. He had persuaded his wife that this little jaunt was purely work-related and that he was only taking his junior along in order to back up the research connection. That he was now eyeing up the drinks trolley whilst a becoming young blonde sat in the seat to his right, only seemed to heighten his sense of freedom.

OsseoTech, as a company, revelled in its reputation for providing top-quality hospitality to clinicians. A reception had been arranged on their arrival into Gothenburg that evening. A senior representative of the company met them at the airport and drove them to the Radisson Blu hotel in the centre. Here they were told to settle in and, once refreshed, come down to be met in the cocktail bar by Erich, the Dental Branch Manager for the company.

Erich greeted them warmly, ordering cocktails and filling them in on the agenda for tomorrow. A tour around the new implant facility would begin the day. This held particular interest for Andy with its emphasis on demonstrating the new surface active implant. The highlight of the day was to be a speed boat excursion across the archipelago to an island, which housed an exclusive restaurant; the whole shebang to be at OsseoTech's expense.

Having thus dispensed with the formalities, Andy and Bernie were left to their own devices. Feeling he had already spent enough time in his SHO's presence and expecting a fairly busy weekend, Andy excused himself and retired to his room. Here he intended to make use of the minibar whilst enjoying a long soak in the bath. Perhaps he might order up a meal in his room. Bernie had seemed happy enough to take herself off, exploring the delights of this beautiful city.

A clearly hung-over Andy joined his fellow guest at breakfast and they exchanged pleasantries while Andy couldn't help noticing how glamorous Bernie looked, sporting tight-fitting jeans, tucked into half-length suede boots, topped off with a low-cut blouse and a sheepskin jacket-beautifully cut. Her blonde hair fell in a pigtail down between her shoulders and to the small of her back. She smelt divine; expensive but subtle. Not for the first time Andy wondered where she got her money from-certainly not from the salary the NHS was paying her.

Having swallowed a couple of Ibuprofen with his orange juice, they met their chauffeur in the lobby, who drove them to the six-storey glass edifice emblazoned with the OsseoTech logo. As promised they spent the morning being shown the technical aspects of implant manufacture. Already aware of the process of osseointegration, (whereby the host bone-making cells infiltrated the highly roughened micro-surface of the titanium cylinder, thus allowing mature bone to lock the root-replacement implant into the jaw), Andy was more interested in the plasma solution Astra had developed in order to increase the speed of this healing process.

This action would enhance rehab for his compromised patients. He asked all the right questions, his extensive knowledge impressing his hosts. Bernie, also impressed, revelled in the reflected admiration for her boss. They made a striking couple.

Andy completed the tour by explaining how he wanted to try these new implants on a particular patient and he received an advance order of 10 implants, free, pending his full clinical report; that should please the managers, he chuckled to himself. After an excellent lunch, they drove down to the harbour where they were kitted out in head-to-toe yellow oilskins, Bernie taking care to leave her sheepskin in the changing hut.

A speed boat trip around the myriad islands of the archipelago followed; some occupied by tiny lighthouses, with other larger islands housing small homes, whilst others sported tiny fishing boats moored up by brightly coloured huts. Everywhere new sights and sensations delighted the couple; sweeping seabirds, herons standing quietly erect on the shorelines, the clear blue sea and sky and sheer exhilaration of the high-speed rush through the waters.

After a while, by now a little chilled, they returned to their hotel for a rest, wash and brush-up. They then returned to the harbour where, in more sedate fashion, they would boat across the water to their exclusive restaurant.

Earlier, calling home, Andy had been surprised when Heidi picked up only to inform him that she didn't know of his wife's whereabouts.

'That's odd,' he thought to himself. 'Where are the girls?' he asked.

'Ja, they are good; would you want to speak to them?'

'No, no. That's OK—so long as they are happy. Will you let Izzy know I called?'

'Ja, I will, of course. Are you having a nice time? How is Bernie?'

Once again, noticing with a smile his employees clipped, Germanic phrasing, he nonetheless called the conversation to a halt and went off to his bath to rest his faintly aching body after the bumps of the boat ride and happily settled into the suds with a glass of red. Later, refreshed, on meeting Bernie in the foyer he was momentarily nonplussed by her beguiling beauty and he soon stopped wondering where his wife might have been. He had happily returned to tourist mode.

Once again then, the pair skimmed across the flat waters, their destination the restaurant, the only building on the small, wooded island. This only came into view as Andy and Bernie made their way up the torch-lit path that wound through the fir trees. An inviting scent of wood smoke and herbs filled the air as they approached the wood-slatted building, bright chandeliers illuminating the gloaming.

Their host, Erich opened the door for them, whereupon they were greeted like old friends and ushered into the warm interior. A glass of schnapps warmed their inner selves. The alcohol rushed to Andy's head and for a moment he felt almost overwhelmed by this sensory assault: the sheer strangeness of this place, the warmth of his hosts and the beguiling scents emanating from the kitchen, whose main feature seemed to be a 6-foot wide, flaming brassiere.

Furthermore, his companion, similarly affected and glowing with vitality and beauty, enhanced the whole, magical experience. It seemed that nothing was too much trouble for the wife and husband who were front of house and chef, respectively. Tiny amuse-bouche of gravadlax laced with mustard sauce accompanied the second glass of schnapps, whilst course after course followed of often unidentifiable portions, some of fish but all spotted with elaborate dressings and reductions, enhanced by sprinklings of herbs and smoked pine.

Plates of wood and stone bore each course to the table, each one accompanied, first with champagne, then exquisite white and red wine. A particular delight for Andy was a slab of rare venison, charred in the flames but pink and rendered to perfection by a dressing of what looked to be melted fat but offset with a startling, palate-abrading horseradish accompaniment. The wine and conversation flowed. Andy found that his young companion was an

43

intelligent, interesting and funny conversationalist and occasionally he allowed himself just to sit back and watch his host, obviously charmed by his companion.

He found he could share his love of music with Bernadine and how the German repertoire particularly interested him. They discussed the mighty fairy-tale set to music that formed Wagner's masterpiece, the Ring Cycle. It seemed they both instinctively understood the Germanic text as it interweaved and illustrated the grandiose music.

At the end of the meal, small, wrapped gifts were brought to their table with instructions to open only once home: a Swedish tradition apparently. Andy realised that a full three hours had passed in this wonderful place. The gentle voyage home, again on a calm sea did nothing to reduce the sense of rapture and good fortune and in this mood, they made for the hotel bar for a nightcap. Here Andy relaxed into Bernie's company.

The whole experience of the day removed any inhibitions he may have had either as husband or senior clinician. It seemed, for this brief time, as though they occupied an alternate universe with all the worries and concerns of everyday, consigned to the distant past. They expanded upon their mutual interests in music and nature and how the two elements became embodied in Wagner's music. In particular, Andy's knowledge of song enchanted his companion.

It seemed they both had a love of Strauss' Four Last Songs. The poetry of the last of these, in which the singer talks of walking hand in hand with her companion into death having spent a full life, inevitably led him to talk about Seb. In describing the lyrics of the last of these songs, Bernadine's grasp of the German syntax brought new meaning and understanding to Andy who, for once, allowed himself to indulge himself in describing his struggles with his son's loss and subsequent grief. How this grief had morphed into guilt and the corroding effect that this had had on his first marriage.

As Andy described the events surrounding this tragic incident, he found himself increasingly moved by his companion's deep concern and attention. He found himself able to unload his deep emotion in a way he could never do with his wife. Isobel, whilst apparently sympathetic, never seemed to grasp the depth of his feelings, always wanting to move the conversation onto safer ground. Andy would excuse this lack of real sympathy by telling himself that, after all, she hadn't known Seb, that to her, it was just an accident.

Bernie, on the other hand, seemed as deeply moved as Andy himself by the story. She didn't try to change the subject or look faintly embarrassed by the revelations. In short, she just listened.

Bernie then explained why she had come to the UK to pursue her career. It seemed she had a difficult relationship with an overbearing stepfather who worked in the German pharmaceutical industry. She then explained that Heidi was actually her stepsister but had felt compelled to help her seek employment in the UK. Pausing, she begged Andy's forbearance as she excused herself.

She returned five minutes later whilst Andy ordered another round. He couldn't help noticing freshly applied perfume.

'Why don't we take these upstairs?' she suggested.

'Great idea!' assented a bemused but enchanted Andy. Refusing to heed his inner voice, he followed Bernie into the lift, noticing the gentle sway of his SHO's hips, the buttocks tightly encased in pale-blue denim. She sat by him on the bed. She told Andy, once again how moved she had been by the story of Seb's drowning. The emotional floodgates opened and Andy held his head in his hands and sobbed. Bernie reached across and their hands met. With her free hand, she reached up and turned Andy's head towards her.

He felt her sweet breath caress his cheeks. They gently kissed. Then, as his emotion evolved into passion, all sense of responsibility, sense of right or wrong, gave way to the irresistible and primal urge as he thrust his tongue into Bernadine's mouth and shared her sweet saliva. She stood and gently smiling at her boss, she eased off her jeans revealing black panties, which, as he lent forward, he found to be inviting him into the hidden damp flesh beneath.

Abandoning all reason, he embraced her, turned her gently onto the bed and entered her.

******

Andy woke with a start. One thought obliterated his hangover. No! That didn't happen—It couldn't happen. As his senses sharpened, the smell of an alien female assaulted him—perfume and the unmistakable must. What had he been thinking? This single act towered over his profession, his marriage—his family. His very sense of self.

Emotion welled in his eyes as he imagined how much Isabel would have loved yesterday—the sights and scents of the Archipelago, the magic of that hidden restaurant, the food. He berated himself as he recalled his treachery in downplaying his wife's sympathies. But now the memory of a truly wonderful experience became sullied, marred for all time. 'What the fuck was I thinking?', he admonished himself.

Showering did nothing to assuage his guilt and, getting dressed, it occurred to him that he now had to meet this girl again, travel home with her, see her on the wards throughout the next week and thereafter. WHAT THE HELL WAS I THINKING!

Down in the breakfast room, his erstwhile lover failed to mirror Andy's anguish. She seemed composed, groomed, smiling, even (or did he imagine this?) a look of triumph drifting, cloud-like, across her beautiful face. What further ashamed him was the unmistakable thrill passing through his loins as he observed her. This realisation heralded another outburst of self-loathing; 'Hell. What's the matter with me?'

'Ah, good morning—Bu, Bernie. Are you OK? I hope you slept well—' Banalities tumbled forth.

'Mr Saunders. How are you? I had a lovely sleep, thanks. What a day! I can't thank you enough for bringing me on this trip. I'll never forget it.'

—*and neither shall I*, thought Andy, stunned by her innocence, her insouciance. Had he imagined it—dreamt it?

'Look,' he stammered, taking his seat, '—about last night—'

'Please, don't give it another thought.' Bernie smiled. 'As far as I'm concerned, it never happened.' Inexplicably a momentary wave of disappointment. 'As far as I'm concerned,' she continued, 'it was a wonderful end to a wonderful day. I have no regrets—and neither should you.' This was her admonishing him now but gently, childlike. 'Let us just say, kleines Geheimnis- our little secret—' Bernie put a longing emphasis on this word, '—our secret is just between us. Nein, not another word.'

So it's come to this, he thought. *She's comforting me, like a child. Get a grip. You're her Consultant for God's sake.*

'Right, fine, OK. Now, we have to be at the airport by 11:00 am. We're being picked up at 10:15 am.'

His attempt at taking control fooled no one. They ate their smorgasbord in silence.

Chapter 9

Isabel surprised herself. She missed her husband. This time it felt different somehow from him being away at work-this time he was in another country, away from her. She thought back to the evening last week when they had come together so happily and she felt very fond. Perhaps she was too immersed in her work so had chosen to spend the weekend at home. She would call her colleague in Germany from home rather than go into the University. She would bend the rules for once. Today she would revel in the feeling of being at home, with her girls and enjoying the sensation of pining for Andy.

Isabel had also been fairly impressed by the Heidi experiment. Although she seemed very-well, German and was very firm with her daughters, she had the knack of appearing and disappearing as and when required. And the girls seemed to like her.

In this cheerful state of mind, she called her friend in Frankfurt. Lisbeth's area of expertise lay in stem cell research and Isabel wanted to pick her brains on the best way to transfer her (as yet, hypothetical) genetically modified stem cells, onto a human adenovirus carrier.

This, she knew represented a necessary step in developing her so-called vaccine. She also wanted to discuss the nature of the crucial enzyme that helped keep the cell lines alive for long enough to extend the research from HeLa to stem cell lines. This exchange of information honoured the spirit of entente cordiale, the unspoken rule that scientists could share their findings, both good and bad.

The call took nearly an hour, not helped by a brief, but irritating break in the line halfway through, but satisfied, she emerged from her study and stepped across the corridor to the drawing room. A sudden movement surprised her. Was that Heidi quickly disappearing down the hall? Strange. A shout of, 'Mum, come and look at this' pulled her back from asking Heidi what she had been doing and, incident forgotten, Isabel clicked from scientist to mother mode. She thought nothing more about it.

The next day, Andy arrived back home. His appearance surprised Isabel. Her husband seemed drawn and tired. Disappointed, she assumed the worst. Hungover again, she thought. But he settled in, having dumped his overnight bag upstairs and, for once, she noted, actually loaded the laundry himself. He gave her an account of the weekend's activities, careful to emphasise the scientific content and skimming over the hospitality.

She bent to kiss him but found herself surprised by his lack of response. He quickly changed the subject. Relieved, he remembered that friends were calling in for drinks later that afternoon and he took himself off to shower and change. Isabel was left with her thoughts. How unpredictable her husband could be but nevertheless she was glad to have him home. Again she thought no more about it and went to the kitchen to prepare snacks.

By the time their friends had arrived (a Shrewsbury dentist, Gareth and his wife, Liz) Andy had slipped seamlessly back into his customary professional good humour. Excellent raconteur, master of the universe, Isabel happily joined in with the banter, relieved to see her husband apparently relaxed again. As always she slipped seamlessly in beside him-the perfect, modern married couple.

Gareth, Welsh and garrulous, kept the jokes and anecdotes flowing but not before Andy had discussed the procedure he had planned for tomorrow in order to try to repair some of the damage caused to the young female in the recent accident. Gareth loved this; loved to share the technical details of the proposed operation; the materials to be used and the rationale behind what was, after all, an unusually early intervention.

Andy explained to his friend that if an attempt was to be made to repair the inferior alveolar nerve it had to be done sooner rather than later. He also shared his idea that whilst the shattered bone was healing he wanted to utilise the window of opportunity—whilst there was high cell turnover—to attach bone grafts and then place implants into these grafts so that the hard and soft tissues would continue to heal and develop around these implants. In this way, form and function would be returned to the patient as soon as possible.

'Why a rib graft?' Gareth asked.

'Well, the great thing about rib is that, provided it is harvested correctly leaving the periosteum intact, then the rib section can be removed in the knowledge that it will grow back again. The rib can be bent and shaped to exactly fit the inner aspect of the jaw. This will provide structure and protection for the particulate graft.'

'Particulate graft?' Gareth interrupted.

'Well, it's like artificial bone-looks a bit like sea salt-which can be inserted between the rib and the jaw like a sandwich filling. I will pack this around the implants before I close the gum tissue back over the whole caboosh.'

'Wow!' Gareth, clearly impressed, welcomed the opportunity to open another bottle of claret.

'I presume I'm driving then?' Liz interrupted, smiling. She knew these two well. She had enjoyed talking to Isabel about her work as a radiographer at the hospital. Isabel had hinted at her mounting excitement over her research but had not gone into any great detail. The result of this happy friendship was that Andy's decline was quickly forgotten and all was laughter. For once Andy got to bed at a reasonable time and seemed to ration his alcohol intake. Tomorrow's operation was clearly on his mind.

******

The operating microscope had been set up in theatre 2 and Andy's ENT colleague was on standby in the event that a micro-surgical repair seemed possible. Andy's choice of a Bach piano suite gently lightened the atmosphere around what was, after all, an elective procedure. San was in early and clearly well prepared. His brief disappointment at missing out on the weekend had been forgotten. He was keen to be involved.

Andy discussed the rib graft as they scrubbed up and reminded his registrar to keep the bone moist in saline gauze before he joined the operation back at the head-end. San's movements were precise as he incised down onto the middle section of the seventh rib on the patient's right side. He carefully dissected the overlying fat and muscle until he reached the thin, tissue-like tube of skin or periosteum, encasing the rib.

Having cut through this he used curved retractors to tunnel beneath to its underside, taking great care to avoid damaging the underlying pleura. He then used bone-cutters to excise a 5 cm length of rib which he then placed in a kidney dish covered by the gauze. Handing this to the scrub nurse he closed the wound in layers and looked up, not able to conceal his pride in a job well done.

'Beautiful-textbook, San. Now get up here—change your gloves—I need you to retract.'

Andy had, by now, cut down on to the injured jaw but was struggling to disconnect the string-like nerve from the dense scar tissue surrounding the area. Everything was a mess of old blood clots and the fibrous tangle of collagen fibres that represented early attempts at healing. The damaged nerve did not readily present itself as two neatly-cut ends which might be suitable for micro repair.

Instead, he saw that the nerve sheath had been shredded by the crushing effect of the shattering bone and the only way he could effect approximation would be by cutting away the shreds and then stretching the nerve to apposition. Andy knew that this stretching would permanently damage the nerve anyway so, reluctantly, he gave up on his attempt and dismissed a nurse to go and release his colleague; their skills would not now be required.

'At least,' he thought, 'I can tell management we tried.'

Putting aside the knowledge that he would now have to tell his patient that she would have to live with a numb lip and chin and possibly the side of her tongue, he carried on. San was able to place the implants in the grafted tissue using a pre-prepared stent and the tissue was closed, only the healing screws protecting the hollow implants, betraying their presence, lying flush with the gum. Andy also took the opportunity to revise a small V-shaped scar on the border of the lip and they surveyed a job well done.

'Thanks, San, really good work-all we have to do now is wait four months and then we can fit her with new teeth. Well done.'

With that, he placed his hand on his registrar's shoulder and they went off for a well-earned coffee. For the time being at least, he had clearly forgotten his promise to his SHO to include her in any implant rehab procedure.

By the time Andy arrived home he had persuaded himself that really, the weekend's events meant nothing. He had spoken to Bernie after the weekend ward round and her attitude towards him had not changed it seemed. He determined to put the whole episode behind him. He remembered why he had fallen so deeply in love with his wife in the first place: her Gaelic good looks, black hair, blue eyes and porcelain skin. His very own Galway girl.

He had also been enchanted by her startling intelligence and wit and again he recalled that early fling in Barcelona where, after a boozy lunch, she had told him how she secretly had always wanted a tattoo and how, giggling like teenagers, they had taken themselves to a respectable-looking parlour and Isabel had leapt at a blue butterfly design. Then with little yelps of pain, then giggles, she had succumbed to the tattooist's needle and he had watched the whole process, fascinated.

Experiences like this had built a protective wall against the current of his guilt and sadness of losing Seb and the ensuing birth of his two little girls had only served to strengthen this barrier. Recently though, the intensity, the demands of their respective professions had threatened to spoil their idyll and he, the stupid bastard, had just made the whole situation worse. He consoled himself with the thought that, yes, he had been drunk, but then again was this not always the excuse he used to escape the consequences of any shortcoming, be it surgery or seduction?

Again, he convinced himself that no harm had been done and as always, his drive home towards the Shropshire Hills had lightened his introspection. He arrived then back home in a better frame of mind where, surprisingly, he found his wife standing alone in the kitchen, gazing out of the window, her back to the door and therefore to him as he entered.

'Hi, Darling,' he called out as he approached her. His wife turned and he was even more alarmed to see tears smudging her make-up.

'Oh, Andy—I've been an idiot—' She came towards him, her arms open to embrace him and once her head was safely nestled in his familiar chest, she let out a sob.

'I've had a call from the University—there's been a security breach and they've traced it back to a call I made.'

'A call? To whom?' Andy asked.

'You know, my friend—in Germany—we're liaising on the same project.'

'Yes, but surely you're always speaking to her—?' Andy was puzzled.

'Yes,' she agreed 'but always from the lab-using secure lines.'

'So?'

'I'm so bloody stupid—' again Isabel gave a sob. '—I phoned her from here—the study. I thought it would be OK. I didn't think about a phone call. I always use the University computers if I need to send an email or anything like that. But I remember now, I thought it odd at the time.'

'Odd?' Andy held her away for a moment and examined her face, 'why odd?'

'Well, the line went dead for a second or two, as though we'd been cut off. But then we resumed our chat and I thought no more about it.'

'What were you talking about?' Andy was more quizzical now.

'This new enzyme—the key to the whole stem cell research—the key to the vaccine idea.' Andy recalled his wife's excitement as she described to him how this enzyme had allowed research to be extended to stem cells and how these might be used in the form of a vaccine against tumour cells.

He also realised, shocking really, that being so absorbed by his own problems he had failed to understand the significance of all of this. His clever, beautiful wife may have stumbled on a cure for cancer. Every research scientist's Holy Grail; the last great stumbling block to universal health.

'So why is the University on your back?' he wanted to know.

'They're not telling me on my domestic line. They've called me in for an interview first thing tomorrow.'

'Look, Darling, it can't be anything too serious. Just a slap on the wrist. You are too valuable to them and they know it. Don't worry—I'm sure it's nothing. Let's go and release the girls, let Heidi off and have a drink.' Thus resorting to his universal antidote to the world's problems, he led his wife into the living-room and towards the drinks cabinet.

******

The prospect of the meeting made Isabel nervous, her enthusiasm and pride in her work at odds with the idea of being accused, apparently, of breaking the rules. Her conversations with Lisbeth, in Isabel's mind, fully complied with the ethical ideal of scientists pooling their intellectual property. She had even considered opening online forums in order to discuss ways forward, especially in the wake of the new technology Crispr, which had helped her refine her ideas for a genetic cancer vaccine.

The Chairman of the rapidly convened meeting seemed, however, to be more concerned about the politics of the University research output. Prof Landon, unusually quiet, confined himself to a comment describing Isabel's work as a 'product' and informed her that her research was a form of political action. The Chairman went on to explain that it was they, the University, that was engaged in a rivalry with foreign interests that patent battles could be anticipated if the research coming out of the establishment had the potential to eradicate or even modify disease.

Isabel argued that research of this nature should be shared. The board, however, reiterated their opinion that her phoning a 'rival' from home had been

52

a mistake. They had considered removing her permit to enter the laboratories. They had 'evidence' that attempts had been made, were in fact 'underway', to hack the University computers and that Isabel's careless exchange of vital information on her home phone had merely seemed to facilitate this 'piracy', as they put it.

In mitigation the board had taken into consideration her impressive work, industry and most recent progress and, on this occasion would be happy to let her continue her efforts, but only after following strict security 'protocols'. After this tribunal, as it seemed to Andy, he tried to defuse his wife's anger by reiterating his view that this represented his predicted 'slap on the wrist'.

Isabel was not about to be so easily appeased. She felt that her freedoms as a scientist, her ethical standards were all being called into question. Andy reminded her that everyone, in whatever profession, had to abide by the rules of administrators. The University had given her five days constituting what they deemed to be 'a cooling off period'.

'Take your time to re-evaluate your goals and aims for your research-understand the consequences of your actions and spend time with your family.'

Thus patronised, she had left the meeting, failing to inform them that her new cell lines had shown real evidence that their RNA would potentially stimulate an immune response in the host, making the creation of a successful cancer 'vaccine' even more plausible. She had shared this information with Lisbeth but had no intention of informing the University in the light of this interview. Not yet anyway. Why the University knew about her phone call was a question left unanswered.

Over supper, she shared an idea developing in her mind as to how she might best use this unexpected break from work, be it under less-than-ideal circumstances.

'Would you mind if I asked Lisbeth to come over for a visit, off the record; as pals. That way I could discuss the way forward with her directly rather than communicate via phone or email.'

'How important is this?' Andy foresaw trouble.

'Well, I feel we're at a crucial point in the development of this vaccine—this 'magic bullet' if you like—and frankly, I don't want the University to know anything about it until I've got it written up. Then I can apply to extend the research to work on human stem cells. I will need the full backup from the University then, of course.' Andy could see just how much this meant to his wife.

She continued, 'If she came to stay here then we could keep it strictly entre nous. What do you think?'

'How would the girls fit in-I've got a pretty hefty week coming up and I'm on call again from Thursday.'

'I see no reason why Heidi can't help out. In any case, all I'll be doing is chatting with Lisbeth and she'd love to meet the girls anyway.'

'I have to say,' Andy was ashamed to admit this, 'I had no idea that your research had come to such a head. I suppose it's got to be great news if the university feel your results are such a big deal.'

'It's just stuff I've been working on for years, but Crispr has helped no end. Using that technology has helped me fill in some blanks in my thinking. Had some real breakthroughs recently.'

'Well, I see no reason why you shouldn't have your friend to stay in any event-she can use the guest suite.'

'Thanks, honey—I'll call her now—on the mobile!' she called back over her shoulder as she left the room. 'Oh, excuse me,' Isabel started as she found Heidi standing just outside the door. She seemed to be making a habit of appearing in unexpected places and at unexpected times.

As always though, Isabel had more pressing matters to deal with and once again, dismissed her nannie's sometimes odd behaviour as being vaguely due to some notion of being Germanic. Perhaps the look that darkened the young girl's features would have alarmed her, even more, had she witnessed it.

Chapter 10

San and Bernadine finished the evening ward round by checking in on Andy's trauma patient. They were delighted to find her sitting up. Andy had taken the precaution of fixing her lower teeth or what remained of them, to her upper teeth, in a process called IMF. He had decided to remove the bone-fixation plates but realised the bone fusion was immature, so he wanted the grafts, implants and bone to have the best opportunity of healing together by effectively immobilising the jaw.

In reality, this prevented the patient from taking solid food whilst even drinking was compromised. Their job today was to ensure and enable fluid intake through a straw inserted into the gap in the lower left of the mouth. Thankfully, speech was difficult, so no awkward questions were asked regarding the persisting numbness in her lip and chin. Satisfied, they went to have a coffee before San clocked off. He wanted to try to get to know his colleague better.

'What made you decide to come to the UK to work,' he asked.

'My stepfather. He works in the pharmaceutical industry and has contacts in the UK and he managed to obtain an interview for me.'

'Why here?' San continued, 'Why not a teaching hospital in London. That would seem the more conventional route.'

'After graduating in Germany, I, of course, knew nothing about the hospitals over here, but my father had some contacts in Birmingham and, how do you say? Zog die Faden.'

San looked puzzled.

'I think—pulled the strings.' She gave a little chuckle.

'So what do you want to do eventually?' San asked.

'I think to get as much experience as possible and then go back to Germany eventually.'

'To do dentistry or continue training as an oral surgeon?' Again a chuckle.

'After what I've seen here, I don't think I am cut out for surgery. All that blood and—betrosen—stress. Andy—Mr Saunders is always so—yes—stressed.'

'How about dental implantology?'

'Well, yes,' Bernadine agreed. 'There's a huge private market for implants back home. Perhaps, with a good reference from Mr Saunders, perhaps I could go into research—like you.'

'I'm not certain if I want to go down that route now (forgive the pun).' Bernadine missed the joke, so he went on, 'After working on that case, with the rib graft and everything, I feel I could go the whole way and become an oral surgeon. I'd love that—' he trailed off, as Bernadine apparently began to lose interest. Perhaps she too had realised that her lack of involvement in the case, had more to do with Andy playing politics. This thought saddened her.

'You seem to get on very well with Mr Saunders,' San persisted. At this, Bernadine visibly perked up.

'Yes, how do you English say, he seems a very—ehrenvollen—honourable man. I like him very much!' They gathered their cups and San took them over to the sink.

'Well, nice to have a chat. If ever you need to talk, you can always come to me-after all, you must be lonely over here, on your own.'

'Danke. Thank you. I always have Heidi to talk to-my Schwester. But thank you anyway.'

With that, she left San with the vague idea that really, he had got nowhere at all. He followed her out and with a shrug thought, *well, at least I tried.*

******

Much to Isabel's amusement, Andy started his day off by going into the hospital for a ward round.

'So much for your day off!' she teased him.

Smiling, Andy replied, 'I'll be back by 10 o'clock. Why don't we get out of here, go for a walk, have a few beers?'

They had promised each other that they would go for a walk up the Carding Mill Valley, then along the Mynd to descend via a lovely, cascaded valley for lunch in the Ragleth arms. This would be a rare treat for them both to get out into the hills together for once. Isabel had decided to accept her five days on the naughty step and had arranged to meet Lisbeth at the airport the next day.

She was determined to put this opportunity to its best advantage by spending some time with her husband. She would then enjoy the friendship of her colleague. No doubt they would be discussing research matters, but at least she didn't have to go into the University. Heidi had been briefed on her child-care duties and so it was with a rare feeling of excitement she pulled on her walking boots and strolled down the hill towards the tourist trap of Carding Mill, knowing however that today, Tuesday would be blessedly quiet.

Initially, Andy said little as they approached the coffee shop for elevenses but seemed to cheer up as was his wont once they started up the sharp incline out of the valley. Isabel assumed this to be his usual pre-occupation with all things surgical.

Once on the Mynd, the sun shone and a light breeze ruffled their hair as they strode along, seeking out each other's hands as their respective minds cleared. The ponies that roamed these hills gave them pause and the white-maned stallion, head of the herd, looked up at their approach and then turned and trotted off across the moor, his magnificent tail and plumage flying in the wind. His trot turned into a gallop as spring-fever spread through the herd and Andy and Isabel stood rooted to the spot as they watched this magnificent spectacle.

Today, they extended their walk past the glider airport to watch a few intrepid paragliders test the strengthening wind as it billowed up the bulwark of the west face of the ridge, allowing a stunning view across to the Welsh border. Today Cader Idris could be seen, the sharp wedge-shaped profile of the mountain clearly visible on the West Coast, whilst, turning a few degrees north, they could just glimpse Snowdon and the Berwyn hills closer to home.

Normally a wonderful view, in today's clear air it was simply stunning and they both stood and gazed before turning and retracing their steps to enter the head of the Ragleth Valley. They hopped and skipped down the rocky path, once stopping to splash their faces and dry mouths in the clear downfall. Heaven. Then as the little ravine flattened out into the valley floor, they quickened their pace, anticipating a pint followed by lunch.

Sitting in the lovely little snug, lit and warmed by a log stove, Andy and Isabel understood their initial attraction a little better, able to appreciate how the stresses of their lives tended to pull them apart. Andy, however, could not entirely erase the guilty memories of the weekend and he hurriedly pushed these aside as he finished his pint.

'I'll get another,' he said and jumped up. 'Let's enjoy this—it'll be the last drink I can enjoy for the next few days anyway!' Isabel smiled inwardly—was her husband seriously reducing his intake?

'I'll have a large white in that case; Pinot Grigio-fab.'

After lunch and after fetching another pint, Andy told his wife that he had been giving some thought as to why the University had come down on her so hard.

'Do you remember when you turned down the research fellowship?' he asked her.

'Yeah, of course—I knew I couldn't devote the time with the family and all that. I was happy enough to carry on my research-be more flexible.'

'Well, that decision of course meant that you couldn't go for a chair at the Uni. D'you think that may have affected how they treated you?'

'Why should they be concerned about that? After all, there are already two professors in biotech at the place, there's certainly no reason for a third.'

'Well, couldn't that mean that they may see you as a potential rival?' Andy went on.

'A rival? In what way?' Isabel pondered this while Andy got her another glass of Pinot.

'After you'd gone to bed last night,' Andy continued, 'I looked up the business interests of those professors. Biotech is big business now you know.'

'Strange thing to do,' Isabel paused, then went on, 'what business interests?'

'Well, it seems that they are involved in a company called EngImmune UK. If your research comes to fruition they stand to make huge profits. Why do you think they came down on you so hard when you committed a so-called security breach?'

'But these very Profs are the ones providing me with the conditions in which to continue my research—we sat and developed the plan together. It's them who are seeking permission for me to take the next step to working on patients' stem cells.'

'Exactly,' Andy replied. 'It's in their interests to keep your brain working on results that will eventually benefit them. Imagine if you develop a vaccine against certain cancers-that would be worth millions if big Pharma got their hands on it.'

Brilliant at cell biology, Isabel really didn't understand big business. She looked puzzled.

'Don't you see? Your Profs will be shareholders in EngImmune. If the company were ever floated on the stock markets they would walk away with millions!' Andy took a triumphant gulp of Hobson's best bitter.

'Why would they see me as a rival? Why would they try to rein me in?'

'They probably didn't buy into your reasons to turn down the chance of a chair-didn't understand or want to understand your need to put family first. They may have thought you were keeping your powder dry to take your results elsewhere. Just a thought.' Isabel mulled this over for a while before answering.

'It's true, I did think the panel were a bit heavy-handed, but I really didn't connect it with my lack of interest in academia—' Finishing their lunch, Isabel realised that these theories of her sometimes over-imaginative husband may have some merit. She would enjoy discussing this with her friend. Deciding to lighten the mood, Andy ordered another round.

'Hey, look, I'm sorry I brought it all up. Today was our day off. Let's go back and open a bottle and really enjoy the rest of the day. What do you think?'

Isabel recognised the look in her husband's eye and laughing, they finished their drinks, got up, said their goodbyes to Wendy behind the bar and, rather unsteadily, made their way back towards the town. Andy really was intent on getting the most out of his day off it seemed.

Chapter 11

The next morning Andy attended a departmental audit meeting. Instead of the usual peck on the cheek, Andy had kissed his wife passionately before leaving home, the memory of their previous evening together still lingering. Isabel, looking forward to meeting her old friend, dropped the girls off at school, after which she intended to drive down the M54 and thence to Birmingham airport. Heidi had been given the day off and Isabel looking forward to the novelty of introducing her friend to Imogen and Lucy.

Once in the hospital, Andy became immersed in his least favourite activity of the month-bloody audit, as he would put it. This month, trauma figures and results were to be examined and Andy anticipated some awkward questions. San had collated all the facts and figures and prepared a PowerPoint presentation whilst the rest of the firm sat around the conference room tucking into coffee and biscuits. The usual suspects came up, annotating 15 fractures of the mandible, five depressed malar fractures and a host of soft tissue lacerations and one bottle injury following a brawl.

Andy's colleague, Stuart Hodgkins, wanted to know which of the jaw fractures had been 'plated-up' or placed in IMF or both. San produced slides of radiographs taken before and after to illustrate his answers. He also dealt very well with questions about which zygomatic arch fractures had merely been pulled back into a stable position or which had required sub-orbital plating. If San struggled, Andy chimed in with help in the spirit of inter-firm cooperation. Bernadine remained silent. There followed the inevitable questions regarding Andy's treatment of the numb-lip trauma case.

Stuart, as head of Department, was accountable not only to the administrators but also to the surgeons who chaired the commissioning meetings, looking at all aspects of theatre use, bed occupancy and treatment outcomes; all in the spirit of attempting to balance the impossible equation of profit versus spending. To Andy, perhaps naively, neither of these objectives should have a part to play in trauma surgery. However, Stuart was required not only to sit on this panel but be answerable to it.

The hot topic currently occupying the commissioners involved the use of the emergency theatres in order to carry out time-consuming repair of facial injuries, whilst, from the medic's and general surgeon's point of view, more important and life-threatening conditions were having to wait in a queue. Andy's S.R had, in this case, managed to transfer the second casualty to the wards.

'Well, what else are we meant to do?' Andy asked. 'Why don't they open up another theatre?'

'There are always costings to consider,' argued Stuart. 'Another theatre suite would need staffing, more pressure on recovery, beds and so forth.'

'But we're supposed to be a regional trauma centre for God's sake, where else are patients expected to go?' Andy became increasingly irritated as he realised, yet again, that in these meetings it all came down to money. 'You can't put value judgements on these issues,' he went on.

'Yes, I agree but what this case illustrates is that there may be a better way to approach facial trauma.' Stuart could see Andy's irritation. 'Look, let's just look at the facts pertaining to this particular case.' Trying to ignore Andy, he pressed on. 'A serious injury is operated on, sight unseen and therefore unplanned, the operators are tired—'

'Hang on Stu,' Andy leapt to his own defence. 'You're not going to start criticising my treatment of this case are you?'

'No, not at all. All I am saying is that if we just dealt with the threat at the point of admission-in this case the bleed from the facial artery-and dressed the main injury giving us time to treat the case conservatively on a day list, with a full complement of staff, properly worked up and planned—'

'What about all the routine stuff?' Andy interrupted.

'Yes, I agree we would need to better plan our resources but, look, back to this case. It appears to me that if we'd planned the case we might have been able to get the plastics chaps in to attempt a micro-repair on the ID nerve.'

'Look!' Andy was by now well and truly rattled. 'That nerve sheath was shot to bits in the initial impact. No amount of fiddling about under a microscope would have fixed it.'

'Yes, I'm sure you're right Andy, but this is what these meetings are all about. To look at what we do and how we can improve outcomes, without criticism.' At this point, Bernadine broke her silence to apparently concur with

Stuart. 'Yes, I have to admit, the whole thing was a bit chaotic. Andy—Mr Saunders—really struggled to get control over the bleeding.' A sharp glance in her direction from Andy shut her up.

'It didn't exactly help that the SHO on-call had no previous experience of dealing with trauma.' Andy pointed out, now furious.

'But that really proves my point. If we dealt with trauma on a more elective footing it would ensure that these outcomes were more, how should I put it?—more controllable.' Then, as an afterthought, 'and of course we would have better-trained staff on hand.'

'Where are they going to come from?' Andy was now regretting everything to do with hiring Bernadine.

'If management insists on these changes—which, after all, would benefit us all—then cash would have to follow allowing us to appoint a senior registrar for example. Really begin to innovate.'

San interrupted.

'Yes and I would love to become more involved. I would have been there to help Mr Saunders if I hadn't been tied up in casualty helping with the other victim of the accident.' Andy acknowledged this and calmed down a little.

'I must say, it isn't the best way to deal with these emergencies. Look, Stu, do you really think we could get more money into trauma provision on the back of this?' Perhaps he should think twice before dismissing the financial aspect of all of this.

'Well, as I say, that's what these meetings are about Andy. All we have to discuss are the protocols for triaging our trauma, so that emergency night-time treatment is limited only to what is absolutely essential and conserve the injury for proper planning.'

Andy left the meeting with conflicting emotions. Firstly he intended to give Bernie a good bollocking, then administer San with a pat on the back. Then, with the lingering thought that these bloody meetings may have some purpose after all he found his SHO and, ignoring her smile, asked her, 'what the hell d'you think you were playing at?'

'I'm sorry,' Bernadine replied. 'I was only trying to contribute to the discussion—be useful in some way—' she trailed off.

'Well, in future, keep your thoughts to yourself and please do not think that our—how should I put it—our shenanigans—' Bernie, understandably looked puzzled at this remark. 'You know bloody well what I'm referring to.' Andy turned away, then, over his shoulder before he left the room, he added, 'just don't forget that whatever reference you expect, it will come from me.' With that he was gone, leaving Bernie a little chastened, to say the least.

Chapter 12

Before leaving his wife that morning and after their passionate kiss, Andy had told her that he was looking forward to dinner that evening with Lisbeth but reminded her of his intention to not drink as he was on call. Privately Isabel had thought to herself 'I'll believe that when I see it!' as she drove off with the girls. Now calming down a little after the meeting, he went to his office where he dictated some discharge letters. His secretary was keen to know how the meeting went. She was only too well aware of her boss's aversion to meetings of all kinds.

'On this occasion, I have to admit that there was some possibility of a good outcome. We may even get some help in setting up a dedicated trauma day-list.'

More work for me then, thought the secretary to herself. She respected Andy and admired his drive but realised that when it came to admin. the buck stopped at her door.

After lunch, Andy embarked on his outpatient's clinic which doubled up as a training session for San.

'Thanks for your support today, San. A lot of what was said made sense. The whole point of your training grade is to prepare you for a future consultancy and if we could operate on our trauma in a more controlled way and during daytime working hours, it would certainly benefit you and your successors.'

'Yes, Mr Saunders. It might also allow us to get more sleep at night!'

'Yep, there is that as well. Thanks anyway, San. Now if I can ask you to start next door, there's some malar wiring and IMF to remove and a couple of new patients to clerk in. Give me a shout if you need anything.' Carrying on with his clinic he heard a knock on the door as San stuck his head around requesting leave from the clinic to attend a call-out to A and E.

'Been an RTA apparently. Seems someone has a facial injury.'

'Yep, of course.' Andy looked up from examining a female patient presenting with a pedunculated haemangioma on her lower lip-rather reminiscent of a large strawberry he had thought to himself. 'Keep me informed.' Half an hour later another knock on the door interrupted him. This time his receptionist was the culprit.

'Sorry to interrupt, Mr Saunders, but a clearly flustered San is asking for your immediate presence in A+E. Apparently, the consultant is struggling to secure an airway.' Tutting, Andy excused himself from his patient and went to the phone.

'What's up San?' His secretary was right. San sounded flustered.

'There's a real panic on, major trauma. The anaesthetist can't get an airway. Female patient. A and E consultant struggling—' San finished gabbling, clearly upset.

'Right. Tell them I'm on my way. Make sure they have a line in. Get bloods and crossmatch.'

Andy entered the resus room in A and E where his immediate impression was one of pandemonium. A trolley occupied the centre of the room. On this appeared to be a female, her clothes cut away, wriggling and struggling whilst nurses attempted to control her flailing limbs. Blood had spread everywhere, all over the floor and smattering the loose coverings over her legs. The anaesthetist seemed to be poking a tube into the distorted mess of her face, clearly unsuccessfully.

Across from this scene Andy noticed a second trolley, this time supporting another figure, with drip bag up and running and ambu mask applied to his (his?) face. What immediately struck Andy though, was the mess of legs poking below the blanket with clearly visible bones protruding through torn flesh.

'What on earth—?'

He quickly crossed to the female; clearly a female, with long dark hair matted with blood, fanning out from the bizarrely deformed face. He immediately recognised the tell-tale features of a major facial injury: the panda eyes, bulging, already the peri-orbital tissues swollen and discoloured as retro-bulbar bleeding distorted the tissues.

The face appeared grotesquely elongated, with the lower jaw, gagged open; the mouth spewing forth a mix of blood and spittle. The patient was obviously struggling to breathe whilst the gurgling sound on expiration betrayed a mouth and throat filling with blood. This woman was drowning in her own body fluids. But why couldn't the anaesthetist get his endotracheal tube in?

'Right, clear the head, let's get a look.' Andy took charge, noting that the A and E consultant had at least got a line in, with plasma and saline flowing, whilst his registrar, (*well done*, he thought), had secured a venflon. Andy palpated the patient's face, felt around the back of her neck and quickly and expertly flitted around the lower jaw, satisfying himself that the mandible at least didn't appear to be fractured.

He swept the mouth with two fingers, much to the obvious distress of the patient and pulled out blood clot, but no foreign body other than sharp fragments of shattered teeth. What he did see, however, was that whatever impact had occurred had rammed her middle facial skeleton down the inclined plane of the base of the skull and effectively cut off her airway.

His first thought was that this patient would need a trachy in order to preserve the airway, but he was also aware of the ongoing complications this action may have further down the line. He then noted, with alarm, the train tracks of blood mixed with a central stream of clear fluid that suggested a CSF leak. God, this was serious. Working around the eye sockets he felt the grating together of bone fragments beneath the soft tissue—'look San, this is crepitus. Get up here!'

As he worked Andy pointed out the classical signs of a Le Fort 3/4 fracture of the middle third of the facial skeleton. Finding himself teaching as he went along, he described the shattered bones as 'God's crash zone-protecting the base of skull and brain from the impact.'

He then hooked his right fore and middle fingers into the mouth and behind the palate, simultaneously bracing the patients forehead with his left hand. The patient's hands clawed at Andy's wrists. 'I'm going to try to disimpact.' Then with a sharp tug, the whole face appeared to come into focus accompanied by a scrunching, squelching sound. A shroud-like image passed across the rearranged features.

'Right,' Andy looked across to the anaesthetist, 'see if you can get a nasal tube in-fast! The tube will stabilise the airway when I let go. Then get her asleep-quickly!' He called across to a nurse, 'get morphine,' to another, 'suction-now-over here.'

The anaesthetist by now had better access and though the patient was still struggling, he managed to secure the airway and started passing Nitrous oxide. The mouth was cleared as far as possible with suction, but Andy noted fresh blood still rising from the back of the throat.

'Christ!' Andy muttered again, thoughts racing through his mind. 'Have we secured her neck?' he shouted to no one in particular. Still, given the balance of risk, he needed to sort the bleeding, pronto.

'You,' he indicated to the anaesthetist, 'brace her neck and head and you two'—to the nurses, 'brace her shoulders. On the count of three we turn her on her side-towards me, all at the same time. One movement. OK?—1—2—3—'

As the patient rolled over, blood spilling onto Andy's brogues, the Airtex blanket protecting some semblance of modesty fell away, exposing the hip and thigh and the top of the white lace panty. Andy glanced and then his blood froze, ice in his veins, the hairs on his neck leaping to attention. He stood, gaping. His eyes saw, but his brain failed to compute. He braced himself against the side of the trolley, feeling his legs give way beneath him.

'Christ,' he said again, 'it can't be—must be some mistake—'

For a moment everyone stopped what they had been doing, clearly disturbed by Andy's shocked face, head turning in disbelief.

'Andy, Mr Saunders—what's up?' San called out.

'I can't believe it—it can't be,' he whispered. Then, shouted, 'someone— please, get Stuart up here, now! I can't carry on here—' With that he stumbled backwards, lent against the wall, his hands held against his face, barely masking the retching sobs that emerged. San came across, placed his hand on his boss's shoulder.

'Andy, what is it?'

'It's Isabel—my wife. For God's sake—Isabel!' He cried out and slid slowly, sack-like, down the wall, his head on his knees, sobbing. Everyone looked across to the now quiet, anaesthetised patient, her thigh clearly visible and, also clearly visible, a distinctive, electric blue outline of a butterfly tattoo.

******

Stuart arrived in A+ E, scarcely believing what the duty sister had told him. Immediately he crossed to Andy, bent and placed his hand on his colleague's shoulder. 'Are you absolutely certain?' he asked him. Between gasping sobs, Andy told him he knew that, as he had disimpacted the middle third, he somehow recognised the face, that what came into focus was the image of—scarcely believable this—his own wife. The glimpse of white knickers he had watched his wife pull on that very morning above the tattoo, the clincher.

'Yes, it's definitely her—Isabel.' Andy collected himself sufficiently to look up at his colleague and said, 'look, Stu, do your best, please help her. I'll leave her in your hands now. Look after her for me.' Sister took his hand and escorted the stricken surgeon back to outpatients, where relieving him of his bleep, she explained what had happened to his secretary. She called for a car to take Andy home while the receptionist explained to the few remaining patients that the appointments would be rescheduled ASAP.

Andy sat in his consulting room, attempting to collect himself whilst outside sister informed his secretary of the unfolding events. The two victims of the RTA had been brought in off the junction of the M6 with the M54 where it appeared the car involved had driven at high speed into the rear of a queue.

The male driver had clearly rammed on the brakes and the force of the collision had caused severe compound, comminuted fractures of both lower legs, whilst the female passenger had been struck mid-face by a malfunctioning, exploding airbag. They both needed cutting from the wreckage. Sister went on to explain the events leading up to the horrific denouement. They both glanced anxiously into the clinic, where they could see Andy, mobile in hand, shaking.

Sister approached him, placing her hand on his shoulder. 'What is it, Andy? Can I help?'

Apparently, he had been trying to contact Heidi, in order to ask her to collect the children from school. His nanny, however, was not answering.

Andy's secretary took over and managed to contact one of the parents to ask them if they would mind looking after the girls; an impromptu sleep-over. She informed her that Mr Saunders's wife had been involved in an accident but didn't elucidate further. The taxi arrived and took him home, leaving the two women shaking their heads.

Once home, all Andy could do was to go straight to the drinks cabinet-a hefty malt might settle him a little. With drink in hand, he tried to recall the awful events as they had unfolded. Tried to think if he could have done anything differently. He paced up and down the kitchen, unable to settle. Eventually, the phone rang. Stuart.

'Andy. I think I have some good news. I've stabilised the middle third with two intra-oral zygoma plates and placed two silastic grafts in the orbital floors. Both orbits had avulsed into the sinuses, but I'm pretty sure her eyes are going to be fine. Two lateral brow fronto-zygomatic plates have also gone in. The haemorrhage stabilised fairly quickly once the maxilla was back in place. As far as the CSF leak is concerned, I've bagged her up with broad spectrums and Flagyl-I'm also certain that will sort itself out. No other signs of brain stem injury. She is sedated and up on ITU. As for the other bloke—'

'Other bloke?' Andy interrupted.

'Yeah, the driver. He's in a right mess.'

'Hang on,' Andy went on. 'Was that the chap I saw in resus, pretty bad leg injuries as far as I could tell?'

'Yes, Andy, apparently he was driving.'

'Are you sure?'

'Yes, absolutely. The police escort described cutting them both out of the wreckage—a bad smash apparently.'

'But, a bloke, in the same car?' Andy repeated himself. 'She had gone down to Birmingham airport to pick up her friend, Lisbeth, a female.'

'Well, I'm not sure about that of course,' continued Stuart. 'But he's got pretty nasty injuries to both legs-been transferred to the orthopods.'

Andy stood bemused, unable to think of what to say. To fill the pause, Stuart went on. 'Now, Andy, take as much time as you need. I'll take over the on-call and sort out the clinics and lists for the foreseeable. I see no reason why Isabel shouldn't make a full recovery. She's in good hands and I will take a personal interest in her follow-up. Give me a call if you have any questions. Meanwhile, get some rest. Are the girls OK?'

Andy told him he had got arrangements in place, thanked his friend and returned to the drinks cabinet. All he could think as he gulped down the warmth of the spirit, hoping it might somehow anaesthetise him, was 'what the hell was Isabel doing in a bloody car with a bloke?' The paramedic's description of the wrecked vehicle had been sufficient to dismiss the idea that this was somehow a casual meeting; a taxi, for instance.

Andy woke having taken antihistamine and the best part of a bottle of malt. He awoke as in a dream, surfacing through the muddy water of drugs and alcohol. He broke surface, damp with sweat. He realised, again with a tremor running through him that in fact, it had not been some unimaginable horror unreeling in images written in gore and panic and shouts, but absolute reality.

He had attempted, successfully—the Lord be praised—to resuscitate his wife following an horrific RTA. She was (yes, it was true) now in ITU. He sat up, reached for a glass of water before the next wave of realisation hit his befuddled frontal cortex; she had been with another man. Who? Who could possibly be driving his wife on the M6? Wasn't she supposed to be with her friend? What had happened to Lisbeth?

He stumbled to the kitchen, flicked on the coffee machine and as the caffeine arrowed through his palate, another, even worse possibility crowded in, could Isabel be having an affair? Surely, not. But then, hadn't he himself broken the marital vows? Why was he so bloody special?

'Right,' he said to himself. 'First things first-I must go and see Isabel. Shower first, then call Heidi to sort out the kids.'

Strange he hadn't seen Heidi-where the hell was she? Questions, questions, but no bloody answers. So, swallowing two Ibuprofens he took his coffee upstairs to the shower. Feeling only a little more human, he dressed in shirt and slacks and crossed to Heidi's accommodation. He knocked on the door. No answer. Where the hell was she?

He called her mobile—no answer. This is nuts, he thought. Think, think! He called the house where the girls were staying and, barely comprehending his own words, he explained that his wife—Isabel—yes—had been involved in an accident and was now in ITU. Could she please take the girls to school, but please don't mention the accident. He would speak to them later.

This done, he left for the hospital and made his way to ITU. How strange it seemed to be treading these familiar, sterile corridors, not as a confidante, an insider, but as a stranger almost; barely able to believe that he was now a relative, a victim, an onlooker.

Waving his lanyard, he swung through the doors, dabbed his hands in spirit gel and entered the space where machines were God, where the only conversation to be heard were the bleeps and sighs of life-support apparatus. The staff nurse, recognising him immediately rushed up to him, needlessly asking him for his calm, his professionalism. She explained that Isabel was 'out of the woods,' but still sedated and intubated.

'Can I speak to Sister—now?' demanded Andy. Expecting this intervention, the nurse tried to reassure him.

'On the ward round this morning, Mr Hodgkins decided to attempt to extubate, withdraw sedation and hopefully transfer her to the wards. He particularly asked that you,' she paused, 'tried not to disturb her at this stage.'

'Can I see her?' Andy was not going to be fobbed off.

He approached the bed to see his once-beautiful wife lying, surrounded by tubes and drips, an airway taped to her bruised and battered face, dried blood still sticking to her hair and neck and beneath her fingernails—betraying her earlier struggles. Her eyes were blackened, bulbous, unrecognisable panda-eyes, thankfully taped closed with micropore. Andy placed his hand on hers and whispered, 'my poor, poor darling,' before bending to plant a soft kiss on her forehead.

Staff nurse dissuaded him from examining the charts and notes and he allowed himself to be led away. Once outside he tried to collect his thoughts. His instinct persuaded him to go straight to his clinic and seek out Stuart and quiz him. But then his other, doctor instinct, supervened and he convinced himself that the professional thing was to leave the place and let the clinical routine unfold.

After all, he knew, a) there was nothing he could do for his wife and b) she was in excellent hands. He decided then to go home, sort the house and kids, locate Heidi's whereabouts and start trying to find out the circumstances of the accident. Find out who the unknown male might be. He would make a 'phone call to the police his priority.

The police were not helpful. It had been a high-speed collision, the vehicle being unable to halt its progress sufficiently to stop it from careering into the back of a tailback. The car hit had been a Range Rover and therefore pretty much unaffected. Yes, the police had tried to question the driver, but he was currently sedated and orthopaedics had no intention of letting them anywhere near their patient.

Back at home Andy still could not contact Heidi. He decided to phone his SHO. She, after all, may know where her sister had gone. To his surprise, Bernadine seemed deeply upset by the unfolding events and asked Andy if there was anything she could do to help. He asked her about her sister's whereabouts.

Bernie had no idea and didn't seem overly concerned where she might be. His next thought was what to do about the girls. He felt in no fit state to manage them at the moment, so he put in a call asking their friend's mother if she could possibly look after the girls for another night. He would meet them from school the following evening and attempt to explain what had happened to their mother. Next, he rang his sister-in-law. Ben answered the phone.

'Hey, how are things, buddy? I heard all about your call-out after our lunch. Bad luck old chap.' Andy was in no mood for chit-chat and cut to the chase.

'Look, Ben. Isabel's been involved in a nasty accident. She's in hospital and I need to be there for her.'

'Bloody hell, how is she?' Ben wanted to know.

'She's not great to be honest-sustained facial injuries and is currently under sedation.'

'Christ, shall I get Alice to the phone? God, she'll be devastated—hang on.' Isabel's sister came to the phone and Andy repeated the news. After she had gathered herself Alice asked what she could do.

'Well, I need to be with her—I can't manage the girls and the bloody nanny has gone AWOL. Is there any chance you can come up for a few days? I need help—' Andy's eyes were brimming, still disbelieving. Alice heard, could sense the distress in his voice and told Andy she could be up later that same day. Ben would look after things at home. She told Andy to try to calm himself; she would get there as soon as possible.

'For God's sake Alice, drive carefully,' was all he could think to say at that particular moment. Relieved for the moment, he opened a bottle of red and used a full glass to swallow a couple of codeine. When Alice arrived later that evening she was only slightly surprised to find Andy distinctly under the weather. They both agreed that it would be pointless to visit Isabel that evening and so she made Andy some supper and settled into tidying up the house.

Chapter 13

His feet appeared to dance on the wave-rippled sand. Pale aquamarine reflected the sun's rays oh so beautifully. This water felt warm matching the breezes ruffling his hair. He turned to his beautiful wife, her ebony tresses dazzling as she gazed into his eyes. Together they pushed, playing, into the sparkling, crystal waves.

A rainbow of fish leapt from the water and spun around their heads, both of them mesmerised by the spectacle. Laughing, hand in hand they plunged deeper. Then the clear ozone air became tinged by the acrid odour of rusty nails as the water thickened around his ankles, his partner now gone, chasing the colours of the rainbow. What was this? His knees had to push through water which now turned red; thick, glutinous waves engulfed his body.

The churning, shear weight of the thick waves now threatened to overwhelm him; he fell, headlong into the bloody morass. Blood clots began to form in his nose, his mouth; he was gasping, drowning in blood! Headfirst now, he spun headlong into the blackening depths, spinning, turning, screaming, his lungs now congealed. At the apex of the crimson tunnel, he saw a face, Seb's face; he reached out his hand and his fingers touched his sons. But then, as before, he lost his grip and Seb was lost once again—

Heaving and panting, covered in sweat, Andy sat up amongst his tangled, damp bedclothes. His head pounded. His mouth suddenly dry. He swung his legs out of the bed, his scrambled thoughts rearranging themselves, as in a jigsaw. The hard truth emerged. He had resuscitated his severely injured wife and she now lay unconscious in a hospital bed.

Worse—no!—he rebuked himself, his jealous heart betraying his love. No, it could never be worse. BUT how had she been involved with the driver of the vehicle? Was she having an affair? Then the contrary thought; he rebuked himself. After all, it was me a few days ago. Why should I care? But my wife-mine! He stumbled to the kitchen, where Alice seemed startled at his dishevelled appearance.

'Bloody hell, Andy. You look rough.' This statement of the obvious did nothing to calm Andy. 'Here, have some coffee. I'm off to pick the girls up to take them to school. Postcode?'

Andy drank thirstily, gulping his coffee. He swallowed the proffered orange juice and attempted to rearrange his senses.

'Alice, thanks. I really can't begin to say how grateful I am. Can we sit with the girls this evening and I'll try to explain what's going on. I'll go into the hospital now-she's bound to be better overnight-find out how she is and see you back here with Lucy and Imogen. How's that?'

'Great. Give her my love if you can and explain that I will come and see her as soon as I'm allowed.' Then, as she turned to pick up her car keys, 'I'd get a shower and clean your teeth if I were you.' Emotions in turmoil, she half smiled as she left.

******

If anything, Isabel looked more grotesque that morning. Three days post-trauma the tissues had swollen to their maximum. The eyes bulged black from the bruised face; her hair still matted with old blood. Stuart had taken Andy to see her and they were both able to see beyond the natural processes of healing and thus concentrate on the main issue; Isabel was still leaking CSF.

Scans revealed that as the middle third had rammed upwards, the pituitary fossa had been fractured in the impact and the subarachnoid space just anterior to the promontory had been breached. Isabel's nostrils were packed in order to protect the leak and broad-spectrum antibiotics were running through the drip. Stuart wanted to withdraw sedation, wake her up, assess her cognitive state.

He asked Andy for his permission. This granted, he reassured his friend. 'OK, Andy. Leave it to me, go and wait in my office and I'll come down for a chat.' He laid his hand on Andy's shoulder, urging him gently away from his injured wife. Later, sitting in the office, Andy was surprised to hear a knock on his colleague's door.

'Who is it?'

To his surprise and chagrin, Bernadine walked in and immediately approached him and knelt by his chair.

'I am so, so sorry.' She gazed into his eyes. Her sweet breath alerted Andy's tired senses. He returned her gaze and softened his heart.

'I just don't know what to do-I feel powerless, hopeless,' he told her.

'From what I heard from San; you were heroic. You were wonderful in what you did for her. You cannot, must not punish yourself.' She laid a hand on Andy's and he did not rush to withdraw this. Stuart interrupted them to find his SHO kneeling by his colleagues' side. If this surprised him, he didn't let on.

'She's stirring now, Andy. I think you ought to come.'

As he stood to go, Bernie hung on to Andy's hand. 'If there is anything you need or just want to talk, please call me.' Then as an afterthought Andy asked her if she had heard anything from her sister.

'No—it is strange. I have left messages but so far she does not reply. But,' she paused, 'please try not to worry-she has done this kind of thing before, you can believe me.'

Back on the ward, the two doctors could see that Isabel had regained consciousness but appeared distressed. Her hands went to her forehead, she groaned.

'She is in pain, Andy.'

Stuart knew, as did Andy, that the CSF leak effectively decompressed the suspension mechanism keeping the brain buoyant and separate from contact with the skull. It was apparent that Isabel's brain, now unprotected and not cushioned as it should be, gave rise to a vicious headache.

'Look, Andy. She will need a spinal tap—I think it's best if we keep her sedated for a while longer.'

'Yes, of course, I understand—do whatever is necessary Stu.' Then, as though unable to suffer the proximity of his prostrate, wrecked wife he turned and left the hospital for home. Even the soothing tones of Bach failed to comfort him on this occasion. He drove as in a daze. His already damaged psyche had suffered another devastating blow.

Back in the familiar surroundings of home, the cruel absence of his wife impelled him to do something, anything to numb the pain. He would look for Isabel's computer. Perhaps he would find some clue to the nagging questions there.

In the study, however, a rectangle in the dust of the desk-top betrayed the machine's absence. Her computer had gone. He searched to no avail and feeling even more useless he retired to the drinks cabinet and poured a large whiskey.

By the time the girls came home, he was only slightly intoxicated but enough to put his sister-in-law on alert. She fussed around her nieces, settled them to do their homework and went to the kitchen to prepare supper.

'Look, Andy, d'you think this is the best way to deal with things? For heaven's sake, I don't know what to do with myself either, but these girls, they need you, they need you to be on the ball. They keep asking me about Isabel and I don't know what to say. I need you to be sober Andy. I need your help!' Thus chastened, he went upstairs for a shower and a clean shirt and came down to sit with his daughters.

'Look, Darlings. Your mum has had a bit of an accident. She's in hospital and our friends are looking after her. I promise you she will be OK, but in the meantime, Alice is going to look after you—'

'Is mummy going to be all right?' Lucy asked.

'Yes, of course. She's just being looked after while she recovers from a few bumps and bruises.'

'What happened, daddy?' Imogen asked.

'Mummy bumped her car on the motorway. She was wearing her seatbelt though and that means she will be OK, darling.'

'Can we see her?' Lucy perked up.

'Not just yet. But I promise as soon as she's better, we'll all go with Auntie, to see her. Look, why don't we buy her a little present at the weekend. How's that?'

This promise of a shopping exhibition in Shrewsbury seemed to cheer up the girls no end, so with perfunctory attempts at normal conversation, they sat and ate their supper. A treat of TV before bed encouraged the girls to submit to an early night and Alice and Andy found themselves alone.

'I just can't believe that Izzy was having an affair,' Alice stated by way of an introduction to the impending discussion. 'Surely, it must have been someone from the University?' she continued.

'The orthopods won't let the police anywhere near the bloke involved and Isabel is back under sedation—so no one knows what's going on.'

'Have you contacted the University?' Alice asked.

'I intend to do that tomorrow. Apart from anything else, her computer has gone missing. The Uni will not be thrilled about that. Isabel got into trouble recently because her work is so sensitive.'

'What was she working on?' Alice asked. 'She's never really told me much about her work.'

'She was developing a kind of vaccine—I hope I've got this right—yes, a vaccine utilising a patient's own stem cells in order to alert the body's immune system to act against tumour cells. She recently isolated an enzyme which allowed the cells to mature which gave her, potentially, more time to alter the cell's genetic material.'

'So, valuable information then if it could be shared with other interests?'

'Well, yes, I suppose so. But I can't see what that has to do with her accident.'

'Surely, a start would be to tell the police about the missing computer?'

'Probably, yes. That's not such a bad idea. But the other mystery is that Heidi—the new nanny—has disappeared off the face of the earth as well. *So that's where the computer has gone,* he thought to himself.

'She's German, isn't she? Alice asked, then, 'Not that that has to do with anything.'

'Yes. She was introduced to us by my SHO, Bernadine. Heidi was her stepsister and, even more worrying, is that she does not know where Heidi is either.'

'Look, Andy—it seems to me you have no option but to contact the police.' Alice glanced at the wine rack. 'D'you fancy a glass of wine—I know I do.' Then she paused. 'Perhaps I shouldn't be encouraging you.' Andy replied he didn't see what else he was bloody well supposed to do and took his sister-in-law's invitation up with alacrity.

The next morning, Andy met the orthopaedic consultant in charge of the unknown male.

'How is he?'

'In a bad way, actually. What appears to have happened is that he braced both legs against the chassis as he saw the collision coming up—probably a reflex braking action. Both legs were severely injured below the knee, comminuted, compound fractures. We've pinned both tibias and fibulas. To complicate things, both knees were dislocated. The right ankle will need to be virtually reconstructed. We're keeping him sedated for a short while, to ensure complete immobility.'

'So, what's next?' Andy's surgical mind took over.

'The major issue is to avoid infection, so he's on massive IV antibiotic doses, broad spectrum and anti-anaerobes. If the fractures become infected then it's amputation I'm afraid. How's Isabel?' By this time, Stuart had joined the discussion and could see Andy getting more and more agitated.

'Well, we've sedated her again. She was very restless, secondary to intracranial hypotension. We may have to operate to close the leak. I've—we've—asked the neurosurgeons for their advice.'

Reeling from the consequences of this update, Andy approached his car asking himself again and again, 'how could this have happened to my beautiful wife?' The never quite suppressed feelings of anger and guilt began to surface again. 'First Sebastien, now Isabel—what have I done to deserve this?'

He looked at the sky as he opened the door. Did he expect God to answer? Speeding down the A49 he decided to stop at the Ragleth arms and once there ordered a pint of Hobson's. He briefly explained to the startled innkeeper what had been going on.

This formality dealt with, he adjourned to the garden to think and attempt to sort out the morass of tangled thoughts plaguing his mind. Initially, of course, the cold, foaming beer did its work and for a few moments, he sat in the weak sun, thinking over the events that had led to this point in his life. At the bottom of the 2nd pint, the awful truth dawned on him that the only thing he had truly lost himself in recently was whilst he was making love to his young SHO.

******

Wishing to avoid a repeat of last night's nightmare Andy had taken the precaution of following his 5 pints of Hobson's, a bottle of Douro and a malt whiskey with 5 mg of diazepam, a drug recovered from his secret hoard of various NHS medications. It was then, the shattering noise of the 'phone ringing that woke him the next morning. For a while, the anaesthetic qualities of these various depressants numbed Andy's brain as he showered away his guilt, his smell, his horror, his sheer incomprehension of what was happening to him.

The caller was Stuart, informing him that a meeting had been called for 2:00 pm that day with the deputy chairman of the hospital trust and which would be attended by theatre sister and the registrar, Sandeep and of course by Stuart himself. No more information was forthcoming, so Andy was left to his own thoughts. His sister-in-law, having returned home from taking Lucy and Isabel to school, seemed unimpressed by Andy's appearance at 10:30 am.

'Scrambled eggs?' she asked, proffering him a glass of orange juice which was quickly dispatched. 'Look, Andy, this is no way to deal with this—'

'What else am I to do?' Andy seemed close to tears, unable to link coherent thoughts together.

'Think of the girls—they need you. Now, more than ever.'

At the mention of his daughters, the tears flowed and Alice crossed the room to hold him in her arms. She was very fond of Andy, admired his dedication to his work and loved him for his support for her sister and her career. She also well knew that he was a different being to her husband Ben, an avuncular, easy-going, happy chap, who loved his work and loved his life. She found Andy to be a more challenging, ambitious man. Despairing of fools but nevertheless a kind and considerate doctor.

'Andy, just try to have a few days off the booze—from what you say Isabel is being looked after. Use the opportunity to spend more time with the girls. Refocus, yeah?' She looked at his unshaven face and sat him down for breakfast. Learning of the planned meeting she advised him to smarten up.

'I hope you're going to have a shave. Remember who you are—a consultant oral and maxillofacial surgeon-stand up for yourself, be proud. Do it for Izzy.'

Thus buoyed, Andy attended the meeting, which, to his surprise, took place in the administration wing. Stuart looked unhappy to be there-he had better things to do. A prim, PR-type lady was 'chairing' the meeting, her grey hair combed back into a bun. Julie, the theatre sister looked uneasy-slightly flushed around the gills. Also present, an apparently reluctant attendee, San sat dressed in his white coat. Stuart opened the discussion by attempting to reassure his colleague that this, 'most definitely' was not a witch hunt. But the hospital had to investigate how it came to be that a senior clinician became involved in operating on his own wife.

'I didn't know it was my wife,' Andy said, stating the obvious.

'Yes, of course, Andy, we understand that but,' he looked awkwardly to his left. '—It's not just that. Concerns have also been raised about—' He coughed. '—how can I put this—the fact that you may have been operating whilst under the influence of alcohol.' At this, Julie dropped her gaze to the desk.

'Et Tu,' thought Andy. His cup rattled against the saucer as he lifted it to his lips. Noticing this Stuart continued,

'And look now, Andy, your hands are shaking. It distresses me to say this, but I don't think you're in a fit state to return to work.' He was interrupted by old Grey Bob.

'Several incidents have been brought to this hospital's attention, Mr Saunders. As you must realise, our foremost duty is to attend to patient safety.' At this, Andy dropped his cup with a clatter.

'Patient bloody safety! What the hell do you understand about patient safety? All you do is sit up here in your fancy offices, pontificating. You have no idea what it takes to deliver a service to your bloody patients.'

Stuart blushed, perhaps seeing his precious departmental funding disappearing in front of his eyes.

'God, Andy. Everyone here is concerned about your health, your sanity. What's the point in refusing to see what's going on here?' Grey Bob interrupted.

'Andy—Mr Saunders—we think it would be better for everyone concerned if you take a month of paid leave. This is not—not, I repeat, a suspension. It is merely advisory.'

'But,' Andy protested. 'Stuart here can't run the Department on his own. With the best will in the world, San here is not experienced enough to step up; sorry, San. And yes, where is our new S.R?'

'We have, how can I say, already taken the precaution of applying for a locum to step into—' a brief smile flitted across her thin lips, '—the breach, as it were.'

'So I don't get to explain, to defend myself?' Andy said.

'As I say,' answered sour-face, 'this is not a disciplinary matter. We are merely advising you to take a break-that is all.' At this point, San tentatively raised a hand.

'Can I say a few words?'

'Of course.'

'It's just that I was present at Mrs Saunders's resuscitation and that Mr Saunders' actions were exemplary. He was highly focused and professional. Without him, I think Mrs Saunders may have died and—' San continued, 'there was absolutely no way that Mr Saunders could have known that he was operating on his wife.' Sourpuss acknowledged this intervention, but nonetheless considered the decision to be final and the meeting was closed.

Andy stood, nodded thanks to his registrar, turned on his heels and left the room. The slam of the door reverberating around the room would be a suitable rebuke to those within, Andy pondered as he returned to his car.

Chapter 14

His soft, padding steps did not disturb the eerie silence of the empty corridors as Andy made his way through the hospital. Normally echoing with chatter, the clatter of trolleys and scurrying nurses and doctors, the silence merely emphasised the contrast between this inner world and the humdrum normality outside the walls. Alas, this apparent calm did not translate to peace of mind for Andy. Thoughts raced around his brain, only temporarily quietened by the benzodiazepines he now resorted to as a matter of course.

Returning home in turmoil last evening, he could scarcely believe that he had been, in effect, suspended. As usual, he had taken refuge in the glorious sanctity of alcohol. Spirits momentarily raised, he had taken up Bernie's offer of a phone call and confided in her. She shared Andy's indignation at the action taken by the hospital. 'Diese Idioten—they do not understand,' was her initial response. She then divulged that she had spent some hours at Isabel's bedside, holding her hand and just chatting to her unconscious form.

This revelation moved Andy to tears and he allowed himself to wallow in this beautiful girl's apparent compassion. He found himself able to ignore the roller-coaster nature of his emotions whenever he thought about her. After the call, he had indulged in private surrender to his overwhelming lust for this Bernadine and, thus spent, his guilty alter ego took charge, urging him to do something, anything to find out what had really happened to his wife.

Perhaps this confused state of mind led him to the current situation which found him stalking the familiar corridors, brief-case in hand, lanyard round his neck in case of challenge, making his determined way to the side-ward containing the driver of the crashed vehicle. Silently he let himself into the stultifying, septic space and took a while to accommodate to the darkness. Lights from the surrounding life-analysing machinery gave only faint illumination to the apparently sleeping figure.

Andy placed his briefcase on the side table and slowly removed the contents. He pulled a face mask over his ears-he needed to stay strictly incognito. He couldn't know that this man would instantly be able to identify him. A vial of flumazenil reflected the blinking lights and Andy took time to draw up five mls into a syringe. He then crossed to the cannula placed in the victim's back of hand, flipped open the giving portal and inserted the open end of the syringe.

Being careful to scrutinise the unconscious patient he started to gently depress the plunger. As he did so he noted the man's lower limbs, encased in bandages with ugly rods emerging from the betadine-stained holes in the flesh, each one connected to a tapestry of wires suspending the limbs from the overhead scaffolding. As the drug began to take effect, the man's eyelids fluttered and blinked awake. Andy, of course, knew that this would only temporarily reverse the sedation keeping this stranger unconscious. He had a small window in which to work. The drug had an immediate and startling effect.

'Mein Gott! Wo bin ich, der du bist?'

'Bloody hell, he's German,' muttered Andy. 'Sprich Englisch!'

The patient repeated his initial question, this time in faltering English. Andy continued, 'Look, I don't have much time. Don't talk unless I ask you a question. Do not waste time in protesting. I know you were driving the car that crashed and nearly killed my wife. What I want to know is what you were doing in that car. What you were doing with my wife.'

Andy ignored the fact that his question immediately identified him. He wasn't thinking clearly.

'Ich verstehe nicht.'

'Yes, you bloody well do understand, so shut up and listen. See this bag?' Andy indicated the bag of fluid dripping constantly into the tubing attached to the patient's arm. 'This stuff contains antibiotics—a lot of very powerful antibiotics in order to stop your leg wounds from becoming infected. If they do become infected you will either die of sepsis or you will need to have your legs amputated.'

'Mein Gott!' the stricken man repeated.

'Good. So you do understand.' Andy turned to the table and picked up another item-this time a fluid-filled IV bag. 'This bag contains saline—looks no different to the bag here,' Andy crossed to the left side of the bed. 'In just a few seconds I can replace the antibiotics with what is for you, useless saline and no one will know. You will soon be back to sleep and your legs, untreated, will quickly become infected. Now, quickly, you have no choice. What were you doing in that car with my wife?'

The German groaned.

'Quick, you have five minutes before you become unconscious again. If that happens, believe me, I will swap the bags.'

This reasoning appeared to impress the patient. He could not realise that Andy would never proceed with his threat, his instincts as a doctor still deeply engraved in his soul. He therefore continued:

'I am working in pharmaceuticals, in Frankfurt and I—how do you say—abgesprochen—colluded—with a colleague of Isabel—your wife. We need to find your wife's research. The password to her computer. Very crucial—important to us. Please, give me—wasser—water, please.'

'Christ, how does he know all this?' Andy thought to himself. Nonetheless, he continued.

'You'll get water when you've finished.'

'I replaced your wife's friend on her flight over here and met Isabel at the airport. She didn't want to come with me, so I-persuaded her-that it was for her own good. To take me to the University. To access the files—wasser, bitte—water.'

Andy crossed to the sink, filled a plastic tumbler and placed it on the man's lips.

'Ah, danke—vielen dank—'

'Was my wife's friend, Lisbeth, involved with you?'

'Nein, no, she was under—zwang—duress, as you say.' He was slowly closing his eyelids.

'Were you seeing, involved, with my wife?' Andy was desperate to know. The Germans' eyes closed. One drop of flumazenil left. Squeeze. The patient offered his eyes.

'Your wife? Nein, of course not. All I—we—wanted was her information, her Forschung—' Then a barely audible whisper. '—wo ist Hy—Heid—'and with that, he was gone.

Andy, leaving the antibiotic drip in situ, gathered his things and left the room.

******

'Andy, good morning. Stuart here. I have good news.'

Once again, Andy had been wakened from his drug-induced stupor by the clatter of the phone.

'Oh, hi. Morning. Good news?'

'Yes. The CSF leak has stopped and we are going to bring her out of sedation today. Would you like to be here?'

'Of course. Yes. Give me time to sort myself out. I'll be there ASAP.'

Andy went down to the kitchen and shared the good news with Alice. 'Can I see her—please?'

'Yeah, of course. Look—I'll call you, OK?' And with that he left the house, leaving Alice, not for the first time, thinking 'what the hell is going on?'

Isabel groaned. The bed back now raised allowed Stuart, Andy and the ward sister to better observe her. Clearly panicking at the fact that she couldn't open her mouth, the interdental wiring locking her teeth together, her hands clawed to her mouth. Andy gently restrained her arms, murmuring to her, attempting to inform her of her whereabouts, urging her not to panic.

'Darling, it's me. You've been in an accident, but you're OK and safe now. Try not to panic. We clamped your teeth shut for a while, but just try to lie still.'

Isabel's bloodshot eyes blinked through her blackened, swollen eyelids, searching for comprehension from side to side. Andy's clinical brain could not avoid assessing the injuries: those swollen eyes, the broken nose, the livid scarring of surgical incisions below the eyes. Almost worst of all, through the swollen, cracked lips, the stark absence of front teeth-lost in the impact—as his wife attempted to speak.

Balancing this initial assessment was the sure knowledge that these tissues would heal. The scars, expertly placed as they were in the folds of skin of the lower lids, would all but disappear. Andy would replace the teeth with implants. The lips would become full and lustrous once again—he tried to stifle his tears.

The only question nagging away at him now was how well the maxilla had reformed into the defining, supporting scaffold for what he knew and loved; the face. That indescribable, subtle alignment of eyes, nose, mouth and shadows in the skin that defined beauty. He knew that even a millimetre or two of misalignment in the facial skeleton would be cosmetically damaging.

Although Stuart had told him, reassured him, that he had reduced the nasal bridge satisfactorily, all it needed was a kink in the septal cartilage to forever alter the shape of the nose. All this, however, would only become apparent as the soft tissue swelling reduced. All Andy could do now was whisper reassurance in her ear and bend down to touch her parched lips with his.

'Sister, let's see if we can get some fluids per-oral ASAP—she must be thirsty—perhaps a wash down as well. See to her hair? Make her comfortable and we'll come back in an hour or so.' Stuart gave his instructions and gently tapped Andy's arm to pull him away from his wife. As they walked back to outpatients, Stuart asked Andy, 'how are things? I have to say, Andy, you look a little rough you know. Are you looking after yourself?' A stupid question which Andy declined to answer.

'Look, Stuart, I'm taking this time off to take a trip. I need to get away for a few days. Alice, my sister-in-law, is looking after things at home and she will want to be close to Izzy anyway. So would you liaise with her? I'll stick around for today and probably travel tomorrow, once Izzy is more with it.'

'Where are you going?' Stewart frowned, surprised to say the very least.

'Ah—just abroad for a few days. I have some business to attend to. Personal stuff you know?'

A raised eyebrow indicated that no, he didn't know, but Stuart decided to leave it at that only adding, 'You know, Andy, you have to use this time to really sort yourself out. It looks as though Isabel is going to be OK, so you need to be fit and well. You're too good, we need you here, in this department, firing on all cylinders. Don't give management any more excuses to bugger us around.' He looked at his friend. 'Andy, please, are you listening? We need you.'

Andy nodded and went to find Bernadine. Andy sat with his SHO in the canteen, trying hard to maintain a professional distance. Why did she have to look so bloody lovely, smell so nice and in a white hospital coat for God's sake?

'Bernadine—I need to ask you for a favour. Would you please try to contact your sister. I need to know where she is, whether or not she intends to return to work. I can't ask my sister-in-law to look after the girls ad infinitum.'

'Ya! I will try—but—'

'But?' answered Andy.

'As I said, she has done this kind of thing before—disappears—then turns up again with no explanation. But I will try.'

'Thanks.' He resisted the temptation to reach across the table and touch her hand, bejewelled as they were by pink nail varnish. 'I thought you weren't meant to wear nail varnish on duty.' He half smiled. Bernie smiled back.

'Well, I don't always get to have coffee with you, do I?' Then, remembering herself, 'how is your wife?'

Andy brought her up to speed with progress, then asked her, 'would you mind keeping an eye on her for me? I'm going away for a few days.' This evidently surprised Bernadine.

'Away? Where?'

Andy toyed with the idea of telling her his plans, but, thinking better of it, replied, 'Just nipping over to a conference in—er—Rome. Taking the opportunity to catch up with some science while I'm on forced holiday!' He smiled, then before getting up, he gave in to the temptation and passed his fingers over Bernie's in a fleeting embrace.

Back at home, Andy went to the study and opened some drawers and found Isabel's address book. Great. He jotted down Lisbeth's address, place of work and phone number. Next, he booked a flight for the next day out of Birmingham to Frankfurt, returning the next day. Satisfied, he filled himself a glass of wine before remembering he needed to go back to check on Izzy later. He rationed himself to the one glass and went to his room to plan his strategy.

'How is she, Sister?' Andy asked, now back on the ward again that evening. He had brought Alice and the two girls along, hoping that they would be able to see Isabel. No matter how she looked, he had bargained that speaking to their mother may allay some of his daughter's anxieties. Sister reported that Isabel had been complaining bitterly of a headache earlier and had asked for the lights above her bed to be dimmed.

'Understandable,' replied Andy. 'Intracranial hypotension following a CSF leak will cause photosensitivity and acute migrainous headache.' Slipping back into his accustomed role, he asked, 'what have you given her?'

'Well, she's taken fluids and we are running some dihydrocodeine through the drip for 24 hours to see how she responds. Otherwise, she is sitting up. I'll leave you two to it—'

Andy approached the bed and placed his hand on his wife's. Her eyes flicked open and a half smile flickered across her battered features.

'Oh, darling!' Andy said, tears once again prickling his eyes.

'Oh, Andy,' she whispered between her closed teeth. 'What happened to me? Why am I here?'

'You were in a car accident—'

'Oh no! Are the girls OK?'

'Yes, yes. The girls, me—we weren't involved.' Isabel clearly had no recall of the incident.

'Where are they now—the girls?'

'I wanted to make sure that you were up to seeing them. Alice is here as well—desperate to see you.'

'I don't want to upset them—how do I look?'

'I've explained to them what happened. I've told them that facial injuries always look much worse than they really are. Shall I get them?' Isabel gave a scarcely detectable nod.

'Sister,' Andy asked as he left the ward. 'Is it OK if I bring the girls in—and Izzy's sister?'

'As it's you—' she smiled and Andy went to the family room. The girls looked up anxiously.

'How is she, daddy? Can we see her?'

Andy took time to tell them, to warn them, how their mother's appearance might alarm, but to say nothing, just smile and try to be as normal as possible. The little group advanced on the bed, where Isabel turned towards them. Tears leaked from the mess of her eyes.

'Oh, oh—my girls,' she murmured.

'Mummy, oh mummy.' The girls stood gazing at the apparition.

Alice interrupted, 'Oh, my lovely Izzy. How good to see you.' Slowly the atmosphere lightened as the small family re-acquainted themselves.

Andy stood, slightly distanced, determined to find out why and how this had happened.

Chapter 15

Not feeling in a particularly holiday mood, Andy nonetheless went through customs collecting some essentials for his trip: a bottle of Glenfiddich, some aftershave and a new shirt. Once aboard the two-hour flight to Frankfurt, he settled into a couple of G and T's and read up on big Pharma. Released from the trappings of his professional life and corresponding relative introspection, he could start to understand the politics underpinning his wife's academic work.

International drug companies, already mega-rich, were always on the lookout for any recent development, new drug, new technique that could be harnessed for financial gain. The possibly unobtainable search for a cure for cancer remained, of course, the Holy Grail. What consistently perplexed researchers concerned the ever-evolving nature of the disease itself. Cancer was in fact an umbrella term that related to the shape or form of the first observed tumours; the crab-like, friable tentacles of rapidly reproducing cells emanating from the central body of the tumour.

The triggers that started this uncontrolled growth were varied and many; the original nature of the parent-cell affecting the tumours behaviour, thus determining the likely course of the disease. Then there were the different cell-types themselves that dictated tumour behaviour-skin cells, brain cells or the slow-growing cells of low-grade prostate tumours for example. Then the site of the initial proliferation was important: was it visible and therefore easier to treat early in the disease process? Or hidden in some deep organ such as the pancreas? Research had highlighted the genetic factors which often lay behind cancers, but the link between this knowledge and a potential cure was evasive, to say the least.

Traditionally, 'cures' for cancer, in all its disguises and manifestations remained brutal. Surgical excision with all the collateral damage to the affected organ that entailed, then the carpet-bombing of radiotherapy, not only killing the tumour but also the healthy tissues and cells the death rays pass through. Not to mention the fact that the radiation altered the genetic material of these formally healthy cells so that they themselves became more liable to undergo mutation.

Then the appalling strategy of slowly passing poison into a patient's body so that not only the cancer cells were killed but also any other actively dividing cell, so that the toll of chemotherapy upon its recipients often caused more illness than the disease itself. Scientists and pharmacologists and doctors all realised that these barbaric therapies would rightly be regarded as such in the future, but meanwhile, these strategies were all that were available. The search, therefore, was well and truly on.

Andy realised that his wife had inadvertently, innocently stumbled in on this underbelly of science, purely over the obstacle of her own naïve belief in the purity of scientific endeavour, the sanctity of research. Her professors, however, had not been quite so ingenue: had realised the commercial potential inherent in cell research and had accordingly bought shares in Endimmune UK.

Aware of this subtle shift into the politics of big Pharma, they had come down hard when Isabel was thought to have breached the strict security cordon they had placed around the University. Big business was here to stay. The communication between his wife and her friend/colleague on her home laptop and the various phone calls had initiated this crisis and Andy fully intended to get to the bottom of it.

Frankfurt was not to Andy's liking: the sterile glass and concrete skyscape did nothing to placate his unease, as he settled into the omni-decor of his hotel. The same dreary mass-produced decorations and so-called wall art depressed him; the views offering none of the spiritual uplift of his beloved Shropshire hills. He decided, therefore, to start his quest immediately. It was only just past lunch, so he rang the number he had found in his wife's notebook.

'Gute Aben—yes, am I speaking to Miss Wagner?'

'Oh yah.' came the reply. 'Mit wem spreche ich, bitte?'

'Andy Saunders, Isabel's husband. Let's speak English, shall we?' A moment's pause.

'From where are you speaking?' Her English was German direct.

'I'm here, in Frankfurt,' Andy replied.

'Can I ask why? Is Isabel with you?'

'No, she isn't. There is a very good reason for that. I don't wish to discuss this on the phone. Can we arrange to meet—please?'

'How do I know it is who you say you are?'

'I will send you details, a photocard, a picture of Isabel that only I could possess. Can we meet in a place of your choosing—yes?' Silence. Andy continued. 'Look, this is very important. Your friend, my wife, has been hurt, seriously, in a car accident. You are the last person she spoke to. I really need to talk to you-please.'

Lisbeth relented. She said she would text details to his mobile. Would he let her know his number? With that, she brought the conversation to an end.

Having achieved this early result, Andy decided to relieve the tedium of his accommodation and went in search of food and some release in this place, armed with a city map and his wallet. Predictably he woke the next morning with his customary throbbing head and limited recall of the night before. As disparate details involving a music bar, copious drinks and a stumbling walk back to the hotel filtered through to consciousness, he took a shower, put on his new shirt, jacket and slacks, shuffled his feet into boat shoes and went down to breakfast.

Following this he rang Alice, then Stuart and was delighted to learn that Isabel was now sitting up and taking semi-solid food through the gap in her teeth. The girls had been in to see her before school. Thus reassured, he ventured out into the glass desert that was downtown Frankfurt and made his way to the pre-arranged meeting place.

Lisbeth was waiting. She stood as Andy approached, recognising him both from the photocard and pictures she possessed of him alongside her friend. She seemed jumpy, nervous.

'Guten morgen, Mr Saunders-Andy. Wie geht es dir, Ah! Silly question, you must be distraught about Isabel.'

'Yes, of course, it's awful, but she is recovering. Thank you.' Andy sat down and ordered coffee.

'What happened?' Lisbeth asked.

'That is what I am here for, to find out. You, as I said earlier, were the last person she spoke with. She was in some trouble at the University.'

'Trouble—what sort of trouble?' Lisbeth replied.

'Apparently, she was in communication with you about highly protected information.'

'Yes. We have been discussing her research. She had achieved great results. We were simply exchanging ideas in order to advance to the next stage. But—'

'But?'

Lisbeth looked down, her cheeks reddening. 'It began to get complicated.'

91

'Complicated?' Andy was repeating himself. 'In what way, complicated?'

'There are people who would love to get their hands on these results—' Lisbeth looked around, apparently anxious.

'What people?' Andy was getting agitated.

'People in the pharmaceutical industry—I have been subject to—some pressure.' She looked around again. 'A gentleman who wanted to know about my research visited me. He told me he worked for a company called CellProcure.'

'What sort of pressure?'

'I had, how do you say—affaire—affair, yes, with a prominent professor at the University. He is married, with children, very secret. This man had details. Records, photos of us meeting. It would destroy the professor's reputation if it became public news. He threatened me.'

'What has this got to do with my wife?'

'This man, somehow—' Lisbeth bowed her head, tears glistened on her cheeks. 'He had interrupted our calls. He knew about the enzyme and the link to continuous cell lines—how this would enable Isabel and me to bundelm sie unsere Resourcen—'

'What?'

'How would you say?—pool our resources—, so that a vaccine could be developed to cure some, perhaps many, forms of cancer.' Lisbeth struggled on, dabbing her cheeks. 'Somehow, he accessed Isabel's laptop with the information we had discussed on the phone—'

'Isabel's laptop—in England? This makes no sense at all Lisbeth. What can you mean?'

'Ja, das ist so. He had knowledge of Isabel's work. He wanted me to access the information. He guessed what information the computer contained but needed to understand it. I told him; I did not know how to access—what passwort-anything—' She turned away and looked desperate. 'I feel I have let my friend down; what happened would, could not have happened without me.' She broke down, sobbing.

Andy looked round, himself embarrassed now. They looked like a couple, rowing. 'Look, Lisbeth, please try not to get too upset. We both have Isabel's interests at heart.'

'Ja, das ist so—of course.'

'But how could this-man-how could he possibly know about my wife's computer?'

'This is where it gets so difficult to understand. This man, he has a daughter, two daughters, working in England. He told me—' She paused. '—told me—Oh, meine Gott. I can't believe it—it is my fault—I didn't tell Izzy—if I had only told her. I thought I could deal with things, myself, here in Germany, but—' She broke down, sobbing uncontrollably. As was becoming his wont, Andy pushed his hand across the table and laid it on Lisbeth's arm. 'Please, please—try to tell me all you know. Just tell me Lisbeth—please.'

She appeared to try, pulled her arm away and sat up, took a few deep breaths. 'Please forgive me, Andy, but one girl, this man's daughter, was called Heidi and—'

'Heidi?' Andy could barely believe what he was hearing.

'Ja, Heidi, the girl who was your nanny. It was she who spied on Izzy.'

'Why, why on earth didn't you tell us?'

'It was too late. Izzy rang me to arrange for me to come to the UK and I thought that I could escape for a while, perhaps explain all when I got to England, to your home.'

'So, why didn't you come?' Andy was keeping or trying to at least, keep his cool.'

'This man showed me the document he was going to send to the University—it contained awful, intimate photographs of me with my lover. He told me, persuaded me, that he would take my seat on the plane to Birmingham. He told me, under no circumstances to call the UK. He seemed to have access to phone lines. He had all the answers.'

'Why the hell didn't you tell him to fuck off?' Andy was seething.

'I knew that once these pictures, this evidence reached the University, it would be the end of the professor's career, his marriage and mine also. All the years of research, work, my career, would all be over.'

'For God's sake, Lisbeth, everyone has affairs, we live in enlightened times.'

'You don't understand, Andy. Here in Germany, things are more-how would you say—hierarchical. This man, my professor, is a religious man. His work, his life, his marriage are wound up in his beliefs. If ever it became known that he was an Ehebrecher—marriage breaker—adulterer you would say-his career would be over and mine too. Sorry, Andy, so sorry. I have been weak. And now my friend, your wife, is in hospital. It is all my fault,—I am so sorry—' She broke down again.

'So why did this—this man—want to come to the UK?' Andy realised the question was rhetorical. As the picture, the little dots, all started to connect he jumped, suddenly realised and mouthed, sotto voce—'If Heidi was this man's daughter, then the sister, the other sister, can only be—' His brain struggled to state the obvious. 'No, it can't be. It's Bernadine, my SHO!' Then, creeping behind like a shadow, the unbearable, unthinkable reality: he had made love to a conspirator.

Reeling from this interview, Andy returned to the hotel and visited the mini-bar, took a Co-codamol and a Valium, 5 mg. He took a while to collect himself, to sift through what had been said. He determined to pay a visit to CellProcure. He found the vast glass complex with the help of Google maps and entered the vestibule. He introduced himself to the receptionist.

'Sprechen sie Englische?'

Ja, Gute Morgen. How can I help?'

'My name is Mr Andrew Saunders, visiting surgeon from England.'

'Ah, das ist gute—do you have an appointment?'

'No, no—but I do have an introduction via a researcher who works at the university, a Lisbeth Wagner.' Andy produced his card. The receptionist regarded this for a while, then picked up a phone and tapped in a number.

'Ja, Ja—das ist richtig—Mr Saunders—surgeon.' A pause. 'Ja—Lisbeth Wagner.' Then to Andy. 'If you are prepared to wait a short while, Herr Gunter, Direktor, will see you shortly.'

'Vielen dank.'

Andy stationed himself on the plush sofa and took in the grandiosity of his surroundings. How far removed from an NHS hospital was his first thought, followed by its corollary; this is where the money is. He contemplated contacting Bernadine but thought better of it-he would save that particular pleasure 'til later. Sitting there in the sun slanting through the cathedral-like glass, his head began to sink slowly forward; surely 40 winks wouldn't hurt. He was startled awake by the receptionist calling his name.

'Please, Mr Saunders. Take the lift.' She indicated over her right shoulder. 'Vierter stock—fifth floor. Herr Direktor will meet you.'

'Vielen dank.'

Five seconds later the doors swished open and it surprised him to be met by a short, red-headed individual, dressed in open-neck shirt and slacks. Not at all what he expected. He noticed that obvious wealth had lent this man an air of solidity. A man loved by his mother.

'Herr Saunders. Willkommen.' He extended his right hand.

'Ah, yes. Danke. Can we—do you—er speak English?'

A chuckle, 'Yes, yes, of course. Please come through.'

He led Andy into a vast office space, all glass, luxuriously air-conditioned. A panoramic view of the corrugated Frankfurt skyline offered itself. A single, vast table occupied the centre ground. Expensive-looking leather office furniture placed around. The director opened the conversation.

'So what is it I can do for you?'

Andy, slightly nonplussed by the effusive welcome and instant contact to the higher echelons of the establishment, wondered how to approach this; head-on seemed the best-perhaps the only option.

'It has come to my notice that a member of your staff has contacted a friend of mine, a researcher in cell biology in, how can I put this?—in what can only be described as unfortunate circumstances.' No reply. Tented fingers framed the Director's still-smiling face. Andy continued. 'This researcher—Lisbeth Wagner—is, I repeat, a friend and colleague of my wife, also a cell biologist, back in the UK' Silence. A smile persisting. 'This lady, Lisbeth, has been approached by this same person. He claims to be employed in your, in this organisation.' The fingers gently opened and closed in a tapping motion.

'Go on.'

'This, ahem, this gentleman has put pressure on Ms Wagner and via her, on my wife with the purpose of obtaining details of their research.' A silence resonated through the glass atrium. Andy pressed on, 'it would appear that this, this gentleman has been able to put his hands on my wife's computer.'

'Your wife's computer? In the UK?' The director burst into life. 'How can this be?'

'Your employee placed his daughter in the UK—in my employ and she was able to access my wife's work.'

Herr Gunter rocked back in his expensive chair. 'Ah, now, Mr Saunders. Now we are entering the grounds of fantasy—nein?'

'I can assure you, Herr Gunter, that this is not fantasy. My wife is, as we speak, seriously injured in a hospital bed.'

'So, now you suggest that this mysterious gentleman is responsible for this?'

'I think, yes, the answer to that question is most definitely yes.'

'How can you say this?'

'Because this same gentleman is currently lying in that same hospital, in the UK, also seriously injured.'

At this, the director leaned forward, lifted his handset and muttered a few words in German. The phone clunked back on its cradle.

'I have made enquiries. In the meantime I must inform you—that, as I am sure you are aware, these allegations are very serious.'

'They are indeed,' agreed Andy. 'But so is my wife's condition, not to speak of Lisbeth Wagner, who is very badly affected by all this.' The phone buzzed.

'Ja, Ja. Vielen Danke.' Then to Andy. 'It seems that—what can I say? A certain—peripheral—' a moment's thought. 'Yes, an employee, we are aware of him. It would seem that he has been absent from work now for some days. We have not been able to contact him.' He resumed the church steeple pose. 'Can I ask you, Herr Saunders, what it is that you intend to do with this—this information?'

'At the very least, I would want to know if a major international pharmaceutical company was aware that an employee of theirs was actively intimidating, yes, attempting to blackmail scientists-researchers-going about their legitimate business. I'd have thought that reputations are at stake. At least the investigating authorities should be made aware.'

The smile vanished. The formerly kindly eyes took on a glassy stare, reflecting the filtered light through the windows. The fingers dropped to the table and met in a white-knuckled fist.

'I repeat, Herr Saunders. These allegations you make are very, very serious indeed. Here you are, a guest in my office, at my company, in my country, accusing me indirectly of blackmail. May I give you a warning?' The smile flicked into life and died just as quickly. 'Some advice if you like. Be very, very careful as to what you do with this accusation—this information, as you put it.'

An image of Isabel's shattered face flashed through Andy's frontal cortex. He stood to his feet.

'I will remind you, Herr Direktor, that I am a UK citizen on legitimate business and with legitimate concerns. I can assure you that I will not be bullied by you or your employees. Thank you for your time. Auf Wiedersehen!' As Andy turned to leave the office, he was astounded and shocked, to see the

Director leap to his feet and in a few short strides block his path to the office door.

'You, sir, are dealing in things you know little about. I will repeat my warning—take care, Herr Saunders. I will only advise you to go straight to the airport and leave this matter to me. We will not be meeting again.' With that, he turned and those cold grey eyes bored into Andy's already mashed-up senses. He left the building, almost staggering down the wide, granite steps as he emerged, blinking into the afternoon sun.

Chapter 16

Stuart came onto the ward just as Isabel first sat up. After asking how she felt, he examined her, crisply professional, his hands skimming lightly over her healing bones. He urged her, gently, to look to the right then to the left, then upwards and downwards. The eyes seemed to function, even though the conjunctivae were reddened and the eyelids still puffed and bruised. She had attempted to leave the bed, but dizziness and nausea overtook her and she slumped back.

'Still early days, Isabel; the leak of CSF will affect your balance for a few days yet. But you really are making wonderful progress,' he told her.

Words squeezed from clamped teeth, Isabel said, 'Where is Andy—I want to see him.'

'Andy went abroad for a few days,' Stuart replied.

'Abroad? Why on earth would he want to go abroad?' She dribbled. Dabbed at her face.

'He mentioned something about attending a conference.'

'Ah yes, a conference, that must be it.' After a pause to swallow. 'Typical.'

Having completed the formalities, Stuart asked her if she wouldn't mind speaking to the police.

'They want to ask you about the accident. How it happened, who was with me?' Isabel's forehead attempted a frown.

'I can't remember. I can't seem to recall anything about the accident. All I know is—' she took another deep swallow-talking was difficult. '—that I was on the way to pick up my friend, Lisbeth, my colleague, from the airport—I can't remember anything else—'

'No worries. Look, loss of short-term memory is something, again, we can expect at this stage. I'll put the police off. Have some rest.'

Isabel's head dropped back to the pillows. She seemed relieved. 'Can I see the girls?'

'I believe your sister is bringing them to see you this afternoon, after school.'

Stuart left Isabel in peace, her eyes closing under the effect of her medication. He had other business to deal with. A prospective locum to interview. Then a clinic, now expanded by Andy's urgent appointments. There were two osteotomies awaiting work-up. He was a busy man and now all this. Head bowed, in contemplation, he didn't notice the SHO, apparently deep in conversation, animated on the office phone.

******

Andy, still shaken by his encounter, steadied himself with a stiff G+T once safe in his room. He took a Valium and considered his options. First, he would make a call to England.

'Bernie, hi—Andy here.'

'Ya, yes, hi—it's me. Andy—Mr Saunders, how are you? No one seems to know where you are.'

'I'm in Frankfurt.'

'Frankfurt? What are you doing in Frankfurt?'

'Look, Bernie. Listen, this is very difficult. I'll come straight to the point. Your sister appears to be caught up in a pretty nasty situation.' Silence. Andy went on, 'she apparently hacked, or help someone hack, my wife's computer. Now it appears she has stolen it from home.'

Much to Andy's surprise, this astonishing statement didn't appear to affect Bernie as much as he thought it might. A flicker of doubt.

'Oh dear, Heidi. As I have said, it is not the first time she has gone—how do you say? AWOL.'

'Why on earth in that case, didn't you tell us before we employed her?'

'She promised me she had dealt with matters—and I knew you were desperate for help at home.'

'But Bernie—for God's sake!'

'But what is that to do with you being in Germany?'

Andy thought hard. Should he tell her that the man lying, seriously injured, in the orthopaedic wards was actually her father? He didn't want Bernadine to race around the hospital causing even more chaos. Still, he had no choice.

'Bernie, listen. Heidi was under instructions, perhaps pressure, from her father who is involved in the pharmaceutical industry over here. I think—in fact, I know—it was this man, your father who was driving the car that crashed—'

Silence, again.

'Bernie? Are you OK?'

More silence, then a soft sigh—

'Mein Gott—I cannot believe this. He is the man who was with your wife?'

'It would appear so.'

Andy was beginning to regret having introduced this subject by phone.

'Andy, I have to tell you. Heidi is my stepsister. You know this. This man is not my father. He married my mother 10 years ago and they are no longer together. He is not a good man.'

'What is his name?'

'Fischer, Gerhardt Fischer. He works in the pharmaceutical industry as a, I don't know how you would say this, Fixierer, a spion, yes, that's it-a sort of spy for the company. He collates data from research all over the world to benefit the company. I am so sorry Andy; I could never think that this could affect your family in this way. I could not guess that your wife's work would be of any interest to this man.'

'Bernie, I am flying home tomorrow. Could I ask you to not tell anyone—I mean anyone—about what we talked about. Wait till I return-please?' Then a thought, '—and please, don't try to see your father—sorry—your stepfather for the time being.'

'This, of course, I will do. I have never trusted or liked this man—the hold he has over Heidi. Everybody.' Andy detected a barely stifled sniff, a sob. 'I am, though, responsible. My step-father used his influence so I could get a job in England. My ambition gave him the opportunity to get to your wife.'

'Look, Bernie. I am sorry too, to bring this news in such a way. Let us meet when I get back and discuss what to do. I cannot see how we can't tell the authorities about all this—but, as I say, hang on till I get back—please?'

'Oh, Andy, it is so good to hear your voice.' Her tone softened to that lilting cadence that seemed to drill down to Andy's core—he imagined her lips, struggling to pronounce the correct English, the soft, sweet breath passing through, lifting the perfume of her skin—

'OK, Bernie. I will see you tomorrow.'

'Andy-Andy, before you go. Take care, be careful—I—' Whatever it was she was going to say next vanished into the air as Andy placed the phone down.

He lay on the bed, the conversation and its repercussions playing in his mind. Most of all though, the image of those lips, slightly parted, arrowed into his loins and he lay back on the bed and abandoned himself to his fantasies.

Afterwards, as he lay resting, he checked on the departure times for his flight the next day. Then, somewhat belatedly, he chastised himself. How could he succumb to his feelings for this girl whilst his wife lay in bed, injured, albeit indirectly, as a result of his involvement with Bernadine. He checked himself, rang home to speak to Alice to inform her of his plans. He then showered, thus purging himself he imagined and dressed to adjourn to the bar. As usual, he felt the need to settle his ravaged thoughts with alcohol. A tankard of the 'foaming article' seemed to do the trick and he ventured forth for the last time to find food.

He decided to embark on a trawl of likely-looking wine bars, sampling wines and tapas; plates of salami, gherkins and mustard sauce all washed down with copious glasses of excellent wine. It came as a surprise to notice that he was actually enjoying himself; relieved for the time being of the responsibilities of duty and marriage.

The remembrance of that soft, German voice lifted him above the everyday, even for a moment, allowing him to forget his injured wife. In this jaunty spirit he visited a steak Haus promising all kinds of the best cuts of prime beef. Perfect. He would indulge himself. Later, full of beef and red wine, he made his way, somewhat gingerly, back to his hotel. He found himself looking forward to lying in bed, indulging in thoughts of Bernie; all guilt now subsumed in his full belly and addled brain.

A muffled 'Das is er,' caused him to look around. Too late. An arm locked around his throat, rocking his head back as he was dragged back and down into an unlit alley. He struggled to stay on his feet. He knew he mustn't fall to the ground. Two men now, grappling, one locking Andy's arms behind his back. Then a glimpse of a balaclavad head in front of him.

'Boom,' the first blow delivered below the ribs with expert force, caused him to fall to his knees and negated his desire to stay on his feet. He collapsed forward at this man's feet. Then a second blow, this time from behind and directed at his kidneys. He folded onto his left side, this allowing his arms to be freed. He instinctively brought his forearms up to his face, rolling into a hedgehog ball as the first kick hit his ribs; one, two, three. He heaved, spat. Became aware of a kneeling figure, the mask against his face.

'Dies ist eine Warnunging. Bleiben sie weg—stay away—from matters that do not concern you. Yah?'

Another metalled toe struck his injured ribs. He rolled over onto his front, crawled onto his knees and vomited. The men disappeared as they had first appeared—silent—gone. He tried to turn onto his backside, to lean against the alley wall, his head gasping for air, now rocked back, heaving.

Every breath daggered a knife through his ribs. He vomited again. He rolled away from the mess and tried to stand, the pain searing through his ribcage. He looked around. No one. His urgent need was to get away from here, to reach the safety of the hotel and this impulse gave him the strength to stagger the two blocks back. Thankfully, the atrium was unoccupied, a low chatter echoing from the bar. Retching and gasping, he made his way to the lift and reached the sanctity of his room, all thoughts of ecstasy and relaxation now expunged.

He sat on the bed, heart rate reducing for what seemed an age. Through gritted teeth, he forced off his jacket and, wincing, removed his shirt. Dark, semi-lunar welts marked the targets on his ribs and turning, he saw the same, on his back to the left of the spine, over the kidney. He drew in a breath and gasped at the pain shafting through his lower chest, confirming the diagnosis of cracked ribs.

Tenderly he removed the rest of his clothes and went again to the shower, this time to wash away the stink of a different kind; violence not sex. The cleansing stream helped to ease him, he tried to stretch to his full height, but pain restricted him. He examined his ribs with trained fingers and found tell-tale indents at the base of the ribcage on his right side. He breathed in, deeper this time, gasped but was able to detect no flexing. His pleura were probably still intact. Allowing himself to pee into the stream of water, he noticed the passing of blood in his urine, rose-coloured, not—thank God—frank blood. Enough though, to alarm him.

He wrapped a towel around his waist and went to his briefcase. A small bottle of diamorphine nestled in the base. There were some compensations for being a doctor, he thought to himself as he took a swig. That and a couple of Co-codamol should do the trick. Now he needed to treat his mind, his addled, disbelieving mind. 'What have I done to deserve this?' Not for the first time he asked this question. Rhetorical.

Crossing to the fridge, he removed the last mini of Johnny Walker's and painfully, slowly, the 50cl bottle of red wine. He positioned the pillows to get comfortable. He realised he would need to sit up to sleep. He knew that if he had miscalculated, any fluid in his lungs would not accommodate him lying prone. Shifting his weight, he took a swig of whiskey with the tablets, leaned back and waited for the blessed euphoria of absence of pain to kick in.

Even more confused than normal, he woke early the next day to stabbing darts of pain leaking through the remnants of the morphine. He had to catch a plane. He had to get home. That was imperative. He tried to stand, gasped and bent double. This was no good. He rang room service and, breaking through the language barrier, stated his strange request for crêpe bandages. Would they kindly send out—he had noted a flashing green cross across the avenue from the hotel? Vielen Dank.

A knock on the door, a puzzled face in the corridor as Andy leaned through the gap and took the parcel. 'Auf der Rechnung-Danke.' He undid the bandages, took one end and tied it to the door handle. Grasping the roll in his left hand— less painful—he danced a slow, stuttering pirouette as he turned and circled the bandage around his chest, tightening as he did so. This took an age, it seemed, as he stopped for short, shallow gasps of air. Having unrolled the entire bandage, he was just able to take the now free end in his right hand and tie a knot with his left.

He stepped back to assess the effect. Yes, this splinting enabled him to stand reasonably erect and support his careful breathing. Next, he took two co-codamol, resisted the urge to finish the morphine and struggled to dress himself. He washed his mouth out. Flattened his hair. He then called to reception to order a taxi, Danke, for the airport. The reception staff didn't appear to register this stooped, dishevelled Englishman stepping gingerly through the foyer. Andy couldn't bloody well wait to get the hell out of there!

Chapter 17

'Oh my God, Andy!' His sister-in-law was, it appeared, not too happy to see this reduced, shambolic figure. 'What in God's name happened to you?'

Andy collapsed, exhausted, onto a high chair in the kitchen, hardly able to work out which part of him hurt the most.

'Were you mugged?'

'No, I was not mugged and no, I didn't fall into a hedge before you ask.'

'Look, Andy, you have to clean yourself up before the girls get home. D'you not think they have gone through enough already without seeing you in this state?'

Andy found he had neither the strength nor the desire to explain the events of the last two days, so, excusing himself, he went upstairs to shower and shave. Having cleaned himself thoroughly he took time to examine his battered ribcage in the mirror.

Breathing made him wince, but, in spite of the pain he could, at least bend and move a little more freely. He noted with some relief that he had at least stopped passing blood. Taking a mix of Ibuprofen and co-codamol he got dressed as best he could and went to his car, thankful, at least that his face had not been damaged. Anyone looking at him would not have guessed at the beating he had sustained.

In the hospital, he contacted Stuart, caught up on his wife's progress and asked his friend to quickly examine him. Explaining away his injuries as a mugging attempt whilst abroad, he resisted the exhortations to get his chest x-rayed.

'What good would it do?' asked Andy. 'Even if a few ribs are broken, there is nothing to be done anyway. And I would like to keep this strictly entre nous, please Stuart.'

'Andy—you know you are going to have to sort yourself out before you return to clinical work, don't you?'

'Yeah, I know. Don't worry—I will. Let's go and see Isabel.'

Isabel was really in no condition herself to criticise or even notice her husband's discomfort, but appeared, nonetheless, pleased to see him. A tear coursed down her cheeks as he lent, carefully, in to kiss her. She either didn't know or couldn't remember where he had been for two days, so no awkward questions needed fielding. It was just enough to be with each other for a while.

Andy noted that a lot of the swelling had receded, exposing the fact that Isabel's once-beautiful face had somehow—(what was the right word)—shifted, in some immeasurable way. He dismissed this thought almost instantly, guiltily. He told himself that these were still early days. Leaving her to rest, Andy left the ward and buzzed Bernadine.

'Hi, Bernie. Yes, I'm back. Yeah. OK is probably not quite accurate, but I need to speak with you, urgently—but away from this place.' He suggested a quiet little Italian bistro, tucked away in one of the many cobbled side streets of Shrewsbury. It would be quiet there; safe.

'Shall we meet there, say 7:30 pm this evening?' Having secured this arrangement, he went home to pick up the girls from school. Initially, they seemed delighted to see him.

'Oh daddy, daddy—how lovely.' They rushed to greet him and flung open their arms for a hug, which Andy rapidly repelled. 'Is everything all right? Are you OK, dad?' Imogen said, noticing her father's obvious discomfort.

'Yes, yes, darling. I'm fine. Let's go home for tea and have a chat. I want to know all about your lessons. And what you said to mummy in the hospital.' They piled in to the 4x4 and once home, Andy noted their initial good spirits beginning to fade a little. 'What's the matter?' he enquired as he served them up with fish fingers and baked beans; a guaranteed thumbs-up for tea. He had sent Alice away to get a few hours on her own. He needed to be with his daughters, alone. Lucy began to cry.

'It's mummy. We tried, we did try, daddy, to be brave, but will she be OK? She looks so, so—' The little girl trailed off, struggling to articulate her fears. Again the distorted, ghost image of his wife's altered face flitted across his mind, but he tried to reassure his little girls.

'Yes, darling. Remember, it is only five days since the accident. It may be a little while yet before she is completely better, but yes, she will be fine.'

Apparently reassured, the girls finished their tea. Andy surprised himself by forgetting his troubles and pain for a while as he entered into the minutiae of domestic life. Resisting the more physical aspects of his daughter's enthusiasm, he oversaw their homework and read to them before they went to bed, admittedly a little early, but with the promise that their auntie would come and kiss them good night when she got home. He retired to his office to consider his next moves, washing down two co-codamol with a whiskey as he did so.

******

She was seated at the tiny bar when Andy shuffled in, a combination of narcotics and discomfort serving to disguise his usual, apparently confident, posture. Bernie jumped up as she saw his stooped figure.

'Andy—Mr Saunders,' she started, apparently unsure as to whether this was official business or otherwise. 'What's the matter?'

Andy seemed to visibly grow as he saw the young doctor, blonde hair tied back in a pigtail serving to highlight the angles and shadows of her lovely face. He advanced and tenderly placed a kiss on her forehead, immediately signalling that this was to be informal.

'Hell, Bernie. I don't really know where to start—let me get a drink first— can I refill yours?' Seated, apparently comfortable, drinks in hand, he started to outline what he knew. He reiterated that the formerly 'unknown male' was in fact her stepfather and that he had been in collusion with Heidi in order to gain details of Isabel's research.

He explained how Gerhardt had effectively tricked Lisbeth into replacing her on the planned UK trip-had in fact blackmailed her. Heidi had overheard Isabel inviting her over. He had been driving the car when it crashed. Again to his surprise, Bernie did not react as he thought she might; not only was her stepfather seriously injured, but he was also, in all probability, a criminal.

'Let me tell you about my stepfather. I have never been close, but he charmed my mother; they fell in love and that was that. But I could not trust him, he knew this and secretly used to threaten me. Heidi was always on his side, was influenced by him. I also knew that he worked for this company, CellProcure in Germany but that his job was, how would you say, im Geheimen—hidden—ah, yes—clandestine. I never trusted him.'

Andy, swallowing his drink, proceeded to tell her about his interview with the director of CellProcure, how he had been threatened and later, attacked.

'Oh, Andy, I'm so sorry. If I hadn't introduced you to Heidi none of this would have happened.'

Andy decided to bite the bullet—after all, things couldn't get much worse.

'Bernie, I have to ask. Didn't you realise you were planted here by your stepfather? It seems an incredible coincidence that Heidi was available, just like that, to become our nanny.'

'No, no—not at all. Oh, Andy, how could you think such a thing. I was so happy, honoured even, to get the chance to come to England to follow my career. I told you that my stepfather used his influence to get me an interview but that was all it was. I wanted to get away from all of that, to be honest with you. I don't think that Gerhardt even realised the opportunity open to him until Heidi came over. And then, I introduced her to you. How could I have known what was going to happen?'

'But Bernie, she was only here for just over a week.'

'I think she got to work on Isabel—sorry, Mrs Saunders, as soon as she got here and Gerhardt took the opportunity. They found out that your wife was in touch with the German scientist.'

They were shown to their table, hidden in an arched alcove. A bottle of wine was ordered.

'Isabel did mention Heidi's strange behaviour at times. But—look. What's done is done. What do we do now? I should have gone to the police as soon as I realised what was happening.'

'No, no—I don't think the police should be involved. My mother would never get over it. Let me, please Andy—'she looked into Andy's eyes and once again he felt the deep stirring, the turmoil in his injured chest. It seemed to him that this beautiful girl was an oasis in a very arid desert. She went on '—let me speak with him, I will tell him what has happened to you. For all his intimidation, he couldn't possibly have known you and your wife would be so badly hurt. Perhaps I can get him to request a transfer back to Germany when he is well enough.'

'What about Heidi?'

'I know Heidi well. She will have gone into hiding. She could be anywhere to be honest with you.'

Andy relaxed a little as the alcohol supplemented the analgesics and he found himself able to enjoy himself a little in this girl's company. 'OK—see if you can speak with him and I will hold back from the police if he can be persuaded to leave the country. He will need to get approval from the hospital of course. There are difficulties—' he trailed off as his concentration dissolved in the flux of drugs and alcohol, in the presence of this woman. He pulled himself up, winced at the effort. 'Now tell me, how are you? What is the locum like?'

Perhaps not understanding that what he had consented to was definately illegal, he allowed the combination of food, wine and compelling company to take its effect. Yet again he found his judgement clouded in the presence of this young woman. It was only the server politely asking them if they would like coffee for the third time that made them realise that three hours had passed. Andy collected himself enough to realise that he wasn't fit to drive, so they sat in the car talking further.

'Andy, I have to tell you I really, really like you and I cannot believe the trouble and pain I have caused for you and your wife. I don't know if you can ever forgive me.'

'Bernie, none of this was your fault. You could never have imagined what was going to happen. You were only trying to help.'

Tears coursed down the young girl's face and Andy instinctively reached across to touch her face, to wipe away her tears, flinching as he did so. 'Oh, Andy—' Perhaps intending to relieve him of his obvious discomfort, she leant across and delicately feathered Andy's lips with hers. Again, the potent mix. The scent of skin and breath allowed him to succumb to her increasingly passionate kissing. Painfully, awkwardly, yet ecstatic, they made love once again.

******

The crashing urgency of the helicopter blades disturbed the early morning peace before the hospital woke from its nocturnal turpitude. The doors at the rear of A+E opened and a hospital bed, complete with patient, came trundling out, accompanied by two paramedics. Drip stands hurriedly kept pace, pushed by nurses. The aircraft's doors opened, the bed bundled in by the crouching staff and the doors snapped shut. As soon as it had come, the aircraft ascended and disappeared into the pale, pink sky.

Chapter 18

Andy and Isabel faced each other across the granite top of the kitchen island, Andy sporting a nascent beard whilst his wife did not quite sport a closely cropped hairdo. In the aftermath of her discharge from hospital a few weeks ago, she had rid herself of the memory of the blood-clotted frazzle that used to be her crowning glory by abruptly cutting it all off.

An act of self-mutilation almost to match that of her features. Temporary dentures hid the gaps in her smile; not that Isabel was given much to smiling these days. Tears constantly formed and then dripped from the ectropion affecting the left lower eyelid. She dribbled at it. The IMF now removed, she was having to practise chewing again and the handicap of the false teeth in no way facilitated this endeavour.

Andy's contemplation of her altered features contributed to the tense atmosphere. The pair of them were struggling to deal with the events of the past six weeks. Andy had been quizzed by Stuart as to what he knew about the evacuation of the German patient, whilst Isabel's picture of events resembled that of a jigsaw as little pieces of memory clicked into place, slowly forming a scarcely believable whole.

How could Andy possibly not have involved the police once he had learned of her kidnap? What had possessed him to act the maverick and take himself off to Germany? How had Heidi come to be involved? Andy naturally avoided informing his wife of Bernie's involvement, but nonetheless, he attempted to comfort his wife, unsuccessfully it seemed at the moment.

'So let's get this right, Andy. You have the hospital wanting to know why the German kidnapper was spirited away. Your friend and colleague cannot understand why the police haven't been involved. What are you thinking?'

'My only concern has been your welfare-everything I did was in your best interests—after all, no one knew how you came to be in that car with a strange man. I had to find out. Try to help—'

'All you've done is make things worse-I mean, look at me for Christ's sake!' Isabel dabbed at her face again, this time removing real tears. '—and don't you think the police are going to want to follow up on the crash report? Of course they will. And my career, my research—what am I going to do Andy?'

'Well, it seems that the German thing is out of our hands now. The BKA have become involved.'

'What's the BKA for heaven's sake?'

'Germany's central agency for police intelligence; they deal in matters of international organised crime.'

'Well, that's great, isn't it, Andy? Now bloody Interpol are involved—'

'The good thing is that they kind of override our police, which, in a way, lets us off the hook.'

'Us—us? For God's sake Andy, I was the one who was bloody well kidnapped—'

A step just outside the kitchen door halted the discussion. Lucy was pushing the door open, peering around, crying.

'Oh darling—' her mother went across to comfort her.

'Mummy, you woke us up-you were arguing again—what's going on? Why are you upset all the time?' Isabel brought her over to the table.

'Look, sweetheart. It's just that we are trying to sort everything out after mummy's accident. Sometimes adults do argue—just like you and Imogen sometimes.'

'And mummy—why do you—' She hesitated, '—Why do you look different?'

Andy interrupted, 'Lucy, your mother has had a serious accident, but she is recovering and doing very, very well. We all have to be patient. And right now, what mummy needs is for you two to help her, go to school and try to be as normal as possible. Mummy will be all right.'

Lucy pondered this for a moment, then allowed herself to be led back upstairs by her mother. Andy sat for a moment; head bowed. He could barely believe that his life had so dramatically been inverted, corrupted. His hand shook. He got up, went upstairs and took a Valium with two co-codamol, came back down and helped himself to a large whiskey.

'How the hell is that going to help?' Isabel had returned. 'And where have my Brufen gone? I have this constant headache and all you can do is take my painkillers. For heaven's sake, Andy.'

Looking around, shaking his head, he looked and felt haunted. He had an interview at the hospital tomorrow and somehow he had to get his job back-he needed the stability of work. Attempting to change the subject, he suggested they go to see Isabel's professors at the University.

'They must be wondering when you are coming back to work, how you are. They are going to need to know that your laptop was stolen for a start.'

'Andy, I can't even think of going back to work at the moment.'

'Yes, I know, but you do need to speak to them, surely?'

'Yes, I agree—but how will you help?'

'We'll have to come clean about how I found out about CellProcure—they must be aware, after all.'

'Give me time to think, Andy, please. My head is throbbing. I need to speak to Lisbeth. I've ignored her texts-she has no idea of what's going on.' Andy decided not to tell her that Lisbeth actually knew a lot more than she was letting on.

******

Privately, Stuart wished that he could get on and do the job that he was employed to do, heal the sick and not sit in bloody boardrooms interviewing his erstwhile colleague for the umpteenth time. He was though, on this occasion pleasantly surprised to see Andy looking respectable; freshly shaved, with well-cut hair and wearing an immaculate suit and tie. He actually looked like a consultant.

'Morning, Andy. Good to see you. Before we go in, a quick update. They will want to know what you know about this German chap. Keep schtum if I were you. They're clutching at straws at the moment. I told you last week that the German police were involved, didn't I? But, how on earth did Izzy get to be involved with him for heaven's sake?' Andy declined to answer this.

'Let's just get this over with, shall we?'

The pair knocked and walked into the panelled room, where again old Grey-Bop was in attendance, flanked by her two stooges. *HR, no doubt*, thought Andy. Introductions over, Andy sat on the opposite side of the oak table to his interlocutors. They wanted to know how he was. How his wife was. How upset they had all been. How on earth had this German fellow got to be in the same car as Mrs Saunders? As suggested, Andy stayed silent on the latter point.

'The real reason for our meeting today, Mr Saunders, is to assess your readiness to come back to work. It seems that the locum is not quite, what can I say?' Grey Bob looked to Stuart, who gently nodded.' Not quite up to scratch, shall I put it like that?' An attempt at a chuckle escaped her dry lips. 'We are of course willing for you to come back so long as you can give us certain reassurances.'

'Reassurances?' Andy maintained his cool, professional demeanour.

'Yes, well, ahem—That you have got over the traumatic events of the last month or so and that you have dealt with your—' She looked across, this time at her HR colleagues. 'Can we just say, Mr Saunders, your drinking issues?'

'Ah, my drinking issues.' Andy resisted the urge to ask them how they would suggest they might deal with the pressures of his work, but again, declined.

'Yes, yes, of course. A temporary blip shall we say?'

'Well, in that case, shall we—' she looked round again, '—Shall we suggest a trial period of, say, six months?'

Andy opened his mouth to speak but a look from Stuart limited him to the simple answer. 'Six months? Yes, that sounds perfect—thank you.'

Once out of the room Stuart shook his hand. 'Welcome back, Andy. Make it stick, OK?' Andy stood for a while, wondering where he could go for a celebratory drink, thought better of it and went home.

******

'Good morning, Mrs Saunders. Please come in.'

Isabel was ushered into the out-patients of the oral and maxillofacial department, where Sandeep was planning to assess her injuries and hopefully prepare the ground for placing her implants to replace the missing teeth. Having removed the fixation wires a week ago, the gums were now healing nicely and all he had to do was to remove a tiny fixation screw that had exfoliated through the buccal sulcus high up. He then planned to take a CT scan, which would enable him to plan the position and angulation of the implants.

Sandeep enjoyed these clinics. Earlier he had seen the degloving trauma case of a couple of months ago and found the grafts had taken well, the mucosa healing beautifully around the implant healing caps. He had taken impressions which would enable him to make a temporary bridge for Andy's patient. She seemed to cope well with the numbness of her lip and the scarring, hidden as it was behind the jawline, was healing nicely.

San, perhaps reluctantly, was taking Bernardine through these processes at Andy's instruction. After all, this represented training in her planned speciality. Isabel expressed her surprise to find Bernadine also present at the consultation.

'Oh, hi,' Isabel addressed her. 'I wasn't expecting to see you here today.'

Sandeep explained the nature of the clinic, that the SHO's training required first-hand experience in this precise scenario; the provision of dental implants in post-trauma patients.

Well, isn't that just bloody typical of Andy? Isabel thought to herself? Insensitive to how she may feel about having her injuries surveyed by the sister of her absconded nanny, innocent or otherwise. All that interested him always seemed to centre around the demands of his work and now this bloody teaching clinic! However, as far as Isabel was concerned, she couldn't wait to be rid of her denture. She found that, together with her altered features, that she just couldn't face her husband, children even and thought more and more of her escape back to the sanctity of her laboratory.

In spite of herself, she found herself surprisingly comfited by Bernadine's gentle professionalism as she took impressions and, indicating the 3D scan, described how the implants would be placed at an angle in order to make the most of the available bone. She watched as San took Bernadine to one side to explain the finer nuances of the transfer of impressions to the 3D model. *They made a fine pair*, she thought.

San then described how the implants would be placed in a few weeks' time and under local anaesthetic. They were going to try to immediately load the implants with a temporary bridge in Mrs Saunders's case so as to rid her of the denture as early as possible. This, San explained, would short-cut the usual healing period of anything between two and three months.

Saying goodbye to San and Bernie she arranged her next appointment and returned home, determined to question her husband further. She had decided to go along with Andy's plan to speak to her profs. as he was now involved in all of this, whether she liked it or not. Her pixelated memory of the accident had been given some focus by the previous evening's phone call to Lisbeth, who seemed to spend most of the call saying how sorry she was, but couldn't, wouldn't speak to her on the phone.

Her friend had seemed frightened, not wanting to talk. Even when Isabel tried to talk to her about the aborted trip to the UK, all she would let on was that she was aware of the German interloper. *So Lisbeth was involved in all of this?* she had thought. Even then she tried to change the subject and asked Lisbeth about her work, but her friend seemed to be determined to say nothing more on the matter. She hung up.

Arriving home and a little relieved at the outcome of her appointment, Isabel forced a smile on finding Andy looking cheerful for once and sober. Initially, she was loath to bring the subject up. She persisted, however.

'Andy, I spoke to Lisbeth in Frankfurt last night.' Andy looked startled. He changed the subject.

'Can't I tell you my good news first?'

He proceeded to tell her about his return to work, how he intended to reduce his alcohol intake. Isabel, however, returned to the matter that concerned her most. Her memory continued to filter facts through and she felt she would go mad if she could not get the picture straight.

'Lisbeth wouldn't talk to me. All she would say was that she was sorry. Sorry about what Andy?' Andy looked hunted, seemed to consider going to the drinks cabinet, decided against it and instead decided to tell her all; about the stolen laptop, Heidi, her stepfather, how he came to be driving the car that crashed.

'Don't you see, darling; this is why we have to speak to the University. If Lisbeth was being blackmailed by an employee of CellProcure, then surely it's a matter of deep concern for your research?' Isabel seemed to consider all of this, as the pieces slowly fell into place.

'But if Heidi was 'planted' as you put it, then surely, your SHO must be involved as well?' Andy sighed. He didn't want the conversation to drift towards Bernardine. 'And speaking of your SHO, why on earth did you allow her to be involved in my treatment. Don't you realise how difficult this is for me?'

'Bernie-er, my SHO, knew nothing of all of this. All she had done was try to help her stepsister by finding her work in the UK. She's as upset as the rest of us—and be reasonable Izzy, I can't just alter the way the clinics work to suit you.' Isabel considered this.

'So, are you telling me that this Gerhardt character got you beaten up as well?' She hadn't given much credence to Andy's mugging story and now the pieces began to form a coherent whole. 'If that's the case, Andy, then surely we must go to the police—'

'I told you, Izzy, the police are involved. The German police are onto it.'

'But can't you see that we're now in the position of withholding vital information—surely you can see that, Andy? Unless we tell the authorities everything we know, then we're in trouble—we're the criminals!' Unable or unwilling, to give an answer to this conundrum, Andy relented and went to the wine rack.

'Let's put that aside for now. I agree though, we have to do something, but, as your doctor, I insist that you are well enough to enjoy a glass of wine—let's celebrate for once.'

Isabel, still thoughtful, succumbed to this line of reasoning and raised a glass. There had to be some pleasure in life, after all.

******

'This is highly irregular, Dr Saunders—'

'Mr Saunders—thank you. I would think you would agree that what happened to my wife was also, ahem-highly irregular.'

'Yes, well, we were very sorry to hear about Mrs Saunders, Isabel's accident. She is sorely missed, but I really don't see how this involves the University.'

Andy and Isabel found themselves sitting in the offices of Prof Landon, the head of sciences and, incidentally, as Andy well knew, a stakeholder in Endimmune UK. Isabel looked uncomfortable. Not only did the Prof keep eyeing her from time to time with a faintly quizzical expression, but she found her husband's presence in her domain, as she saw it, disturbing, to say the least.

'It is my opinion,' Andy continued, 'that the sequence of events leading to my wife's accident was instigated by your insistence that Isabel should be disciplined for communicating with her colleague in Germany.' Prof Landon did not seem to be impressed by this argument.

'We had every right to discipline Isabel. We were very aware that her private communication, both by phone and by email I might add, represented a potential breach of security.'

'Breach of security? Surely, Isabel has every right to share her intellectual property with her colleagues. Is there a contractual issue here?'

At this Isabel had to interrupt, 'Andy, thank you, but remember I work here and Professor Landon is also a colleague—'

'Yes, yes of course I understand. I just want to ascertain the facts. So Prof, is Isabel prohibited from sharing her intellectual property?'

The Professor looked uncomfortable. He wasn't used to being interrogated.

'I think the issue here is the fact that matters sensitive to the University and its work were discussed out with the Department.'

'So, are you telling me that none of your lecturers or researchers may work from home then?' Prof. Landon reddened.

'Of course, our staff are free to do their 'homework' if you will, it is just that Isabel's work was becoming, ahem, how can I put it? Was becoming—was reaching a conclusion that would be potentially game-changing.'

'Forgive me,' Andy was now in full flow. 'I think the term you are struggling to find is 'valuable'.' Prof. Landon raised an eyebrow.

'Well, 'valuable' is a fluid term. Of course, any scientific breakthrough has its—erm—'

'Price?' Suggested Andy. At this Isabel could take no more.

'Andy, I see no point in discussing this further. All I'm concerned about is getting back to work. I need, I have to, get my brain working again.'

'Yes, darling, of course. But—' and this to the Prof. 'The fact is, Professor, that other people were also aware of the 'value' of Isabel's work. Her accident directly resulted from the intervention of what I can only call hostile elements in the pharmaceutical industry.' If the professor had felt uncomfortable before, then he was now positively agitated.

'Hostile elements?'

'Have you heard of a company called Cell Procure?' The Professor was now angry.

'Look, Dr—Mr Saunders, I think this line of questioning has gone far enough. All I am interested in now is facilitating Isabel's return to her work.' A pause.

'Well, then, good. Let's get back to work, shall we? See if we can put this unfortunate affair behind us.'

In the car on the way home, Andy expressed his desire to expand on his apparent success.

'Did you see his face when I mentioned Cell Procure?'

'Andy, surely you're not suggesting that my professors had anything to do with my abduction, are you?'

'What I am saying is that they probably have as much to gain from marketing your cancer vaccine as anyone else. After all, we know they are shareholders in Endimmune UK.'

'Please, don't call it a cancer vaccine, Andy. I'm not even sure if the carrier material will initiate a good enough immune response. I *have* to return to work.'

'Purely from a clinical point of view, Izzy, you are not remotely ready for work. We need to get your implants in, sort out your occlusion and let your ectropion settle. That might need another operation and you are still getting problems with balance and memory. There is a way to go yet.'

Isabel sighed. 'Yeah, I know. And I need to spend more time with the girls. It's just that I am so eager to get going again.'

'First things first.' Andy laid a hand on her knee.

Instinctively, she pulled away. *Talk about the pot calling the kettle*—she thought.

The interview at the University cemented Andy's suspicion that they had all become involved in a level of intrigue above the mere investigation of a car accident or a stolen laptop. This was abduction, kidnapping, espionage, clearly instigated by big Pharma. It also looked as though Isabel's professors were involved in some way. The problem for Andy was that he continued to be side-tracked by his own inner struggle.

He wanted to return to work but was fearful. He remained disturbed by the change in his wife, not only-the least consideration in fact-the cosmetic, the aesthetic issues, but also by her change in mood. She was now irascible, prone to wandering off, deep in her own thoughts and even tetchy with the children. This feeling of alienation only served to heighten his wholly unsuitable but implacable feelings towards Bernadine.

He longed to see her, to talk to her, to kiss her, to feel her skin electrifying his. He realised these feelings were outrageous and unforgivably selfish, but this inner conflict only had the effect of drawing him towards the sunlit uplands of intoxication—of narcotic relief even. He needed a drink, dammit. And in the background always, always the nagging inner rat of guilt-guilt that he couldn't save his son, now exacerbated by the fact that he couldn't help his wife in *her* hour of need. And yes, of course, the now added burden of his feelings for Bernie.

Back at home, he succumbed to the least destructive of his desires and opted for a glass of wine, which Isabel declined to share with him. Alcohol had no attraction for her at the moment. Andy then retired to his study, his mind, for a while at least, finding clarity under the influence of the grape. What occurred to him almost immediately was that, so far as the accident was concerned, he was out of his depth.

He realised that he was not Sherlock Holmes, about to bring big Pharma to heel. He wanted to unburden himself so that he could concentrate once again on his career, his calling. He decided then to contact the police. He called Stuart, who gave him a contact, the same CIO that had wanted to interview the German before he was spirited away.

Andy was directed initially to the chief inspector involved in the crash aftermath. He started off by admonishing Andy for failing to be in touch sooner. Andy pointed out that the orthopaedic surgeons had blocked initial questions, whilst he, Andy, had been too close to the drama. Too emotionally and physically involved with his wife's injuries, to be held in any way answerable for the initial delay in response.

Responding to questions about his whereabouts the weekend before, Andy defended his trip to Frankfurt by claiming that he had been trying to ascertain the whereabouts of their nanny. Only after meeting with Lisbeth had he become embroiled in what appeared to be organised corporate crime. The CI suggested that he may not have heard the last of this matter but told Andy that he would escalate the enquiry.

There were, after all serious matters here. Activity outside the confines of competitive intelligence. Acquiring commercial secrets that may have monetary value, hacking, wiretapping, physical assault and kidnapping. The CI seemed to enjoy listing the possible breaches of the law as he listened to Andy's story.

'Thank you, Sir, for your information. No doubt the SIS will be extremely interested in what you have to say. Meanwhile, Sir, if you don't mind, I would strongly advise you against travelling to Germany again for the foreseeable and Sir, ahem, if you don't mind me saying so, leave the investigations to the professionals in future.'

Thus admonished, Andy nonetheless felt better for unburdening himself and now felt able to concentrate on the next hurdle: scheduled for on-call duty next weekend he realised that this would severely test his stated intention of not imbibing whilst in charge of the bleep. With this in mind, he stopped off at the Ragleth for a pint of Hobson's.

Chapter 19

'Well, Izzy, I have to say I was very concerned about Andy. I enjoyed being in Shropshire again and seeing the girls, but his drinking seemed out of control to me, I must admit.'

Alice and Isabel were catching up on the 'phone. Ever since Alice had returned home Ben and she had spent time discussing the paradox that was her sister and brother-in-law's marriage. They had seemed a successful, happy and vibrant family but one that had disintegrated so easily. Ben suggested a trip to see Andy but had been secretly relieved when his wife put him off. After all, the principal activity the brothers-in-law enjoyed included the imbibing of good claret. He did though, provide a sounding board for his wife who also expressed severe doubts about the long-term damage done to her sister's face, teeth and mentality.

'But look,' she went on. 'How are you? That's what is most important right now.' Isabel listed her current ailments: her dentures, her droopy, leaking eyelid, residual bruising, difficulty eating, lack of appetite anyway, dizziness and lapse of memory.

'Apart from that—' Even Izzy managed a laugh. Her sister continued,

'I can't believe what happened with Heidi and your laptop.'

Isabel continued to explain to her sister that Andy had at last gone to the police and that now the whole thing would be investigated. '—And it seems that Andy is even sticking to his resolution to quit drinking when he's on-call. Who knows, there may be light at the end of the tunnel—'

The two sisters carried on chatting in this way and Isabel found relief in the fact that she could relax a little in the gentle to and fro of harmony with her beloved sister. She looked up as Andy stuck his head around the kitchen door.

'Sorry to interrupt love. Seems there's been a nasty accident. I'm off to A+E. Will let you know what's going on once I've assessed things. See you later. Cheers'

Isabel noted with pleasure the clean shirt, jacket and glint in her husband's eye as, so far as she was concerned, he got back to doing what he did best.

On arrival in A+E, a clearly distressed SHO confronted Andy. 'Oh Andy—sorry—Mr Saunders—it's awful, come on through.'

Once in the resus room, the usual scene confronted Andy; paramedics and the resuscitation team all attempting to stabilise a clearly severely injured patient. Apparently a young female, she had sustained a severely gashed head and face and what looked like an avulsed right orbit. The central laceration extended from mid-forehead to upper lip, effectively dividing the nose into two. San was at the head end, holding gauze swabs to the wound in an attempt to stem the haemorrhage.

As Andy approached he clicked into auto-pilot, assessing that venflons were in place with fluid replacement commencing. The patient, clearly distressed, exhibited classical signs of traumatic shock; pale and shaking, struggling to breathe. Andy quickly assessed the injury, noting fragments of bone protruding through the midline cleft. Regarding the eye, he left well alone.

'Has the ophthalmic team been called? Quick, we have an open globe injury on the right with retro bulbar haemorrhage on the left. What happened here?' He turned to the senior nurse.

'Apparently kicked in the face by her pony—an 18th birthday present for heaven's sake! You think we can save her sight?'

'That's not for me to say I'm afraid—we need the optic guys-quick!'

'OK, let's get her into the scanner-we need to find out the extent of the skeletal injury. The brain may be involved here. Call the neuro boys as well please!'

Andy, once confident that the patient was stabilising ordered up immediate theatre space and called the senior anaesthetist.

'We need to get the airway secured, then into theatre. Straightaway.' He took Bernie to one side. 'Look, I need your help here. Excellent experience for you but you have to put emotions to one side—OK?'

'Yes, Andy. OK.'

'San, I want you in theatre as well now.'

Half an hour later, Andy, now scrubbed up and able to assist his ophthalmic colleague eased the right globe back into its bony orbit. Andy noted a superior orbital rim fracture now the eye had been replaced into the protection of the bony walls of the orbit. The scans showed frontal bone fractures, un-displaced with no apparent cranial intrusion, whilst the nasal bone had been cleaved in two; canthal tendons now untethered. Comminuted fractures to the left orbital floor accounted for the bleed behind what appeared to be an intact left eye.

Finally, Andy noted a midline maxillary fracture. The teeth appeared intact with a midline fracture down the hard palate. Apart from the mess of the left orbital floor, the injuries seemed almost surgical in the neatness of the fracture lines, testimony to the direct force of the blunt injury.

Having, for the time being, dealt with the eye injury and eliminated the need for the neurosurgeons, Andy got to work. The rule was, as he explained to Bernie and San, to get the hard tissues, the skeleton, back in place first before any attempt was made to close the soft tissue injuries. He explored the wounds over the frontal bone and along the right supra-orbital rim and cleansed the wound edges. He noted fragments of straw and muck among the shards of bone. The whole thing needed thorough debridement.

This itself took half an hour, allowing Andy to visualise the now clean bone edges. Using micro-plates, he secured the eyebrow bone and the forehead bone. He could then concentrate on the nasal bridge which he stabilised with a 'T' shaped plate, bent along the long axis to reform the nasal profile. Now he could tension the canthal ligaments, floated apart on their bony islands. This he achieved using wire threaded through the reconfigured nose.

An intraoral approach allowed him to plate up the anterior maxilla below the nasal septum. He could then reseat the nasal septum into the groove along the top edge of the palate, having also placed a plate across the midline suture, also through an intra-oral incision. Having packed the nostrils in order to stabilise the septum, he could now concentrate on the left orbital floor.

As he incised along the lower eyelid, his hand began to shake. This incision, referred to as a blepharoplasty, represented the most delicate incision max-fac surgeons were called upon to make and the more he tried to control the tremor, the worse it became. He paused.

'Is everything OK, Andy?' Theatre sister again.

Bernie looked across at him, her blue eyes sparkling over the top of her mask. Emotion or encouragement? He couldn't tell. He passed his scalpel back to the scrub nurse, lent against the operating table and took three long, steady breaths. 1-2-3. 'Come on Andy,' he murmured to himself. 'You've done this tons of times-it's routine.'

He took up the scalpel again, aware of sweat forming over the top of his headlight. He separated the delicate skin folds, then incised again through the circumorbital muscle, directly down onto the fractured bone of the lower orbit. He gave tiny flexible retractors to San to keep the access open. Another few breaths. Now he could see that the eggshell floor of the left orbit had shattered, allowing the soft tissue encasing the left eye to herniate into the space that was the maxillary antrum or sinus.

Andy was not in the mood to go through his usual spiel about God's crash zone. Using a wider flexible retractor he gently teased the contents of the orbit up into place, gave that to Bernie—'hold that completely still'—and measured the defect in the orbital floor. Turning to the scrub table he precisely cut a matching rectangle of surgical plastic and inserted this under Bernie's retractor. Taking this from her he allowed the orbital contents to settle back into their rightful place. Taking a tiny pair of tweezers he took hold of the outer skin of the eye and tested it for full movement. 'Great,' he murmured.

He could now place and fix another bone plate along the lower rim of the bony orbit and start to close the wound. Andy remembered, had a vision of, his wife's ectropion and realised how crucial the next few minutes were. If this closure couldn't be achieved perfectly, he would disfigure this young girl for life, even more so than she appeared to be already.

He took the 6-0 ethilon suture and started to thread this, invisibly along the inner margin of the eye lid. All he needed to do was create a zip-like, continuous suture all along the lid which he could then tension at either end and thereby close the wound invisibly. However, his hand began to shake again. As much as he steadied himself, the fine needlepoint seemed to swing from side to side. He was not able to control himself.

He handed the suture holders to San under the pretence of teaching him and trusted him to complete the delicate task under his supervision. This San did, expertly, much to Andy's surprise. This allowed him space, some time to collect himself, to breathe again and turn to the more straightforward task of closing the facial wounds.

Dressings in place, he left the theatre, pulled off his gloves and dumped his gown in the basket and retired to the coffee room. There he sunk his head in his hands and quietly wept. Once again he asked himself how things should have turned against him so suddenly. The familiar lethal combination of sadness and guilt flooded through him. The one thing he could be proud of, trusted in, was his surgical ability and now, even that appeared to be deserting him.

San and Bernie came into the room and studiedly ignored their boss, perhaps appreciating his anguish having operated on such a tragic case. They busied themselves with coffee, also absorbing the recent traumatic events. Bernie certainly had never before witnessed such an affront to young life at such close quarters.

Hearing their murmured conversation, Andy gathered himself and called them over. He would lose himself in the professional obligation to teach these young doctors.

'When you write up the clinical notes, they must be contemporaneous. This means that they must be a true and accurate record of events as they happened. It is a good idea to write these immediately, recalling what happened and when. What was done at what time, what materials were used, a list of pre-and post-op medical interventions and a summary of the results. Where ever possible explain the reasons for decisions made.

Describe the condition of the patient at completion. Then write up a follow-up and treatment plan, sign and date it. Remember you may be asked precise details of the case in six years' time. You may need to explain why certain actions were taken. Medico-legal lawyers are increasingly adept at finding holes in the clinical record which may uphold a claim for negligence. OK?'

They drank their coffee in silence, eventually broken by San who wanted to know the prognosis for this girl.

'Visual acuity is the main concern here. The facial skeleton came together well and of course, she will bear a visible scar for the rest of her life. But neurologically she should do well. I am pretty sure the left eye will be fine, but replacing a prolapsed orbit is a different matter. The ophthalmic team will of course be following her up carefully. By the way, Bernie, what actually happened to her?'

'It seems that she received the pony as a birthday present. She was putting it in the stable and walked behind the animal and bent down to clear a hay bale. The pony was aufgeregt apparently and kicked out a hind leg and caught her full on the face.'

'Owfger?' interrupted San.

'Ah, yes. Sorry. I think nervous, agitated, you would say.'

'Good grief. Imagine how the poor parents must feel.' Andy understood a little of their pain. 'I'll go and talk to them. And San, thank you very much for picking up the slack in there-you were really impressive—well done!' To Bernie, he said, 'I'll catch up with you later.' Having checked on his patient in recovery, Andy went to seek out the parents.

******

Isabel contemplated her features in the bathroom mirror. She did not enjoy the experience. The face looking back at her was not one she recognised. For one thing, one lower eyelid drooped, revealing the pink, moist inner surface which, more or less constantly, leaked tears. She had had her implants placed by San, (irritatingly assisted by Bernadine-why did she feel so antagonistic towards this girl?) which were now healing, but she still had to wear the hideous denture.

San had explained that the placements were not stable enough for immediate loading, so a temporary bridge was out of the question. The dip in the upper vermilion border of her lip also concerned her, but Andy had assured her that this could be revised at a later date. The most disconcerting aspect and she suspected, a permanent change, was the faint but discernible shift in her features. No longer regular and therefore attractive, appealing, they were just plain wonky!

Nothing one could put a finger on but undeniable nonetheless. This depressed her. It seemed to affect Lucy and Imogen as well, who were both recently misbehaved and uncommunicative. Teachers had been in touch concerned about the drop in formerly high standards. Andy, their father, was all over the place. And, to make things worse, she had received notice from the University that a branch of the police, SIS, had been in touch with Prof Landon and intended to interview them both regarding the accident and the claims of international interference.

She realised that the only thing that brought her any joy was the prospect of getting back to work. She felt an almost missionary zeal to correct what she perceived was her involvement in the whole episode. She needed to redeem herself-to complete her research, so that, at least, people—patients—might benefit in the future from this mess.

She experimented with some make-up, tied what was left of her hair back and resolved to sit down with her husband and enjoy supper together; perhaps even go out for a meal. When she suggested this on Andy's return, his response was not what she had hoped for. He didn't even seem to notice her attempts at cosmetic improvement. Instead, he launched into a report of the case he had been called out to.

'Oh, Izzy, it was truly awful. This poor young girl is probably disfigured for life. Very possibly blind in one eye at least.' Andy went on to describe the injuries in more detail and what he had done to alleviate the worst effects. Also confessed to his loss of control, his loss of confidence. 'I couldn't complete the procedure, Izzy. I had to leave it to Sandeep.'

Isabel startled herself by not responding to this news as she might once have done. After all, she, too, was altered—disfigured even and Andy didn't seem to be as concerned as he obviously appeared to be about this unfortunate girl. The very fact that she thought this seemed to make things worse and all thoughts of an attempt at a normal supper together, soon dissipated.

Neither of them could enjoy the release of a drink together—for different reasons—so she changed the subject by telling Andy about the investigation by a branch of MI5. This news did nothing for Andy's mood and he retired to his study only to emerge later to try to spend some time at least with his daughters.

Back in the hospital the next day, he joined the ward round to see the young girl who was sitting up, fully awake and apparently quite cheerful, with her right eye dressed in bandages. She either hadn't seen or didn't care about the livid scar dissecting her young face from forehead to upper lip but seemed to be more concerned about the welfare of the pony. She explained to anyone who would listen that the poor beast hadn't known what it was doing. Shouldn't be made to suffer for her injuries.

Apparently, as one of the nurses confided to Andy later, the parents, visibly distressed at the outcome of their largesse, had threatened to have the animal destroyed. Satisfied he could do nothing more to help the girl, for the time being, Andy dismissed San to outpatients and asked Bernie to join him for a coffee.

Once alone, Bernie told him how impressed she had been by his performance the previous day, how upsetting she had found the whole experience.

'Well, Bernie, this is the nature of trauma surgery. It is always deeply concerning for the victims, but one has to distance oneself from the emotional aspect, try not to get too involved.'

'But Andy, I noticed that you too were affected—'

'Ah, well—that's different. That is something I am dealing with. Perhaps I've spent too long away from the work. Need to get my eye back on the game. That's all.'

Bernie, of course, did not believe a word of this and went to reach out to comfort him.

'Not here, Bernie. Not at work. In fact, I've been thinking-this whole thing has got out of hand. I need to concentrate on my work, my wife, my children. I can't be carrying on with you in this way.'

'Carrying on? Is that your cool English expression for what is happening between us?' She leant forward and placed a hand on Andy's knee causing him to look anxiously from side to side.

'Look, Andy, you have to understand. Not only do I admire you enormously for what you do; your skill, your dedication. I also feel responsible for what has happened to you and your family. You need to understand that I am here for you—that—' she paused, 'that, in fact—' She looked up into his eyes, '—ich liebe dich Andy—I love you.'

******

Andy found that it was only a short step from Co-codamol to morphine so far as he was concerned. This latest episode had him reaching for his secret stash. Privileged access to the dangerous drugs cabinets was a 'perk' for the head of max-fac trauma. It was a relatively simple matter to slightly over-prescribe for his post-op patients and spirit away these smaller increments over time. He preferred diamorphine elixir as he had no intention of injecting himself.

He kept a glass phial for the job in his safe at home. For emergencies only he liked to kid himself. Diamorphine, (or heroin, to use its more common nomenclature), he had found, settled the perpetual stamp-stamp of thoughts through his brain, especially in the small hours. It even quietened the inner rat; the gnawing of guilt and remembrance.

He had ignored the faint tremor, betraying his intake, that always affected his hands the next day, until of course, it had reared its head mid-surgery. The other advantage of this particular drug was that it lessened his craving for alcohol thus allowing him the luxury of social imbibing only. This, of course, went down well with all concerned. The morphine also helped ease the lingering discomfort from the beating.

With a glass of red wine over supper, which Isabel was glad to note appeared to be his sole intake, the couple tried to reprise the plans for supper from the previous evening. They discussed tactics for the upcoming interviews. Andy advised Isabel to rely on the loss of memory angle and thereby avoid any awkward questions whilst he would fall back on his obligation not to discuss clinical matters outside the hospital.

Feeling both a little more relaxed, they decided to have an early night. So thus settled for the night, he was alarmed when the phone rang. After all his on-call rota had finished. A clipped voice wanted to know his name.

'Who is this please?' Andy climbed out of bed and retired to his study, attempting to leave his wife undisturbed.

'This is an operational officer for the SIS. Could I confirm your name, address and phone number please?' Andy was in no mood for this nonsense-if anything he felt faintly euphoric-free of all earthly cares, as it were.

'Well, you should know. You rang me after all,' Andy responded, somewhat playfully.

'Sir, I repeat. This is an officer from the special investigations service—MI5 if you like. I can assure you this is no laughing matter.' Andy demurred.

'What can I do for you?'

The officer described the events of which Andy was only too well aware.

'We need to ask you some questions, Sir. Would you give an indication of your whereabouts over the next few days?' Andy had no intention of alerting the hospital, so suggested that any meeting took place at his home.

'We would normally wish to be more formal, Sir, say at a police station of your choosing. I will make the arrangements.'

Andy did not like this one bit. He attempted a version of the 'who do you think I am?' gambit. 'I am a senior surgeon at the Shropshire Hospital's Trust,' he informed the intruder. 'I am constantly required to be available to attend trauma patients.' A brief silence.

'Very well then, Sir, this is only what you might call a preliminary enquiry, so I see no reason I should not meet you at your home. Let me know your availability and a fellow officer will accompany me.' Andy reached for his diary, agreed on a time, gave contact details and went to put the phone down. 'Oh and Sir, before you go. I must remind you that on no account are you to leave the country. We may ask you to surrender your passport.'

Andy was about to remark that he had no intention of leaving the country but wisely thought better of it. Before he returned to bed, he went to his safe to help himself to a couple of mls of precious elixir. After all, he reassured himself; he needed to settle his nerves.

Andy woke the next morning with the usual feeling of dread. Whilst his clinical mind rationalised these feelings as the after-effects of the morphine, this knowledge did nothing to improve his general mood. The balmy effects of the last evening's intake had well and truly dissipated. Things did not improve on greeting his wife, who was up before him and already at work in her office.

The University had supplied her with a new laptop, this time secured with an in-built tracker that would alert the authorities if it went beyond the boundaries of this address or that of the University. Prof. Landon had been in touch and suggested that, whilst she convalesced, she should catch up with her work from home. He had also warned her against making calls, or sending emails, linked to her work. Needing no second invitation, Isabel had already engrossed herself.

'Would you mind dropping the girls off on your way in?'

This request did nothing to improve Andy's mood who replied, somewhat sarcastically, 'Let's have breakfast together, first? Would that be OK?'

Apart from anything else, he was keen to at least try to re-establish some semblance of family life.

'I'm not hungry, to be honest. Why don't you carry on and we'll catch up later.'

Andy considered telling her of last night's conversation with SIS but thought better of it and went to sort the girl's breakfast out. Resisting the urge to go to the safe, he swallowed two Co-codamol instead and washed them down with strong coffee. Thus fortified, he called Lucy and Imogen down. They too seemed to have caught the low mood of the place and bickered with each other and resisted Andy's efforts to get them ready for school. Normally so cheerful they seemed to have lost their enthusiasm for seeing their friends, perhaps missing their mother's normally close attention. Still, once in the car, Andy chivvied them along and tried to pretend that things were normal.

'Try not to worry about mum, girls. She's had a terrific shock and will take time to get back to normal.' They met this optimistic remark with silence and, glancing in the driving mirror, Andy couldn't help but notice the looks passed between the two girls.

Eventually, Lucy, usually the most forthright of the two girls, ventured a question, 'Daddy, will mummy get to look—' she searched for the right words '—normal again?'

'Girls, your mother suffered some nasty injuries and she will take a little more time yet to fully recover. You must both be as understanding as you can with her. Give her time. I know it's difficult but—'

Lucy interrupted, 'Yes, daddy. I think we know that but, will her face always be—', again a pause, '—always be—' She looked at her sister. '—well, crooked?'

Of all people, Andy knew the answer to this question but was unable to share this with his daughters just then. Instead.

'Yes girls, of course, she will look like your beautiful mummy again. Try not to worry.' Reassured or not, he dropped them off at the school and carried on to the hospital.

Chapter 20

'Thank you for agreeing to meet us at your home,' Officer Luke Arnold introduced himself, apparently ignoring the fact that it had been Andy who had requested the home meeting. He introduced his assistant, Ms Laker.

'Ms Laker will take notes. Otherwise, this meeting is very much an informal affair. We are just attempting to establish what went on around your wife's unfortunate accident. Can I start by asking you how you first became involved in these events?' Andy went on to describe how he had been called out to an RTA in his capacity as the on-duty head and neck trauma consultant and how, having managed to secure the female patient's airway, he recognised her to be in fact, his wife.

'That must have been singularly difficult for you, Mr Saunders.'

Andy agreed that indeed, the whole affair had been even more traumatic than usual. He went on to describe how he transferred the care of his wife to his trusted colleague, Stuart Hodgkins.

'I am interested in what you knew about the circumstances of the accident, Sir. How, your wife—I do apologise here Mr Saunders-I realise how difficult this must be for you but, as I say, how your wife came to be in a vehicle with a person unknown to you?'

'All I was aware of at the time was that there had been another person involved in the same accident, who had also been admitted.'

'The driver of the vehicle, as it turned out, I believe?'

'Yes. But of course, I didn't realise this at the time. It was only later that we were told that two people had been removed from the same vehicle.'

'Who told you this?'

'The attending paramedics at the scene. They confirmed that the German was in fact driving the car.'

'The German?'

Andy paused; Ah yes, the German. Officer Arnold continued. 'May I ask how you knew the driver was German?'

Andy's mind flashed back to the side-ward and his certainly unlawful methods of extracting this particular information.

'Ah yes, the gentleman concerned was conscious on admission and yes, I believe he was, how can I say—expressing himself, indeed, in German.'

'I believe this gentleman was seriously injured,' stated officer Arnold.

'Yes. The attending orthopaedic surgeons confirmed that his injuries were consistent with bracing his feet against the brake pedal in an attempt to avoid the collision. The paramedics confirmed that he was in fact driving the car.'

'Do you mind me asking, Sir, how your wife came to be a passenger in a vehicle driven by this German gentleman?' Andy realised he needed to keep his wits about him. This fellow was no mug. Andy thought on his feet.

'I know that Isabel-my wife-was communicating with a colleague in Frankfurt,' he said. 'That she had arranged for her to come to the UK.' Officer Arnold glanced at Ms Laker.

'I also understand,' he continued, 'that your nanny was German. Is that right?'

How on earth did he come to know this stuff?

'Well, yes, but this could have been purely coincidence,' Andy parried.

'In my experience, Mr Saunders, coincidence only occurs in fairy tales.' He allowed himself a faint smile directed, once again, at his assistant.

Do I tell him that my SHO is also German? Andy considered.

'I think I can explain that erm, coincidence. My Jr in the Department, Bernadine, is German. It was she who introduced her stepsister, Heidi, to us— my wife and me. She knew that we were looking to fill such a vacancy.'

'Stepsister, you say?' Andy once again found himself on the back foot.

'Yes, it was only after I had spoken to my wife's colleague—Lisbeth Wagner—in Frankfurt that I realised the connection.'

'Well, I'm grateful you mentioned your trip over to Germany. Could I ask what made you undertake such a trip? Your wife, after all, was seriously ill in hospital.'

'I knew my wife was being well looked after and that there was very little I could do to help her. I thought it might be helpful to speak with her friend.' Officer Arnold coughed.

'Excuse me. Forgive me, it seems a little—erm—extreme shall I say, to travel all the way to Germany to talk to this lady, Ms Wagner, you said. Why didn't you just call her? On the phone or her mobile?'

Andy again realised he could not divulge how it had been uppermost in his mind to find out the identity of the German driver, who his contacts were.

'I was so distressed, officer, so traumatised if you like, by what had happened to my wife and my ignorance in treating her, that I needed to get away; to collect my thoughts.'

'Again, forgive me, Mr Saunders, but—' Again he paused as he looked through the windows towards the Shropshire Hills. 'You live in such a beautiful place. Why would you go to Frankfurt of all places in order to—er—get away, as you put it?'

Bloody hell. This interview was altogether more difficult than he had anticipated.

'I had the advantage of my sister-in-law, Alice, being here at the house. She had already planned to visit, to babysit while my wife's friend, this Lisbeth Wagner, came to stay.'

'Ah, so this Wagner woman was actually meant to be here, in England?'

'Yes. I told you. My wife had gone to the airport to pick her up,' explained Andy, now thoroughly disorientated.

'But your wife was in a vehicle with this unknown German gentleman?'

'Yes, but of course, I didn't know this at the time.' Andy's cheeks were now glowing.

'Let me get this right. Your reaction to the news that your wife had been in a serious accident involving an unknown male was to fly to Frankfurt to meet this lady who was actually meant to be here in England?'

Andy was now visibly discomfited. The officer continued, 'So again, forgive me but I want to get this clear. Your wife was unconscious, later sedated and the injured driver was also in no condition to communicate with you or indeed, anyone else. So how did you know that this Wagner woman was still in Frankfurt.'

How indeed? Andy thought on his feet.

'She, Lisbeth, had rung home, spoken to Alice—my sister-in-law. Saying about how the trip had been cancelled at the last moment. She seemed very upset, according to Alice.'

'Mmmm. Cancelled by whom?'

132

'I could, of course, have only presumed it was my wife.' Officer Arnold considered this for a while.

'In that case, Mr Saunders, why was your wife still, by your account, travelling to the airport?' Good point well made. God, this was exhausting.

'All I am aware of,' Andy replied, now exasperated, 'as I think I have explained, is that my wife's colleague phoned here, apparently very distressed. I obviously thought that she must be aware of what had led up to these events.' Light at the end of the tunnel? 'I was so concerned to understand what had gone on that I took the opportunity to fly to Frankfurt.' Ah, at last, Andy thought. Perhaps this man will leave him alone now.

'Thank you, Mr Saunders, for your help with our enquiries.' Again, he glanced at his colleague. 'I will consider what you have told me and no doubt I—we—will be in touch again.' Andy clearly did not relish this prospect. 'But, before we go. Can I ask you one last question? I understand you were the victim of an assault whilst you were in Frankfurt. Is that correct?' How on earth did he know this?

'Yes indeed. A trivial matter, really. Certainly not worth reporting. An attempted mugging I'd have thought.'

'Was anything stolen, any attempt made to extract money or indeed, your mobile phone?'

'No. In fact, the whole thing was over in seconds. Just youth, I think. A random attack.'

'A random attack?' Officer Arnold repeated. 'Very interesting. As I say, Sir, I have no doubt we will return to these matters. We'll let ourselves out. Goodbye, Mr Saunders.'

Andy waited until they had left, then took himself upstairs to the safe. He sat on his bed and swallowed five mls of diamorphine. Waiting to calm down, he decided to call his brother-in-law, Ben, to ask him to ask his wife to stone-wall any enquiries that may be made about a certain phone call from Germany. Returning to his bed, he lay down and welcomed the warm relief as narcotic-induced sleep overwhelmed him.

******

Andy woke with a start. It was the middle of the night and Isabel, who had taken to snoring heavily since her accident, was lying beside him. He realised that it was not his wife that had woken him, but the realisation that the effects of the morphine had worn off and that he was now amid morphine-induced insomnia. A true paradox. He lay sweating and anxious. That bloody investigating officer had run rings around him.

There was no way that he couldn't see through him. He went over the interview again and again and the more he examined his responses, the more he realised he had no option but to come clean. Well, not entirely clean, but at least confess that he had extracted information from the injured German and that this information had inspired him to travel to Frankfurt. After all, he consoled himself; he had received facts that could only help in the wider investigation; he could divest himself of weighty knowledge and let them get on with it. They had much bigger fish to fry.

Thus, kicking this recurrent cycle of thought off and into the clichéd long grass, his mind temporarily emptied, allowing a tidal wave of fear and loathing to come washing, uninvited, into the vacuum. The usual culprits, but that knowledge itself did nothing to ease the turmoil. He gave up on sleep and went downstairs. He took two Co-codamol with a draft of whiskey and turned towards his office. He realised that Bernardine was on call. He text messaged her.

'Can you talk?'

'Yes,' came the reply. 'I'll be in my room in 10 minutes. Speak then—Ja?'

Andy told her, in whispered tones, the events surrounding the interview. He went on to suggest that he might go back to the officer and give him the information he had been reluctant to disclose.

'At some point, Bernie, I am going to have to tell them what I know about Heidi and your stepfather. I see no other way.'

'Andy, to be very honest with you, I must tell you that I feel—I care more about you than I care about them. I know that my stepfather is involved in these matters. I've already told you that I never trusted him. And of course Heidi, she is completely under his influence. I gave her an opportunity-with you-to prove that she could make a choice, to reform even, to make the right choices for once. But all she did was repay me-and you-by stealing your wife's computer. Spying and—how do you say?—hacking. I am very ashamed of her.'

As usual, Bernardine's soft, lilting, perfectly accented voice stilled Andy. He allowed the conversation to drift away into regions that should not play host to the usual exchanges between a consultant and his junior. The effects of the heroin, the nagging of the guilt, his memories, his inner rat all coalesced into a honeyed miasma of love for this beautiful girl. At last, he felt able to return to his bed and sleep once again.

Back in his office the next day and safe from scrutiny Andy took the card Officer Arnold had left with him and called his number.

'Good morning, officer. Mr Saunders here. I wonder if I could have a word with you off the record, so to speak. I have some information that I believe could help you with your enquiries.'

'What sort of information?'

'This is strictly, must be, off the record. It is information gained during my duties as a clinician and, as such, confidential. It is a matter of patient confidentiality if you will.'

'Very well. Where shall we meet?'

To Andy's surprise, the officer agreed to his suggestion that, as the interview was to be informal, that the back bar of the Ragleth inn might be suitable. After all, a pint of Hobson's could only help oil the wheels.

Later and having taken their pints to the snug and fended off Wendy's natural inquisitiveness as to the identity of the stranger, Andy and the investigating officer from the SIS settled down, with Andy determined to reassert what he saw as his natural authority in this second interview.

'The information I would give you now is strictly confidential because it was obtained in my role as a senior clinician in the hospital concerned. It will be apparent that the information concerns my involvement and treatment of a patient under my care. As no criminal activity took place during these interventions, I am certain that you will honour my testimony in this regard.'

Officer Arnold did not look so certain but took a draft of his ale nonetheless and wiped his lips.

'Go on.'

'You asked me yesterday how I came to know certain details regarding the injured driver, his relationship with my wife and his connections with the pharmaceutical industry.' Andy emptied his pint and called for another.

'Go on.' Officer Arnold repeated. Andy waited for his pint and then resumed;

'I went to see the driver of the vehicle—the orthopaedic consultants had asked me to check over his facial skeleton-he had a few bruises, but I ascertained he had sustained no serious injury. Whilst I was examining him, he came to and was obviously confused. Didn't remember he was in the UK.

I gathered he was German, but he spoke excellent English. He told me he worked for a company called CellProcure in Frankfurt and that he had become aware that my wife, Isabel, had information of benefit to them.' He took a long draught of his beer. 'He explained that he had managed to, how can I put it, get information from Ms Wagner, Lisbeth—my wife's colleague—and taken her place on the plane over here.'

Officer Arnold seemed to absorb this information with studied concentration. Andy continued.

'He then, apparently, abducted my wife, thus explaining how he came to be involved in the accident.'

'Are you telling me he told you all this whilst lying in bed, severely injured?' Andy finished his 2nd pint.

'Of course. How else would I know?'

The officer pondered this. 'So what made you go over to Germany? That still puzzles me.'

Andy paused before answering.

'Well, our nanny, my wife had grown quite fond of her and I knew, through my SHO that she must be involved in some way. Bernardine—this SHO—had told me that Heidi was her stepsister and that this man was her stepfather. I wanted to find out how this Lisbeth woman also came to be involved; it was her who told me that Heidi had stolen my wife's research.'

From his hoped-for moral high ground, Andy was becoming aware that the more he talked, the less credible his story. He decided to draw the interview to a close.

'Another pint?' He asked his apparently sceptical new friend.

'No, no thank you. I've had quite enough.'

'You won't mind if I do?' Andy asked, fully intending to have one anyway-his mouth was rather dry for some reason.

'You won't mind if I interview this SHO—Bernardine you say—just to clarify a few points?'

'No, of course. She is very sympathetic towards my wife and her involuntary involvement in all this.'

Andy realised he would need to have a word with her before this proposed inquisition took place.

'Well, thank you, Mr Saunders. This has all been very interesting—very helpful.'

'You agree that I have no interest in this affair, other than the welfare of my wife?' Andy was keen to get this particular monkey off his back.

'I will, of course, be providing this information to my colleagues in Germany. No doubt they will wish to corroborate your story. Apart from that, I thank you for your confidence and I will wish you good day; enjoy your beer.'

As he left the hostelry, Andy found himself not entirely reassured. Having taken the precaution of walking home, Andy pondered the situation. From whichever angle he viewed his life, the prospect appeared clouded by storms of indecision, chronic anxiety and loss of his treasured routine: the innate trust in his surgical capabilities. He also realised that he had stirred up a hornet's nest. He had now included his convalescent wife in the conspiracy theories around Heidi, the missing computer and her co-conspirators. His mood was not improved upon entering the kitchen:

'Where the hell have you been?' came the happy greeting. Then, as Andy approached her, she recoiled at his hoppy breath.

'I thought you were going to reduce your drinking—you promised. Now look at you, the girls aren't even back from school.'

Andy didn't offer the excuse that he had been attending an informal meeting with an investigation officer of the secret services. This news would be very unlikely to improve her mood. Instead, 'I'm not on-call why shouldn't I enjoy a drink on my afternoon off?'

'Because it would be nice for once if you could be around and compos mentis for the girls for once—that's why!' Trying to defuse the situation, Andy approached his wife, who recoiled from his advance.

'D'you not even think that I might want to have some time to myself. I need to get to grips with work—it's not all about you!'

'Yes, I realise that I do, but we both have responsibilities—to our careers, I mean. Why not think about hiring another nanny?'

'Great advice coming from you, Andy. You're the one who started this mess by introducing Heidi into the household.'

'For heaven's sake Izzy, you can't blame me for that—it was your friend in Germany just as much to blame. If you hadn't used the home laptop to swap work with her, none of this would have happened.'

'Oh, that's great! So now the whole thing is my fault. For Christ's sake, Andy.' She started to cry. This time Andy did manage to console her and thought better of his decision not to tell her of his interviews.

'Look, darling—the whole thing is out of our hands now. You know I told you that the German intelligence services were now involved—the BKA—well I've now been interviewed by their UK equivalent. I've told them all I know. You and I are the victims here. I repeat, it's now out of our hands.' Isabel seemed only partly reassured.

'What about my work, Andy? They're sure to follow up on what happened at the University. Prof. Landon's involvement—'

'Well, so what if they do?' Andy stood back, both arms extended, his hands rested on his altered wife's shoulders. He contemplated her face. The professional concerns confused with the personal—could they ever be disentangled?

'If there have been criminal goings-on and the university was aware, then surely it can only be a good thing if it all comes to light. After all, you are the innocent one in all of this, the victim as you pointed out. All you've done is use your incredible brain to come up with a possible answer to the ultimate clinical conundrum; the cure for cancer, for heaven's sake. I'm proud of you Izzy. All you've got to concentrate on is getting better and getting back to what you do best, so you can carry on with your wonderful work.'

Isabel seemed to succumb to this soliloquy and rested her head on her husband's shoulder, leaving Andy to ponder the question: yes, he *was* proud of her, sorry for her even, but he asked himself—did he, could he, love her again? The appalling shallowness of the question caused him to shudder with revulsion at his own weakness.

******

Later that evening, again self-anaesthetised as a buffer against the advancing train of unanswered questions, an awful truth settled amongst the debris clouding his mind. Bernardine, his SHO, his lover, must be an accomplice in this ghastly story. It was far too much of a coincidence that she would have introduced her stepsister, in all innocence, to his wife, the very person whose research CellProcure wanted to access.

The company who would go to the extreme of sending its representative, the girl's father, to blackmail Lisbeth and eventually kidnap his wife. Bernie *must* be involved. Could she even have been planted by her stepfather in the first place, employed by Andy in order to get to his wife? Surely not. It was she, after all,

138

who admitted that her ambition had led to all this. She couldn't be involved—it was too incredible, something out of a poor thriller novel.

But, as the old surgical diagnostic sieve proved; what was left after sifting through all the facts could only represent the correct diagnosis. He had to speak to Bernie first thing. With that thought uppermost, he lapsed into deep, drug-assisted sleep.

On waking Andy attempted to collect himself by partaking of a shower followed by breakfast, which comprised two Co-codamol, a Brufen, 400 mg and a Valium 5 mg. He would grab a coffee in the hospital canteen where he had arranged, via text, to meet his SHO. Bernie seemed immediately concerned by Andy's appearance.

'What's up? You look awful!'

'Thanks, that's all I need.'

'Look, Andy, before you start, I need to get something—' she paused, struggling for the right words. '—How would you say—von meine Brust. From off my chest.' She tapped her white coat.

'Go on.' Andy was also struggling to find the right way to introduce his questions, so seemed happy to listen.

'I feel I must offer my resignation. I can no longer work alongside you, Andy. I must return to Germany. Try to leave you to sort out all of this mess I have created for you.'

Andy had no immediate answer to this. In fact, the coffee splashing on the table betrayed his inability to assimilate the words emanating from this girl's mouth. His hands shook. He could understand the text, but his brain was refusing to accept its meaning. Bernie, therefore, carried on.

'All this is my fault. If I hadn't introduced my stepsister to you, none of this would have happened; your wife's injuries, the trouble I've caused you here, at your work. I know that my stepfather was involved in some bad things back home, but I never associated that with your wife's work.'

Again, Andy found himself on the back foot. His intention had been, after all, to quiz her. He hadn't expected this turn of events.

'Are you telling me that you were not acting under instructions from your stepfather? That you weren't sent here deliberately by him to gain access?'

'Oh Andy, how could you possibly think that. All I ever wanted was to pursue my career here in the UK.'

'So how do you explain the coincidence of Heidi knowing about my wife's work?'

'Gerhardt, my stepfather, has many ways of getting what he wants. He saw my presence here as an opportunity. An opportunity to get access to your wife. It was easy for him to find out that I worked for you and that your wife was carrying out the research his company was also involved with. He sent Heidi over, in my care, knowing she would find a way—and then—' Bernie bowed her head, a tear rolling down her cheek. '—and then, I was so, so stupid to introduce her to you as a nanny—I led her to you—forgive me.' She sobbed again. 'I caused all this to happen.' Andy, yet again found his resolve weakening. His confused and battered brain committed another volte-face.

'You didn't know, couldn't know, that she would intercept my wife's calls, access, then steal, her laptop—'

'No, of course, but it was I who gave her the opportunity.'

By now, visibly distressed, Andy couldn't help but reach across and hold her hand, bending his head to look into her eyes. This tableau confronted the theatre sister, Julie, entering the canteen for a quick coffee. Neither of the two lovers, employee and employer, thus engrossed, noticed her look of deep concern as she carried away her cup of coffee. Neither did they know or indeed seem to care, that she had every intention of reporting the scene to HR.

*****

After Andy's morning outpatient clinic, a call from his colleague, Stuart prevented him from jumping into his car. He intended a quick getaway.

'Andy, hi. Glad I caught you. A quick word if I may.' Not best pleased to be scrutinised by his friend and colleague, Andy paused.

'Oh hi, Stu—what can I do for you?'

'Well, Andy. Look, this is very difficult. We've received a complaint—well, several complaints actually and HR have been in touch. They want to speak to you. As a matter of some urgency, it would appear. This is most unfortunate, Andy, but they want my presence at the meeting again. Look, I'm so sorry, Andy.'

'What's it about?'

'They wouldn't let on. They do though, expect you to attend first thing tomorrow morning.'

'What happens if I refuse?'

'Andy, you know very well that that would not be wise. I don't think you have a choice.' Andy gazed across the car park, clearly in two minds.

'Andy, come on. Think clearly. We have to sort this out, once and for all.'

'Sort what out? Can't they bloody well understand I'm under stress?'

'Perhaps that's what they want to discuss—offer help?' Andy gave a mirthless smile.

'Fat chance—'

'Anyway, I'll expect to see you at 9 am, yeah? And—' to Andy's back as he clambered into the vehicle. 'Andy—smarten yourself up a bit-please.' Andy started up his car and drove off.

Isabel had also had a difficult morning. A phone call from the University had left her reeling. It had transpired that the SIS had been asking questions at the University and that Prof Landon had been detained. No more information had been forthcoming and Isabel had been summoned to a meeting the next day. When Andy arrived home, Isabel asked if he could look after the girls the next day.

'No, I'm afraid I can't. I have a meeting at the hospital. Attendance imperative.'

'Andy, I also have a meeting at the University. Why does my work always have to come second?'

'It doesn't, Izzy. I help out as much as I can, but you know how it is—I'm a full-time consultant—I can't mess around.'

'—and I can?' Isabel replied.' Andy, I *have* to get back to work. I can't stand just hanging around here all day playing housewife.'

'Playing'—so that's what you call it now is it?'

'You know exactly what I mean, Andy. We're going to have to find a carer for tomorrow at least.'

'I could ask Bernadine. She's off tomorrow. She won't mind I'm sure—after all, it's her bloody stepsister who ran off!'

Chapter 21

For once released from mothering duties, Isabel hired a taxi to Shrewsbury station and from there caught a train down to Birmingham. She still found herself struggling with balance from time to time and didn't want to risk driving. In fact, she wondered if she would ever want to drive a car again. She was now experiencing flashbacks to the collision and even driving in the taxi, she felt exposed.

However, once there, she reacquainted herself with her laboratory and her colleagues, who all gathered around, offering sympathy and incredulous gasps as her story unfolded. She promised them she would soon be back in harness and went up to her professor's office. She found a very stern-looking Prof Taylor who asked her to take a seat.

'Thanks for coming in,' he told her. 'You will have heard that Professor Landon has been suspended and that he is now under investigation by the SIS.'

'Why on earth—?' Isabel asked.

'Before I go any further, forgive me. How are you? I could not believe it when I heard of your accident.' Isabel had no desire to relive this particular experience and after a brief résumé of her recovery asked her senior to continue.

'It would seem that Raymond was involved with a biotech company in Germany called CellProcure.' At this Isabel stayed silent, only a barely lifted eyebrow betraying her emotion. The Prof continued.

'Yes, elements at CellProcure were using clandestine methods to obtain intelligence about research being carried out in this university. It appears that we were one of their targets. And yes Isabel, the work being carried out by yourself and your colleague in Frankfurt was of particular interest, apparently.'

Isabel remained silent. 'It would seem—I hardly find this credible, but there you are-it would appear that Raymond, Prof. Landon, was involved in what one can only refer to as espionage. He was, apparently coercing with CellProcure.

Apparently, as a shareholder in EndImmuneUK, he stood to make an awful lot of money if this potential cancer treatment was ever developed.'

At last, Isabel spoke.

'You will be aware in that case, that my accident was a direct result of this conspiracy. That my laptop was stolen and an agent from CellProcure was driving the vehicle when it crashed.'

'Yes, indeed. The investigating officer did suggest that you and indeed your husband, were inadvertently caught up in this appalling mess.'

'So, what happens now?'

'The agent responsible for the cyber-attack on your home phone, the theft of your laptop and the accident which involved you, was abducted back to Germany under the auspices of CellProcure. I suppose they were hoping they could keep their involvement under wraps as it were—'

Isabel did not let on that she was already aware of the sudden airlifting of her abductor from the hospital. The professor continued, 'He is, though, now under investigation. The only good thing to come out of this is that the University is now absolved of any involvement in this—this espionage, which of course means that you are free to carry on with your vital work as soon as you feel able.'

'What about my colleague, Lisbeth Wagner?'

'Well, it would appear that she was also under some pressure from this operator. It transpires however that she has done nothing that would be regarded as criminal.' Prof Taylor appeared to be well-informed.

'Did this investigating officer tell you all this? Surely, it's confidential?'

'Well, again it seems that he questioned your husband at some length and while it appears that he has been somewhat—' The professor coughed. '—somewhat misguided, shall we say, he too has done nothing that could be deemed criminal. With your involvement, so tragically for you, in all of this, I think the officer thought we should know that we are not under further suspicion. I've no doubt he will communicate with you directly, but in the meantime he wanted us to get back to some sort of normality.'

'Will Prof Landon be prosecuted?' Isabel wanted to know.

'Very likely, yes. There are questions around insider trading. He has also been involved in industrial espionage—a very serious crime. Which, of course, leads me to my final question.'

'Which is?'

'As I say, I—we—the University, that is to say, are very keen to get you back to work. It would seem that you are now close to publishing a paper which, to say the least, will put this University on the map for all the right reasons. If you can overcome the stem-cell transfer problem, then we may well advance the so-called fight against cancer, significantly.'

'And the question, Prof?'

'It seems that the German universities are keen to distance themselves from this conspiracy. They have offered a joint chair in cell biology-together with this university—in order to advance this research. We are also aware of your initial reluctance to become too involved in academia, that you had turned down a fellowship in order to put your family first. We have, of course, every sympathy with this point of view but are now in a position to ask if you would be prepared to put yourself up for this position?'

Isabel struggled to keep control of her lower jaw as her mouth gaped open in astonishment. 'Me? Go for Professor? I can't believe it.' The professor smiled.

'Let's put it like this Isabel, after all you've been through I am certain that you will receive the full backing of the University.' Barely able to assimilate all of this information, she thanked her professor and went to find a strong coffee.

******

It could certainly be said that Isabel's husband's interview was not going so well. Back in the familiar boardroom, Andy found himself facing the usual panel, but this time augmented by a severe-looking fellow in a dark suit. He was, rather worryingly, introduced as the Accountable Officer for controlled drugs. He also noticed, again with alarm, the presence of Julie, the theatre sister.

Once again, proceedings were begun by a short word from Stuart who described the considerable stress, both professional and domestic, that Mr Saunders had been under recently. Ever present, old Grey Bob dismissed this pre-emptive claim for clemency in short order.

'Mr Saunders, it appears once again that your ability to carry out your duties has been compromised. I acknowledge the comments of Mr Hodgkins—' she glanced at Stuart—'but my primary concern has to be the health and safety of patients and colleagues. We have received several-how can I put this?—statements of concern regarding your performance.'

144

This time she turned and indicated the theatre sister, who looked as though she wanted to be elsewhere. Grey-Bob continued. 'It was reported that you had to cede control of operating to a junior during a recent procedure.' Andy glanced at Lucy. 'That you actually could not continue with your work, that you requested an inexperienced junior doctor to complete a very delicate task.' Andy could not let this pass.

'I will remind you that I am here to teach; that my registrar is not inexperienced but rather that he is here to learn.'

'Yes, of course, but my understanding of the situation is that you were unable to continue—' At this, Andy shot another look at his former friend. Grey-Bob noted this.

'I will remind you, Mr Saunders, that employees have a responsibility to raise any concerns about another employee whose behaviour may and I repeat, may represent a risk to health or safety of employees or patients. In this case, it would seem to apply to the well-being of a young girl with serious facial injuries.'

'I will not have this!' Andy reddened. 'That young lady received prompt and expert care. I defy anyone to have achieved a better result.'

'That, Mr Saunders, is not the issue here. My concern is and this is a very delicate matter, my concern is that you have been underperforming as a result of being unfit to practice.'

'Unfit to practice?'

'Yes, Mr Saunders. It would appear that you have attended outpatients smelling of alcohol. It is also a matter of record that you have also attended at operating theatres under the influence.' Again, a glance in Lucy's direction. 'Yes and worse it may appear.'

'Worse? What can you possibly be implying?' This time Grey-Bob turned to the dark-suited gentlemen. 'Please continue, Mr Wright.'

'Yes, thank you, ma'am. Yes, it has come to light—,' this time he directed his comments to Andy. 'That certain stocks of controlled drugs have not been accounted for.' Andy blanched. 'Yes, it seems that certain medications have disappeared and not been signed out. In each instance, it appears that the incidents are closely related to medication prescribed by yourself, Mr Saunders, for the management of certain patients. This includes the case recently alluded to.'

Stuart looked at his friend—disconsolate. Grey-Bob continued, 'Thank you, Mr Wright. Now ,we could confirm our suspicions that you are abusing alcohol and narcotic drugs, by requesting blood and serum tests. However, we do not want to submit you to these interventions if you are willing to submit to counselling.' Andy resembled a stag, well and truly cornered.

'Counselling?'

'Yes, assisted counselling, perhaps CBT. Managed withdrawal.'

'Bloody hell,' Andy muttered to himself. 'She's got this all lined up.' Grey Bob continued, clearly enjoying herself. Perhaps she too enjoyed perpetuating the myth of the hospital dentist.

'We don't want to impose disciplinary action, so it would be better for all concerned if you agreed to a period of leave, shall we say?'

'So, you're suspending me?'

'No, Mr Saunders, we are not suspending you. We are merely suggesting that you take a period of voluntary leave on the condition that you submit, as I say, to professional help.'

'Do I have a choice?'

'Mr Saunders, no, I don't think you do have a choice. At least if you intend to continue your career here in your capacity as a consultant.'

'Do I have an opportunity to appeal?'

'Appeal? Mr Saunders, I repeat that you are not being disciplined. All we require is that you cooperate with Occupational Health. We must remind you that you are held in very high regard in this institution and that all we want is to get you back to work, where you belong, as soon as possible.'

As the meeting dispersed, Stuart grabbed hold of Andy's arm. 'Look, Andy, I didn't bring this up at the meeting, but I saw you in the canteen with Bernadine. Lucy as well. I had to persuade her not to mention it. What the hell was that all about? You're old enough to be her father, for heaven's sake. Andy, just take this opportunity to get some rest—sort yourself out for God's sake—and leave that bloody girl alone. What are you thinking?'

Thus diminished, ashamed and admonished, Andy, skulked off home, his tail well and truly between his legs. Here he was greeted by, of all people, the aforementioned Bernadine. As he walked into the front room, he was initially surprised, then thrilled to see his daughters clearly enjoying her company. She had built an island of cushions, on which all three were comfortably perched, with books and drawing materials all around.

Ripples of laughter lifted his mood immediately. Bernie's shining smile turned towards him and his heart lifted, took flight from the former depths of despair. He couldn't bear the thought of losing this girl, her resigning, going back to Germany. Excusing himself, he went to the kitchen and instinctively reached for the red wine. 'Bloody hell, how am I ever going to sort this out?' He drank deeply. The familiar warm relief washed over him as the alcohol worked its magic.

When later Isabel returned, she was surprised and perhaps a little disturbed to find a scene of domestic bliss. First, she heard laughter from the sitting room and on entering, was astounded to find her husband sitting in the middle of the room, surrounded by cushions and happy females, one of which was her husband's employee.

'Hi, everyone!'

'Oh hi, Mrs Saunders.' This cheery greeting from Bernadine seemed to perplex Isabel who really didn't know what else to say so instead she returned to the kitchen, took off her coat which she then hung across a barstool. Her rather chastened husband followed her.

'Oh hi, darling. How did it go?'

'Andy, what's going on? Why is she still here?'

'I've only just got back myself and the girls seemed so happy, I kind of joined in.' This cheerful response did nothing to reassure Isabel.

'You've been drinking, haven't you?'

'Oh no, Izzy; not you as well. I've had a hell of a day. Don't start all of that again.'

'Do you want to know how *my* day went, Andy?' Bernadine interrupted this tense exchange.

'Hi, look shall I be getting away now? Your girls are lovely, Mrs Saunders—so well-behaved. Any time I can help you, if I'm not at work, please let me know.'

'Yes, thank you—Bernadine, isn't it? Yes, thank you for looking after my, er, family. See you again. Goodbye.' Bernadine left the kitchen, resisting the urge to glance back at Andy. The tension hung heavy.

'So darling, how did the interview go?'

'Don't 'darling' me, Andy. What's going on?'

'What do you mean; nothings 'going on.' I've had such a ghastly day it was actually quite nice to return home to happy children.'

'Well, that's great, Andy. And why do you think it is that they haven't been happy? Answer me that!'

'Look, Izzy. I don't know what you're getting at—'

'Your bloody drinking—that's what I'm getting at, Andy. That and your lack of interest in your family.'

'Izzy, I'm going to get a grip-I promise you-in fact, it's out of my hands now-I'm going to *have* to get a grip.'

'What do you mean?'

'Effectively, Izzy, I've been sacked.'

'Sacked!'

'Well, not sacked exactly, but laid off.'

'Laid off?' Isabel could not help repeating herself.

'I've been given enforced leave. Referred to Occupational Health for counselling.'

'What the hell, Andy?' He could see no point in not coming clean, so he continued.

'Some stuff has been going on at the hospital—drugs gone missing—and they're accusing me.'

'Andy, for God's sake. This can't be true. Are you telling me that the hospital is accusing you of stealing drugs? Drugs now, Andy? What are you thinking?'

'Well, that's just it, Isabel. I haven't been thinking, have I. Ever since your accident—'

'Oh, so now it's my fault—'

'No, Izzy, don't be silly. All I'm saying is that the shock of seeing you, of treating-resuscitating you for God's sake—and all the other stuff. It's just all got too much for me. I only took painkillers and a bit of Valium here and there just to help me deal with things.'

'Valium, painkillers, on top of the booze—Oh, Andy.' He omitted to tell her about the morphine.

'But look, Izzy, the hospital is helping me-they want me back at work as soon as I've sorted myself out'

'—and how exactly Andy do you intend to 'sort yourself out?' You've been drinking already for God's sake.'

'Yes, I know, I know. But look, I promise, I will get help. I won't let you all down. I've thought about signing up for a week or two at the Priory-there's one in Wrexham. It'll be like a real break-give you time to be with the girls and get well again. I know if I stay here amongst familiar things I won't be able to stop drinking—It's all too much Izzy—'

He slumped on a barstool, took his head in his hands. 'Oh, Izzy, I'm so, so sorry. I'm not the man I set out to be. I've let everything get on top of me—work and Seb, I can never get Seb out of my head—Oh, Izzy.' He started to sob, shoulders heaving. 'I should have rescued him, Izzy, saved him. I was too weak, too cowardly—and then what happened to you—It's all too much.' His wife's reaction shocked him to the core.

'So here we have it. It's all about you, isn't it, as always, Andy? What about me? I'm the one who got smashed in that car, remember? I'm the one always has to put my career on hold. And did you ever think to ask me how my interview went Andy? Instead of gallivanting around with that German girl—you seemed perfectly happy then, Andy. And now you're telling me you're an addict and need to go into rehab, for God's sake. And who's going to pay for that, Andy? I suppose you will come to me once again, begging bowl in hand, wanting to dip into Grandparent's legacy. Whilst you take a little holiday away from your family and duty. Leaving me, as usual, to clear up your bloody mess!'

Andy looked up, shaken by this outburst. His wife continued, 'D'you really want to know, Andy, how this afternoon went? Well, after I'd been told all about German interference in my work and you playing the little detective, I was asked if I wanted to put myself up for a chair, for heaven's sake. Probably the biggest opportunity in my entire career. All I wanted to do was get home and celebrate with my husband and all I get is you playing happy families with your bloody SHO and then breaking down like a little child when I challenge you!'

'For God's sake, Izzy. Don't be ridiculous. Why didn't you just tell me—a Professor, for heaven's sake. Oh, Izzy, I'm sorry, come here.' He negotiated the kitchen island and went to hug his wife, who reacted by pushing him away and storming upstairs. Hearing the study door slam, he went to reassure his daughters who were happily watching the TV, oblivious to the glass-shattering sound of a marriage falling apart.

Chapter 22

In the cold light of day, Andy considered the monumental events of the previous day. He realised he had to deal with his demons but also still had the moral sense to understand that this would be easier said than done. He had been, of course, surprised and delighted by Isabel's news, but equally dismayed by her totally uncharacteristic assault on his already shattered psyche.

Understanding, from a purely clinical point of view, the depths to which his addictions had sunk, he also realised that he needed help; expert help. He knew he wouldn't detox without third-party coercion. Added to these concerns was the fact that a few weeks in the Priory didn't come cheap. He had the choice of either raiding the family savings, such as they were or indeed, as Isabel had predicted, go to her inheritance with begging bowl in hand. This latter was unlikely to be welcomed by his wife in her present state of mind.

He would also need a referral from his GP although he didn't relish coming clean to his friend; admitting the full extent of his fall from grace. However, he didn't have a choice. If he wanted to return to his beloved surgery, he had no other options.

He called the GP surgery to make an appointment: hurdle number one negotiated. Now he had to confront his true feelings for Bernadine; time to man-up he told himself. Family must come first. I will speak to her: hurdle number two. He rang her mobile.

'Shall we meet tomorrow lunchtime in the Italian again?' Yes, Bernadine agreed to escape hospital duties for lunch. 'See you there.' Even this brief conversation lifted him, gave him cause to smile. He only just avoided stumbling right there and then, threatening already to tread on hurdle number two.

In the light of all this, it was perhaps not unsurprising that Andy did not sleep very well. Eventually abandoning the marital bed, he succumbed to the inevitable, got up and retired to his study where, clear-headed at last, he plotted a map through the next few days. It helped to write things down. Perhaps he should approach this as he would approach any other clinical conundrum; develop a treatment plan, accept the need for intervention and just get on with it.

After a stiff dose of caffeine, he woke the girls and actually enjoyed their warm, early morning presence and gentle sisterly banter. Leaving them eating breakfast, he took a cup of tea to his wife, gently kissed her on the forehead and though only half awake she was aware of his whispered apology for yesterday's argument and the trouble he had caused her. He informed her he was getting the girls ready for school.

Like a man released from his inner turmoil having confronted his demons, he relished the sweet smells carried on the early morning May breeze. The little family crunched across the gravel and made the familiar drive into Shrewsbury. Returning along the same route, he found time to take in the stunning profiles of the Shropshire Hills as they, too, welcomed the sun. Bach, once again, provided blissful counterpoint.

Back at home, he became aware, once again of the familiar tremor in his hand as he cleared the kitchen; the plates and dishes rattling as he loaded the dishwasher. He acknowledged the gnawing presence of that constant ache, the yearning that he knew caffeine would not appease. He went to the safe and with a sigh, rather like that of a lover leaving his beloved, emptied the last few drops of the precious elixir. Back in the kitchen, he supplemented this with 5 mg of Valium and another mug of freshly ground coffee.

Now able to face the day, he retired to his study and put on a linen shirt, jacket, slacks and loafers-the consultant's weekend uniform-and went into Shrewsbury, where once more he enjoyed the simple pleasure of strolling alongside the River Severn. Again, like a prisoner enjoying his last day of freedom, he drank in the sights and sounds of normal people going about their business: the school eight surging down the river, followed by their rowing coach shouting advice and rhythm through his megaphone.

He observed the dog-walkers and even a troop of cygnets skimming the water after mother swan. He had forgotten what normal life looked like, this knowledge fuelling his greater desire to do whatever it needed to get himself well again—to become equipped once more to do justice to his training, to become the father he wanted to be.

Later, after another coffee in town, he visited his friend's practice in the old town and made the necessary arrangements for his voluntary admission to the Priory. He was now ready for the final task on his list, namely, to meet with and deal with, perhaps the most pressing addiction; his feelings for his young SHO. He began to realise that her intoxicating presence was just another in the list of artificial stimulants he had become used to using in order to quell his persistent inner rat. Bernadine was just another drug on the list he needed to address during his planned detoxification programme.

On descending the steps to the old restaurant, he quickly realised how difficult this process was going to be as he looked across at Bernadine, already ensconced at the bar, her beautiful blonde hair cascading down onto her elegant shoulders which only half-turned as she shone her beatific smile towards him as he approached. He bent and bestowed a kiss on her perfumed forehead; how could she smell so sweet after a morning in outpatients? How stark the contrast with the same kiss bestowed on his wife earlier in the day.

Clearly with a mind to enjoying this last taste of freedom he ordered a large glass of Chianti and bought his young friend an Appletizer. He started to tell her of his new-found resolve, instigated by his enforced lay-off, but Bernadine apparently had other things in mind.

'Andy, you know what I think of you—you understand my feelings and that is why I must tell you that I will return to Germany. I cannot continue and see the man I love destroyed in this way.' Andy tried to intervene, unsuccessfully. 'Nein, meine Liebling, let me finish. All I have done is cause you pain and trouble. Look at what has happened—your wife—your career. It has to stop.'

'But, Bernie, none of this is your doing. You didn't instigate the spying, the hacking. You didn't know that your stepsister was involved, that she would steal the laptop, that your stepfather was a criminal for heaven's sake—' In his muddled mind, Andy clearly had ignored the open goal now gaping in front of him. All he had to do at this juncture was accept Bernadine's resignation and apology and withdraw, dignity intact. Perhaps, however, it was indicative of how far his addictions had taken over his powers of reasoning that he allowed the conversation to continue.

'Yes, von coures, I know. But had I not introduced her to you—'

'Bernie, thank you, but you don't have to do this. You will do well here in the UK; continue your training by all means. You will get an excellent reference from the hospital—you don't have to go back to Germany—not yet anyway.' He took her hand in his. 'I know, Bernie, that our relationship is not right—that circumstances perhaps made me act inappropriately, but that was me, my responsibility.'

Little did he realise or even want to comprehend, that the open goal had been missed; the hurdle well and truly flattened. Instead, he explained how the hospital had given him sick leave, how he intended to address his demons. How he had taken the big step to admitting himself to the Priory.

'I just don't think I could bear the fact that you had left the UK because of me. I know how difficult the next few weeks are going to be and, selfishly I know, it comforts me to know that you will still be here. Perhaps I could talk to you, from the hospital if things get tough. You wouldn't be—I don't know—you wouldn't be judgemental. Why don't you see out your contract and review the situation then?' He squeezed her hand, looked into her blue eyes, '—Please?'

'Let me consider—think about it, Andy. Now tell me more about this Priory—'

The opportunity well and truly missed, the pair tucked into spaghetti vongole and for the moment were allowed to forget about the outside world: its pressures, responsibilities and scrutiny. They could lose themselves in the quiet warmth and embrace of mutual regard, perhaps even yes. Love.

******

To Andy, Isabel's reaction to his decision to admit himself into the Priory did nothing to endear her to him. Or indeed cause him to regret any part of the conversation he had recently enjoyed with his SHO. Isabel clearly regarded this decision as evidence of failure; the stigma would hang over her and the family. Why not mitigate these effects by attending an out-patient program if he couldn't just 'get a grip'?

'—and don't even get me started on the cost of all this. I hoped that this money could be used for the girls' schooling. There's even talk of allowing girls into Shrewsbury School. Have you any idea of the fees at that place? But think of the start it would give them in life. But no, all you can think about is yourself and your needs yet again.'

All this did, of course, was reinforce Andy's fundamental belief that his wife didn't understand the depth of his despair, the self-loathing and the consequent self-medication. Bernie had been far more sympathetic in his view, more understanding and dare he say it; more loving. On reflection, however, he also realised that Isabel herself was undergoing her own trauma, even before her accident; the acute and ever-present anxiety of the balancing act between being a mother and a scientist.

Despite this, Andy convinced himself that in order to help her and thereby his family, it was imperative that he addressed his own issues first and as a matter of priority. Even his GP friend had been more sympathetic than his wife and had to counsel him on what he could expect at the Priory. He had discreetly arranged a referral to the shortest detoxification program available.

Thus it was that Andy presented himself a few days later at Priory Coleg in Wrexham, where he prepared himself to embark on a 28-day detox program and rehab. He felt prepared for the hard work; the pain, the commitment. He had to embrace what he anticipated would be humiliation, submission; in fact a complete reversal of the behavioural tenets by which he had been guided in his professional life to date. In short, he needed help and he knew it.

After settling into his remarkably comfortable room (the program in fact was far more costly than a similar stay in a five-star hotel) he unpacked and prepared for the first meeting with the Director. He was told he would undergo an initial period which usually lasted 7 to 10 days of medically assisted withdrawal and detoxification before intensive individual, then group therapy, in order to address the source of his addictive behaviour. This phase may include the use of CBT, EMDR and/or CAT, all under the auspices of his allotted addiction treatment team.

When Andy asked what form the medical assistance would take and the director replied that benzodiazepines would form the bedrock of the anxiolytics to be used, Andy declined to inform him he had already been self-prescribing these in the form of Valium, which he had begun to consume rather in the manner of Smarties. He also declined to inform him of his use of diamorphine. This interview left him with absolutely no illusions as to how difficult this process was going to be.

******

Isabel had welcomed the new nanny and introduced her to Imogen and Lucy. She had batted away the girls' suggestion that they would like to see more of daddy's friend, Bernadine. Instead, she left the girls in the brisk and efficient care of the new employee and retired to her study. The news of her impending route to a chair had completely changed her view of her career. Until now, she had considered her work, not exactly as a side-line, but had always put the considerations, the happiness of her husband and two children first.

She had realised that she was a victim of that inbred societal rule that dictated that the woman's place remained in the home. Instead, she had been presented with a once-in-a-lifetime opportunity to genuinely address one of the few remaining medical conundrums: how to control or even cure, the insidious curse of uncontrolled cell division, i.e.; cancer.

This objective, it seemed to her, was far more important in the greater scheme of things. It ran contrary to the introspection required for bringing up a family and supporting her apparently vulnerable husband. After all, he had taken himself off to address *his* issues, why couldn't she equally follow *her* destiny.

With this new resolve firmly established at the front of her mind, the University had equipped her with a newly encrypted laptop. Strict instructions on how not to communicate the results of her research over the 'phone had been provided along with a guide template as to how to progress her work on the stem-cell/adenovirus carrier for her 'vaccine.' All she had to do now involved sorting out the details, laying a road map for her continued research.

She realised that in this new spirit of cooperation from the University she would be able to advance her research and obtain the necessary permission to use actual patient's stem cells. She considered that she would be fit to travel into Birmingham in roughly 4 to 6 weeks, about the time it would take for Andy to complete his particular bout of self-indulgence, as she saw it. In the meantime, she would be on hand to monitor the relationship between her children and the new nanny and pick up any slack.

She had even stopped worrying about her asymmetric features, convincing herself that Professors in oncological research did not worry about what they looked like. She felt the self-righteous tug of vocation. THIS would define her life; not Mr bloody Andy Saunders!

******

The first few days passed relatively peacefully in the Priory for Andy. Yes, he would have murdered for a drink on days one and two, especially as dinner time approached. After all, he reasoned, wasn't it a human right to enjoy a glass of God's own fruit juice with food? Orange juice just didn't cut it so far as he was concerned. However, the novelty of the situation had seen him through these early days, berobed as he was by the determination of the evangelist.

On day three, however, he had slept poorly, finally waking up with a killer thirst, a throbbing headache and, he noticed as he slurped his tea, a distinct tremor, noticeably worse than before. He felt wretched. Trying to pre-occupy himself with work, (he had determined to spend his time during his enforced stay, catching up with the theory of microsurgery, fully intending to embark on a course as soon as he got out of there) he opened his laptop and found he couldn't concentrate.

He went for a walk, attended an assessment clinic and as lunch approached, longed for a glass of something chilled; anything to just settle his nerves. He started to worry about everything; his work, his children, the SIS investigating officer. Shit! This was awful.

As the next few days passed, he saw himself as a reduced, shrunken human being. He had stopped shaving, stopped washing his hair. After all, what was the point? Who cared what he looked or smelled like? His sleep had become sporadic; what sleep he managed interrupted by the old, recurring nightmare of the swirl of sea, sucking Seb away from him, drawing him into a vortex of whirling water which morphed, always morphed, into thick, metallic, cloying clots of blood. He would wake from these episodes, bathed in sweat, crying out, longing for some kind of peace, some release from his torment.

The chlordiazepoxide was only touching the surface of his anxiety. Had no effect on his tremors or his self-loathing. The fact that the attending clinician had diagnosed a bad case of AUG did nothing to assuage his guilt, his dread of what the future held. The only advance in this bloody awful process had been his admission, spluttered out during one of his clinical meetings, that he had also been abusing opioids; after all, he had reasoned, how much lower could he sink?

The upshot of this confession was that he was prescribed naltrexone which counteracted his longing for the morphine-assisted release from anxiety; that overwhelming feeling of well-being.

After two weeks of this, he began sleeping better. He started to enjoy his food a little more, stopped throwing up after meals. His constantly throbbing headache began to ease. As the weather improved, so did his mood as he was allowed to walk in the sunlit gardens. The smell of grass, the simple sound of birdsong, began to ease through the muddle of his mind. He began to think more clearly.

He still would have loved a glass of rose after one of these walks or a whiskey before sleep, but this desire, the need had lessened and he found himself enjoying a sweet cup of tea instead. He also began to look forward to the next phase of treatment which represented a break in the boredom if nothing else. Visitors were also to be allowed access in the next few days. Perhaps the light at the end of the tunnel? A better future he reasoned.

Chapter 23

Meanwhile, the SIS officer questioned Bernadine. What was her relationship with Heidi, Gerhardt Fischer? How did she account for the extraordinary coincidence that these two had been involved in Mrs Saunders's abduction, but that she, Bernadine, who after all had introduced the former to her boss and his wife, remained ignorant of the espionage and movements of her stepfather? The fact of her very real innocence in these matters enabled Bernadine to convince the officer of her denial.

Andy only learned about this interview after he had met his nemesis, Officer Luke Arnold once again, this time in the common room at the Priory and again accompanied by his silent assistant. He had not been impressed to learn that his first visitor in his incarceration was to be the indefatigable policeman. He started by informing Andy of his admiration for Bernadine.

'Yes, it's clear to me that she had no part to play in what turned out to be a conspiracy. I was most impressed with the girl. She was clearly devastated at the damage she had inadvertently caused for your career and marriage. It was true that she had benefited from her relationship with her stepfather, but only in so much as he kept her well-funded over here in the UK.'

'So that accounts for the clothes and perfume,' Andy ruefully reflected. The officer continued. 'She clearly thinks very highly of you.' Andy, however, was keen to change the subject.

'Thank you for that, but I'm sure you haven't come all this way to discuss the merits or otherwise of my junior staff.'

'No, indeed. I just felt you needed to be aware of the progress of the inquiry.'

He explained that Gerhardt and the CEO of CellProcure had been arrested, the former still in recovery in the hospital in Germany. Prof. Ray Landon had also been implicated in the conspiracy. It transpired that the CEO and Gerhardt had been lone actors. But they had found this useful idiot, Landon, and got him to do their dirty work in the UK. To somehow get Gerhardt's daughters involved.

The CEO (whom Andy recalled with a shiver running down his spine; the way he radiated menace at the end of that interview in Frankfurt) used his considerable influence within the company to manipulate others to do his bidding. They had ascertained that Professor Landon was a weak link in UK academia and included him in their activities. They preyed on his greed and stupidity. The wider pharmaceutical industry in Germany, however, was horrified by the disclosures.

'In that case, how could they possibly have arranged for the transfer of Fischer from the UK to Germany?' Andy asked.

'It seems that CellProcure, under the guise of this CEO, was intent on damage limitation. It was relatively easy for him to liaise with the UK via Prof Landon and use his influence with the NHS and thus arrange for the transfer, citing better facilities in order to save his legs. It was all done clandestinely so as not to alert the wider community. It was of course the Prof who facilitated your SHO's placement in the UK, again using this influence with the NHS. This action, of course, led to the introduction of her stepsister into the Saunders's family and all that flowed from it.'

So that confirms Bernie's story, he thought to himself, with some relief. Not wishing to expose any more of his feelings for her to this man, Andy contented himself by remarking that this incident had 'certainly upset our orthopods!'

'So what happens now?'

'All three have been charged under the official secrets act and will face multiple charges including industrial espionage and cyber-crime. The CEO, Herr Gunter will also face charges of inciting criminal assault—which, of course, brings me to your involvement in all of this.'

'Here we go,' thought Andy.

'There is no doubt that some of your behaviours have not been consistent with those in such a position of authority. However, you have been subject to several appalling incidents that would test the resolve of any reasonable man. This must be taken into consideration.'

'But?'

Ah, yes indeed, but. God, this man is infuriating, thought Andy.

'I think that I have indicated previously that none of your actions, whilst foolish, do not amount to criminality. I think it may be deemed appropriate that the criminal behaviours of these three will be mitigated by future international

159

cooperation in the joint search for a cure for cancer. I understand your wife is to become Prof Saunders. Is that correct?'

'There's a lot of work to be done before that eventuality.'

'Nonetheless, she will become a significant benefactor of these developments, it is to be hoped. As for you, Mr Saunders, I also understand that you voluntarily undertook to undergo—' he glanced round at the sterile walls, '—treatment at this establishment and that, again speaks of a degree of character, shall we say.'

For God's sake get on with it, thought Andy.

'It is felt that you have undergone punishment enough, Mr Saunders and that we will not be involving you further in our enquiries.' With that, the Officer stood, shook Andy firmly by the hand and took his leave, leaving Andy, once again with plenty to think about.

******

Bernadine had obviously been busy. She had paid a visit to her boss's home, asking after the welfare of Mrs Saunders and wondering if she could help with the girls. Perhaps unsurprisingly this approach had received the cold shoulder. She had also managed to communicate with Andy in Wrexham and, initially dismayed by how downbeat he had sounded, she happily took up the opportunity to visit him once allowed.

In preparation for her visit, Andy had smartened himself up, shaved, dressed in a clean shirt and had even applied aftershave. Bernie however was still shocked to see this handsome man's drawn features, horrified to see the weight loss and the unaccustomed self-effacing demeanour. Her presence though, as always, lifted his spirits and they walked through the gardens discussing their future plans. Bernadine reiterated her desire to return to her country of birth, resisting Andy's pleas to the contrary.

'Look, Andy, you need to get yourself well again, get back to work, attend to your family. My presence here will only distract you. You know my feelings for you and that fact alone dictates that I must go.'

Andy had reached for her hand after this and pulled her close and looked down into her face, attempting to fill his empty emotional tank; to refuel his belief in the purity of love. The new, different trauma of the last few weeks had not, it seemed to him, lessened his desire for this girl; his belief that they could and should be together.

The experience had seemed to expose the middle-class shallowness of his previous existence. The necessity for the large house, the SUV, the shallowness of the societal hierarchy that seemed to inform his chosen profession. Why not live in a modest home, teach his children the true nature of human interaction, without the artificial encumbrance of elite schooling and all it implied? He would still be able to operate, to help people in distress through no fault of their own. Who needed the bloody politics?

During the long hours of enforced isolation during his initial recovery, he had thought long and deeply about what was really important to him. He had examined the intricacies of his marriage, understood that Isabel, through no fault of hers, had failed to understand the depths of his grief for his lost son; had not understood the source of his feelings of guilt.

He had spent long afternoons listening to the symphonies of Mahler. The massive final movement of the third symphony had rescued him when he was at his lowest ebb. He determined that he would spend more time pursuing this passion once out of this place. He would join a choir again. Perhaps get involved in the local amateur Operatic Society. The problem with all of this remained the fact that whenever he thought about music, felt the transcendent power of healing, he associated these feelings with his love for Bernadine. Another paradox.

Nonetheless, he also understood that he admired his wife's scientific brain, her dedication, was thrilled by the prospect of her ascent to the top of academia. The question that nagged away at him, however, remained unanswered. Was admiration a good enough substitute for love? What Isabel's accident had proven to him was that his genuine attraction for her had been, apparently, only skin deep. The deep irony of this observation did not escape him.

He felt ashamed to admit that he had been drawn to her looks. Her confidence, her physical presence had also been a factor-*but* did he love her? Even this admission had left him feeling ashamed, paradoxically adding to his already overflowing list of reasons to be guilty. However, in the depths of his confinement, he realised he had found the answer to that essential question.

His recent counselling sessions enabled him to dig deep into his psyche; helping him to understand that his addictions were really a smokescreen. That short-term elation masked the actual source of his unhappiness. He needed to come to terms with the loss of his son, but he also needed someone who would understand why this had been so much a part of his life until this point.

This train of thought led to the inevitable question: was not his regard for Bernadine also a function of her beauty, her youth? But no; he had seen, as through a clear glass into the true spirit of the girl; that brief interaction with his daughters, her reaction to his rudeness in that first operation, her generosity in her concern for his injured wife.

Again that link with music; her instinctive understanding of the poetry of Strauss. He had a glimpse of innocence-perhaps even a future. But now that, too, was a chimaera. She had stated her wish to go back to Germany and that was that. This knowledge threatened his initial good recovery and he languished in his room, drowned in self-pity—that awful precursor of addiction.

His third visitor (how ironic he had thought) was Isabel herself, whose presence did nothing to assuage these feelings burning away inside him. She seemed ashamed to be there. She also saw the same diminished figure that had confronted Bernadine earlier, but instead of an outpouring of concern, sympathy or love even, had instead responded with an aloof repugnance almost. His enquiries about the girl's well-being met with a summary of their progress at school, their apparent ease with the new nanny, her concerns with her ongoing question: 'who was going to pay for all of this?'

The only time she had brightened up was when she discussed the progress of her research, the imminent publication of a paper to be entitled 'Immunological stimulation in targeted oncology.' She had even discussed the possibility of taking an apartment in Birmingham during the week in order to allow her to concentrate on her studies.

When asked how the girls would fit in with this arrangement, Isabel failed to notice the apparent contradiction with her financial concerns set alongside the idea that the girls might attend public school. She had continued to sing the praises of Shrewsbury School, anticipating the allowed entry of female students.

Andy spent that night, again sleepless, disturbed, anxious. His rehabilitation seemed to have taken a backward step. He resolved to send an email to Bernadine in which he described his true feelings, his hope for the future, his alienation from his former wife. He told her that he wished to return to a simpler lifestyle in which he would concentrate on his work and bring up his girls as best he could. He even told her that he had come to terms at last with the loss of his son and that he fully intended to put a stop to his damaging behaviours. He explained how he hated the idea of Lucy and Imogen being 'farmed out' as he saw it. He reiterated his love for her.

In this way, by perhaps having removed some of the burden of hiding his true feelings, he was able to reset his determination to fully engage with this process. He underwent individual and group counselling. He allowed therapists to address the true source of his addictive behaviour. He learned about the 12 steps to full recovery. He began to understand the depth of support he would receive once discharged.

During a phone call with Stuart, he had been reassured that he would be welcomed with open arms back into the hospital. The fact that he had voluntarily entered this rehab. programme had impressed the administrators. Stuart had informed him that the NHS had declared themselves happy to contribute to the necessary expenses. The final accolade was that he had also been accepted onto a course in micro-surgery.

The fact that the conversation had then gone down the route of planning for future head and neck reconstruction represented even more evidence of a return to more normal relations with his old friend. They had even strayed into the territory of inter-speciality rivalry and discussed how they intended to return this particular specialised branch of max-fac surgery to its rightful owners and away from the ENT and plastic surgeons. Their mutual enthusiasm for this prospect seemed to fuel Andy's desire to embrace the future.

In this way, the next few weeks passed uneventfully. Andy found himself stronger by the day, more confident. He slept well and attended the gym and enjoyed the freedom of the swimming pool. He communicated happily with his children via their mobile phones.

Only latterly, as he approached discharge did he find himself increasingly unsure as to how to approach his marriage to Isabel. Had she implied that she wanted a separation when mooting the idea of an apartment in Birmingham? Had she been unable to fully express a desire to start again? All he realised now remained the need to get out of the Priory as soon as possible and begin to address these issues.

The day of discharge dawned bright and sunny. He had arranged for a taxi to take him back to Shropshire but first, having packed his bags, turned to give a farewell nod to the room that had witnessed the agonies and recovery of the last weeks. He had a strange feeling of inversion as he left what had become a prison. At the same time, he was able to recognise the transformation that had taken place within its four walls. He was, therefore, fond and knew that he would remember his time there for the rest of his life.

Much to his surprise, he had become a very popular inmate. The staff had recognised his professional background and skills as a clinician. He had even been able to impart some of this knowledge to the doctors and his fellow patients. As he recovered he had regained a little of his natural composure, his physical presence. He considered himself cured. They had even arranged a farewell party for him and he found himself running a gauntlet of applauding staff, councillors and fellow recoverees before he could walk down the steps of the clinic and feel the healing warmth of the sun embrace him.

Walking across the gravel of the car park he searched around for his taxi realising that he was early and leaned against a fence post, dropping his suitcase to the ground, relishing the sight and sounds of the fields around him; the growing sense of well-being and freedom. He glanced back to the old Georgian building that had been his home for the last 28 days and said a silent prayer of thanks.

He bent his head to the ground, picked up a fragment of gravel or two and playfully tossed them in his hands. He became engrossed in his own thoughts, oblivious to the sound of steps on the gravel as someone approached. Some third sense alerted him and he turned to see who the person might be, interrupting his reverie, his new-found peace.

'Hello, Andy. Ja, ich bin es—it's me.'

Andy stared, unable to speak, scarcely able to ingest, to comprehend, this vision of smiling beauty approaching, hands held out in anticipated embrace, hair wafting in the summer breeze.

'Yes, Andy, it is me. Welcome back. You and I have work to do, a life to embrace and if you will have me, I would like to do this together—meine Liebling. Komme hier.'

Their embrace seemed to melt into, to belong to, the serenity of that summer day. There was, indeed, much work to do, but in the meantime Andy allowed himself to believe in the rapture of that precious moment.

Part 2

Chapter 24

The Unison C natural non-chord scored for the whole orchestra declared the opening of Haydn's mighty oratorio, 'The Creation.' The two lovers sat, together, in the nave of St Chad's Church, situated at the apex of the quarry gardens near Shrewsbury Centre.

Sitting hand-in-hand they were absorbed in this depiction of the beginning of life on earth; out of the emptiness of space, infinity even, this flare of sound, emerges the Representation of Chaos. The bass soloist recited the words 'In the beginning, God created the heaven and the earth.' His statement then resolving into the shattering C major of the opening chorus '—and there was LIGHT.'

So absorbed were the pair in the concert that they didn't notice the slight figure, seated in the back pew's, observing them throughout. The applause gave cover for this person's departure into the shadows as Andy and Bernadine stood to leave.

Happily repeating the bass lines from the concert, resonating sotto voce, Andy allowed Bernadine to lead him to their favourite restaurant, hidden away down the cobbles of the old town. They received their customary greeting and were led to the discrete table beneath the brick arch. Water was brought to the table and the couple reminisced and laughed together, able for this brief time to leave the upheaval of their lives confined to the past if only for a few moments. Music, love and hope filled their hearts. They would lose themselves in the intoxication of new love, they would deal with the concerns of the real world tomorrow.

The next morning found Andy sitting in the square chatting to his old mate, Gareth.

'Yeah, I'm sorry I missed the concert. I heard it was thrilling.'

'Yes, it certainly was,' agreed Andy. 'A lovely choir and four wonderful soloists. I even found myself wanting to sing the bass part.' Andy sipped at his coffee, a brief silence betraying his friend's unease. Not usually lost for words, Gareth found himself in a difficult situation.

'Look, Andy, everyone sympathises with all you have gone through, but settling down with this young girl seems a little—how can I put it? Inappropriate somehow for a man of your professional standing. And Izzy—God knows she's been through enough herself—what about her?'

'Isabel made it perfectly clear that her work meant everything to her now. She is happily ensconced in her flat in Birmingham and seems perfectly happy for me to see the girls whenever.'

'What about the house?' Gareth asked.

'Isabel has put it on the market but still uses it on weekends. I'm not quite sure what she will do after that—' Andy trailed off.

'You do realise that Liz is not too happy about the situation either?' This reference to Gareth's wife, one of Isabel's best friends, did nothing to cool Andy's ardour.

'It's difficult, I know, but Bernadine makes me happy Gareth. I can be my true self at last. Now I'm not drinking, I realise how messed up I've been—now I can finally deal with Seb's death and without her, I don't think I could ever have managed that.'

'What about your work; the hospital?'

'I've had a straight talk with Stuart and he has backed me. Can see I'm a better person now, more able to concentrate on my work. Now we've got funding for the new trauma centre, I can really get involved with the micro-vascular stuff—'

Gareth seemed immediately on safer ground, discussing clinical matters. 'So what does that involve?'

Andy also visibly perked up as he described connecting arteries and veins together under a surgical microscope, so that 'paddles' of tissue; skin, muscle and even bone, could be 'plugged in', in order to replace a facial defect left by trauma or ablative cancer surgery. In this way, the two old friends chatted for another hour, before Gareth asked about his friends' new living arrangements.

'Well, we've found a nice little apartment overlooking the quarry park. It has two bedrooms, so the girls can come and stay—'

'What do they make of all this?' Interrupted Gareth.

'They love Bernadine. Actually, she's a natural with them—talks on their level in a way—and she helps with their German homework.'

'Mmm—well, I suppose you know what you're doing. Are you still in counselling?'

'Yep. Following the 12 steps religiously. Enjoying work and enjoying waking up feeling refreshed and eager for the day. Enjoying life Gareth—you should try it!' Gareth ignored this attempt at humour.

'How's the singing going?'

'Great, thanks. I've got an audition with the town choir next week and I'm working up an aria for that—'

'Bloody hell! That I have to hear—'

'Ha ha. No chance Gareth. Not ready for public performance yet. But I'd love you and Liz to come to a concert if I get in.'

'I'm not so sure Liz will be too keen. I'll always support you though, you know that.' As they finish their coffee, they stood to go and failed to notice a figure just dipping behind the town hall stone columns as they left the square.

******

Isabel had finally found her fach. She loved her little bolt-hole in Solihull and found she could work all day at the lab and with her laptop, continue her research once back in the flat. Her stem-cell transfer experiments continued, now uninterrupted by the domestic pressure she had now escaped. Although she missed the girls, she knew they were happy in weekly boarding and so she could look forward to spending time with them at weekends, when she could give them her full attention.

She had now come to terms with her soon-to-be-ex-husband's behaviour and what she saw as his love tryst; his mid-life crisis in all its glory. She even tolerated the girl's relationship—such as it was—with that German girl. They seemed to get on well with her and that's all she worried about at the moment. She had bigger fish to fry. She had a thesis to write. A potential route to a coveted chair opening up in front of her. At the moment, that is all she cared about. Her husband's fall from grace, as she viewed it, was his concern.

Back in their apartment, Bernie and Andy prepared supper. Bernadine was happy to support her man's determination to stay away from alcohol and they had got into the routine of drinking non-alcoholic fruit cocktails and fizzy water. Andy's new zeal—determined to keep his demons at bay-overcame the occasional longing for the pop of the cork. For the time being, at least, his intoxication with his lovely former SHO was satisfaction enough.

'How was practice today, sweetheart?'

'Yah, gute. Very good. Damien has given me some treatment plans to work up and am placing my first implant on Friday.'

Bernadine had left the hospital and Andy had used his contacts to find her an apprenticeship in a new, all singing and dancing dental clinic in the town. This suited Bernadine perfectly: she had realised that the blood and guts and drama of maxillofacial surgery was not for her. Also, once the marital shit had hit the proverbial, it seemed politic to leave.

'Well, we are seeing the girls on Saturday, so perhaps we can go to the Italian on Friday to celebrate. How's that?'

'So long as it's with you, meine liebe dich, I don't mind what we do.' She shimmered across the small kitchen, stood on tiptoe, held Andy's head between her palms and gently kissed him on the lips. This sweet assurance expunged any tremors that may have threatened to disturb his new peace of mind; this happy state of equilibrium achieved after so much turmoil. He returned Bernadine's embrace and together they settled in for the evening.

******

'Wow, Daddy! Thanks—that's great.'

Andy had indulged the girls with an inflatable canoe and so, full of excitement and the promise of adventure, the small group made its way down the quarry gardens to the edge of the River Severn, close to the pontoon that marked the boundary of the Shrewsbury School rowing club. Once inflated and using the pontoon as a launching pad, Andy tentatively pushed off, with his eldest daughter, Lucy, as his experimental crewmate.

The pair pushed the vessel out into mid-stream, testing the buoyancy. Slowly they gained confidence and their shouts of delight carried back to the banks of the river where Bernie stood with Imogen, who was also squealing with delight and shouting for her turn. Now synchronising their paddling, the two, now expert mariners, came up alongside and swapped with the uncertain couple, perhaps now, not so keen.

'I'll take Imogen out then,' Andy told Bernadine. 'Then I'll come back and get you and show you how easy it all is.'

Lucy helped Bernadine lay out the picnic blanket and gleefully piled into the delicacies held within. There was lemonade, ham sandwiches and cake. The sun shone. The slightly damp companions joined them for a happy picnic, whilst Bernadine allowed herself to be guided back to the river by a now confident Lucy.

Andy lay back in the sun, Imogen happily munching on cake and watching the antics of her sister and Bernie in the boat. He wondered how life had come to this ideal: the almost magical transformation from the chaos of the previous year. He pondered on his failed marriage and, whilst accepting his burden of guilt, he allowed himself to revel in this newfound happiness. Yes, he felt for Isabel; all she had endured with the accident, her abduction and his eventual breakdown.

But it had been her choice to put her career first, move to Birmingham and had seemed perfectly content for him to have access to the girls. He had also found—rediscovered—his mojo back in the hospital; regained his former poise and command of his surgical calling. He also now had time to pursue his love of music, his singing: had found a voice coach to tame his unruly bass and had gotten to grips with a proper, full-blooded opera aria and was looking forward to showing off in his upcoming audition.

These pleasant thoughts and the joyous cries of his daughters and lover, served to once again smother-even calm-the ever present undercurrent of unease, always bubbling away beneath the apparent calm of the surface. Perhaps he had not quite forgotten the effect that his nightmares had had upon him and how these linked into the smell of blood whilst he was operating.

After all, he had struggled to put these negative feelings into the back of his mind. Suffered the agonies of withdrawal. Prostrated himself almost before the counsellors and his fellow clinicians. If he had noticed the still figure, standing on the opposite bank, gazing intently at the happy group, then perhaps these ripples might have threatened to splash over and become a tsunami, would in fact completely wreck his happy reverie.

Chapter 25

Gerhardt swore. Not for the first time that day. His prosthesis refused to follow his commands. He struggled to stand on his one, reasonably good leg, whilst attempting to balance on the below-knee artificial limb. High technology perhaps but fucking useless as a leg. He swore again. Gerhardt Fischer had had a tough year.

Having been tried and found guilty of industrial espionage, along with his CEO, Herr Gunter, he had been sentenced to a 10-year prison sentence. As if that were not enough, he had undergone a below-knee amputation on the right side, where a full ankle reconstruction had failed. The left leg, whilst still severely injured, had survived the accident in Birmingham. The courts had not viewed these injuries as mitigation and so it was that he found himself in the hospital wing of a so-called 'white-collar prison' undergoing rehabilitation.

Almost by definition, Gerhardt now had plenty of free time in which to assess his life and the misdemeanours that had brought about this sorry state of affairs. Whilst most people might consider themselves fortunate to be alive; might even be repentant for their crimes or perhaps use the enforced isolation in order to re-educate, concentrate on getting fit again, Gerhardt did not consider himself 'most people.'

Instead, he was angry. Angry with the authorities of course. They hadn't needed to view his collaboration with Mrs Isabel, bloody, Saunders as abduction. And why throw the book at him for industrial espionage? All he had been trying to do was get hold of some useful research details from that bloody woman, at the behest of the company he worked for, CellProcure. The fact that his boss, Herr Gunter had also been found guilty of industrial espionage had not helped his case either.

He cursed again when he thought of that balding, little fat, self-satisfied bastard. He had got a lesser sentence when the whole plot was actually instigated by him. It had been him, after all, who had arranged for Mr bloody Andy

Saunders to be beaten up. Why had he escaped punishment for that? Why were the two thugs responsible still at large?

These various thoughts plagued him throughout his waking hours; sharpening his thirst for revenge rather than improving him. He would show them. He *would* get those bloody research results, no matter what. No matter what he had to do. He would sell them to another biotech company and get the credit.

After all, he still had plenty of contacts. Still had strings he could pull. One advantage of being in this low-security wing was the access to a 'phone, mobile and laptop. He still had his contacts in the UK. Also, he still had Isabel's computer, courtesy of his step-daughter Heidi. But even this was of no use without the bloody password. He had to get the password.

With these thoughts curdling in his brain, he managed to stand and make a few, lurching steps from the bed to the barred French windows of the ward, from where he could at least gaze on the outside world for a while.

******

On the micro-surgery course, Andy had trained the tremor out of his fingers. At first, peering through the eye-piece of the microscope, his suture holder tip had completely swung side-to-side, completely out of the field of vision. The thought that he could manipulate the tiny suture needle through the walls of a blood vessel was laughable.

Over time, however and purely by concentrating on the tip of the needle, the tremor subsided until he could at least hold the forcep and suture within the field of vision. He next had to learn how to manoeuvre the tiny thread through the walls of a plastic tube, which was hollow and meant to represent a real-life artery or vein. The tube was, in fact, smaller than a length of very fine string.

Over weeks of practice, he was able to effect a vessel re-connection on a donor's vein, so that it was water-or blood-tight. He then progressed to assisting a plastic surgeon in real life in connecting an artery during a free-graft operation. The next step then entailed bringing these skills to his surgical repertoire back in the hospital.

Until recently, patients with facial defects would have to go through a series of painstaking tissue transfers which entailed only partly separating the donor tissue at its source, then attaching to the recipient site whilst still connected at the other end. This would entail weeks of waiting for the blood supply to stabilise, often holding the patient in uncomfortable positions, before allowing the graft to be separated and sutured into the defect. Newer treatments involved fusing grafted bone, with skin grafted over; again involving painful, multiple operations.

This new micro-technology allowed the surgeon to take a section, in reality, a wedge-of tissue, which included the skin, muscle and bone all together in a complex graft, from, say, the hip or the small of the back with the vein and artery still attached. At the defect, the surgeon would dissect out a similar connection of artery and vein, bring the graft to the site and then, under the surgical microscope, connect the vessels in a 'plug-in' procedure.

This would mean that an immediate blood supply would be available to the graft, which would be sutured into place. These procedures were complex and lengthy and some operations might take up to 13 hours. The graft (and patient) would then need to be under careful observation in ITU to ensure circulation through the graft was maintained for at least the first 24 hours. If the tissue became pale or grey, then the surgeons would be back in the theatre again, attempting to repair the failed connection.

All this attracted the attention of the administrators again. Politics intervened. Cases strictly rationed. Today, though, Andy had got approval for a young man who had the misfortune to grow a very aggressive tumour in his upper jaw. The ameloblastic carcinoma was of dental origin and needed to be excised in its entirety, together with a surrounding bed of healthy tissue, in order to provide the patient with any kind of healthy future.

Andy had had to go before a panel comprising administrators and general surgeons, in order to justify the operation. The patient, he explained, was a young student with a bright future and the procedure would leave him with a significant cosmetic and functional defect. His speech, ability to eat, to smell and appearance would be significantly compromised. Until this new technology had become available, he explained, he would have to wear an obturator—in effect a plastic plug attached to a denture-in order to replace the palate and cheekbone, while the whole thing would be barely concealed beneath a skin-graft. The eye on that side would drop. His appearance would be horrific.

Now, however, he could take a paddle of latissimus dorsi-the muscle overlying the lower ribs on the back, together with the rib and skin and repair the defect, all during the same procedure. The cosmetic result would be comparatively and significantly better, with a well-placed pair of spectacles rendering the whole thing scarcely noticeable. Andy had argued the case well and duly given the go-ahead for today's operation.

The removal of the tumour was relatively straightforward. Andy used saws to cut through the midline of the hard palate and then separating the cheekbone through the zygomatic arch, this enabling the whole cheekbone to be removed complete with the tumour. Externally, access to the site was achieved via a soft-tissue flap incised carefully through the skin crease in front of the ear and round under the hairline in a question mark shape. The surgeon would then replace this over the top of the grafted tissue, thus masking the defect.

Andy took care to dissect out branches of the greater palatine vessels which lay exposed on the floor of the operating field. Swinging the microscope over, Andy then connected these vessels to the protruding bundle of vessels from the graft harvested from the young man's back earlier. Releasing clamps higher up the palatine vessels sent life-giving blood into the pale graft, this pinking up nicely as blood flowed through. The bulk of the graft settled in; Andy then closed the soft tissue flap over. Andy had designed the graft so that the skin from the small of the back actually formed the roof of the mouth.

He stood back and seemed pleased with the result. He asked his assistant, now senior registrar Sandeep, to monitor the case overnight in ITU, giving him strict instructions to contact him straight away, if the pulse through the graft failed. This done, he left and drove home, aware that his hard-won peace was, once again, being disturbed. Even Bach failed to extinguish the smell of blood.

After such a long procedure, he felt its cloying presence. An almost animal smell with a metallic overtone. He felt his clothes reeked of its miasma. More than ever, he needed the escape of the grape. He longed for the fruit and vanilla spice scent of a newly uncorked bottle of red; in sweet opposition to that other red. The tinge of alcohol promised release from the stresses of life.

After this marathon procedure, this contrast seemed ever more disturbing. After all, he felt, he could put up with the surgical claret if he could later enjoy the vinous variety. He needed that release; celebration even. Fruit juice didn't cut it so far as he was concerned. Vein v vine. This conundrum unsettled him as he let himself into the flat.

Bernadine welcomed him as always, her very presence, her smell-yes, that again-but sweet, intoxicating in another way. Her presence, as always, reassured him, settled him. He went into the front room and put Bach on again but louder. Might that glorious music erase the memory of the operation?

'Are you OK, meine Liebling?'

'Yes. Just knackered. That operation took 10 hours. God, bending over that microscope is absolutely exhausting.'

'Well, I'll leave you to recover in here with Mr Bach. Supper is on and I'll bring you a fruit cocktail.'

The proffered drink did not, it must be said, do much to settle Andy's nerves. He sat back and let the opening chorus of St Matthews Passion do the job instead. Back in the tiny kitchen, Bernadine decided that this was probably not a good time to tell Andy of a strange feeling she had experienced of being followed on her way back from the surgery.

Andy did not sleep well. Knowing that he might be called out during the night to rescue a failing graft did not exactly beckon the Angels of sleep. However, he woke to see his companion lying, her back to him, her long blonde tresses cascading over the pillow.

He snuggled close, the warm scent of her skin stirring in his loins. He snuggled closer; she stirred and only half turned to him, her morning breath awaking his senses even further. She pushed up on her elbows, looking into his face, once again filling him with joy and wonder that this beautiful girl would offer her body to him. All thoughts of work, stress and responsibility fled his mind as Bernadine gently straddled him and eased herself onto his erection. The two lovers were in complete union now, their love sealed in the hot house of lust. The inner rat subdued in the musty aftermath—

It was then, a happy, breezy consultant who let himself into ITU.

'How is he, Sandeep?'

Sandeep, as always totally dedicated to the job at hand, had been monitoring the pulse oximeter attached by a tiny lead and microchip to the bulging graft representing the patient's new palate.

'I've been able to view the graft and thankfully it's a very healthy pink; well perfused, Andy. He's doing well.'

'Let's keep the sedation going. Collect bloods, U's and E's—Usual stuff, yeah?'

As always his instructions were largely pointless as his SR had already attended to the basics of post-op care.

'Great stuff, San. Let's go and get some coffee-you need some rest—I'll deal with the clinic today, OK?'

Sandeep nodded and followed his boss to the canteen. Although he respected Andy's skills as a surgeon and recognised his clinical acuity, if pushed, he would have to admit he had lost a little respect for his immediate senior. After all, he considered, consultancy to him was not purely about clinical expertise, but a greater moral responsibility attached to this prominent position; this honour even.

Responsibility to his patients, of course, but also to his staff; clinical and otherwise. They all looked to him for moral leadership. Then there were wider societal issues to be considered. A consultant held a position of some standing in society; again there seemed to San to be a political responsibility that went with the job and all it entailed. That he had left his family to go off with that German SHO bothered him. How could he have abandoned his two young children? His poor wife, so badly injured in that awful episode. Then he had witnessed at first-hand Andy's breakdown and rehabilitation. It had been him, San, who had stood up for his boss at these awful hearings.

Nonetheless, he strolled along the corridor, just a respectful step behind Andy, hands thrust in his white coat pockets, as they discussed the merits and otherwise of the previous day's work. He would do his duty, have coffee with his boss, but all he really wanted to do right now was sleep. He had been up now for over 24 hours.

Chapter 26

The experience, as she entered the house, was akin to a slap in the face with a wet fish; not quite sufficient to knock her over, but more than enough to upset her sense of equilibrium. Isabel had let herself into the house on Friday, having escaped the bank holiday queues on the M6 and now back in the relative peace of Shropshire. She had been looking forward to the weekend: looking forward to seeing her girls and relishing the escape from the University.

Instead, she now stood in the old kitchen, alone, memories flooding her brain; not the most recent, the rows, the angst but rather the sense of adventure she and Andy had so enjoyed when they bought the grand house with the help of her grandparent's legacy. The joy of bringing the little new-borns home, the idea of building what? Yes, a home. And yes; she missed Andy: his physical presence, his urgency, his smell. She even missed the deep growl of his voice as he hummed his way around the old home.

In short, she recognised the sharp blow of grief. Grief for all they had had. She had been too keen to escape what she saw as the confining bands of marriage, of motherhood. Too keen to immerse herself fully in her research. She had given up on their marriage too easily, allowed Andy to 'shack-up' with that German girl. What was he thinking? What was she thinking? A tear escaped her damaged eye and plopped on the marble top.

The house, too soon, had lost that elusive 'feel' of home; the faint taint of last night's supper, Andy's aftershave: instead the quiet of emptiness, of abandonment. Her shoulders shook as the wave enveloped her. She determined to write to Andy. Before she collected the girls. She would put the lights on, give a blast of heating, have a bath, warm the atmosphere with perfumed steam, the smell of pasta sauce: anything to banish the silence, the oppressive emptiness.

******

The Old House,
Upper Stretton,
29 Aug

Dear Andy,

Please forgive me for writing to you in this way. Much bitterness has passed between us over the last year or two and I now understand that we are both to blame. I believe that we have been too hasty in giving up on our marriage, our family. I had become obsessed with my work, the prospect of a chair; all still important, but not sufficient to give up on our life together. I also realise that I have changed, physically and emotionally since the accident and I think I allowed the shock of all that to overwhelm me; us.

At night I wake up, crying, missing your body next to mine; your long legs entwining with mine, even your habit of pulling the duvet off me! I also understand that you have worked hard to overcome your demons and I did not acknowledge that commitment. Your progress in your career has impressed me. I miss you, Andy.

As for my work, we have the altered stem cell vaccine ready for stage I clinical trials, but I have a feeling that the genetic code derived from cancer cells may be too unstable, will mutate too quickly to make the vaccine viable in the larger population. No matter, what really concerns me is our little family, our children; I miss what we once had. We were good once, weren't we?

If you are now happy and settled, please don't worry. Ignore this letter and I will understand. On the other hand, you know where to find me.

Your loving ex-wife,

Isabel.
XXX

Isabel's letter surprised Andy, to say the very least. He didn't really know how to take it. Surely she couldn't be serious. Had she been drinking? He dismissed this idea. He would think about it later. May even discuss the matter with Bernie. Would that be a bad idea? He couldn't think about it now. He had an audition to rehearse for. He arrived at Shrewsbury School where he took voice-coaching once a week with the resident teacher in vocal studies.

He ran through his preparatory scales, his mind still preoccupied with the letter. The lessons addressed Andy's tendency to bellow; to hone the sound into a more focused voice, remove some of the vibrato. He had chosen an aria from Haydn's Creation to sing to the choirmaster: 'Now Heaven in fullest Glory shone.' Difficult at the best of times, but frankly impossible if he couldn't concentrate.

Why had she written in that way? She rarely allowed herself such sentimentality. He, too, missed the feeling of family; the big house, the noise of the girls running about, the security and dare he even admit it: the responsibility. At the moment he was acting like a kid; in love, in a flat, going out for meals, seeing his daughters when it suited him. And then, the clinching factor: the lovemaking, the beauty of a young girl who seemed obsessed with him. But he asked himself; could that not, too, be transient? A sharp mischord alerted himself to the fact his teacher had gotten fed up with him; his lack of focus.

'Andy, you have to concentrate. Your top is all over the place today. Do you want to reschedule? Is it work?'

'No, no, I'm sorry Nigel. It's me—let's run that opening line again, OK?' The lesson continued, Andy now attempting to refocus.

******

Gerhardt lay on his bed, the prosthetic thrown on the floor for the time being. He had Isabel's laptop on his one good knee pondering on what he could do to access the information held within. He thought back to how close he had been to getting the information he so wanted.

How he had replaced Lisbeth on the flight into Birmingham, how he had met Isabel in the airport, waving a placard with her name on it. How he had persuaded her in the arrivals hall that he worked for the University. Had been sent to pick her up to take her there. Convinced her to leave her car at the airport and climb into his car. He hadn't completely thought through the process of how he might persuade her to give him the information he had come for, but all the tricks of the trade were in his repertoire. All he had to do was get the car to a quiet place.

Having driven past the exit for the campus, Isabel had become alarmed, kept asking stupid bloody questions. She had even reached across to grab his arm, causing him to look away at the crucial moment. When he saw the queue ahead, it was too late. He rammed on the brakes and hit the tailback. And now look at him. He had lost his leg, his job, his very credibility. He fully intended, however, to get it back; by fair means or foul. And Gerhardt, being the person he was, understood the process would likely be foul.

******

Andy left the letter in his drawer. He would worry about it later. Right now, he had things at the hospital to worry about. His young cancer patient had been struggling. Although the graft had taken, the swelling around the face was taking time to settle. He complained about the pain from the donor site on his back. He couldn't eat. Kept gagging at the feel of the graft protruding into his mouth. He couldn't taste or smell. He complained throughout the day and night and now the nurses were complaining to Andy.

Yet again, the politics of the job overwhelmed him. This patient would have to spend a lot of time in bed, in rehab and bed occupancy concerned the administrators more than the welfare of the patients.

'Are these complex procedures really worth the hassle, Andy?'

Stuart and Andy were enjoying a cup of coffee together in the canteen.

'Surely, a free graft is better than a prosthesis, especially in such a young man,' Andy reasoned.

'Yeah, I know. But we don't work in isolation, Andy. That operation took nearly 13 hours and questions are being asked again at the audit meetings. We are going to have to justify ourselves all over again: the time, the use of ITU, the beds, the rehab.'

'But surely, Stu, we're here to heal the sick, by any means at our disposal. We have to use these new techniques even if they are time-consuming at first.'

'No offence, Andy. But you can be a little naïve. As head of Department, it's me who has to justify what you do and you know what it's like: 'oh, the bloody dentists are at it again!'

'Well, they can fuck off, Stu.'

'Great idea, Andy. Shall I tell them that at the next meeting?'

The two colleagues chuckled at the thought, but the conversation had rattled Andy and leaving the hospital that evening, his first thought had been to stop off at the Ragleth and get himself a pint. Surely, one pint wouldn't hurt, would it?

But no, he would resist the urge and go back to the little flat, discuss plans for the next weekend when the girls were coming over. Tonight, he and Bernie would go to the new Carluccios in the square. He might even raise the subject of Isabel's letter—

'Meine Liebling—you OK?' Her hand reached across and touched Andy's, the electricity between them still crackling. Perhaps he wouldn't mention the letter after all.

'I'm sorry, darling. Just had a few issues at work—nothing really important.'

'That hospital. They don't realise what they have in you; your dedication, your skill—'

'Thanks my love—it's just the age-old balancing thing, money versus patient care. They don't seem to understand that health provision isn't—can't be—managed like a business. Profit versus expenditure. It's just not like that—'

Andy still enjoyed coming out to dinner, but somehow it just didn't seem the same without that delicious thrill of the first drink, the perusal of the wine list. Fruit juice could only take one so far and that destination did not sit well with Andy. He loved the girl opposite him, lusted after her, but nothing seemed the same without that extra little kick. After all, he had had no desire to revisit the drugs; just a drink. Surely that wouldn't do any harm. And then he had to go to that meeting and confess all, as though he were a real addict. It didn't suit him to unburden his inner feelings in front of all those relative strangers.

Bernadine brought him back to earth, discussing the upcoming weekend.

'What shall we do with the girls?' she asked.

'Don't forget I have that audition on Saturday morning—'

'Ya. I also am not around 'till lunch. I have an implant case booked in as well.'

'Well look, I'll call Isabel and see if I can pick the girls up from the school early afternoon. How's that?'

'That's lovely. Try to stop worrying now, my love and enjoy the meal. Yah?'

Yet again her blue-eyed gaze melted his heart and, for the time being at least all thoughts of hospitals, marriage and child care took a back seat. They couldn't know that the girl with the cropped hair, back turned towards them, had also heard their conversation. As she stood to leave, Bernie glanced towards her, a slight shiver of recognition thrilling through her. She remembered the feeling of being followed the other day.

'No, surely not—it can't be. I must be mistaken.' Andy's voice calling from the door pulled her attention away.

******

'Ja, das ist so.' Gerhardt listened intently as his daughter, Heidi informed him of her overheard conversation. He sat in contemplation. His dislike of that bloody English surgeon deepened even further as he thought of him serenading, and worse, his stepdaughter. He'd show them. He'd get the password—get his own back. He made another phone call.

******

Isabel regretted sending the letter almost immediately after her conversation with Andy. Typical of him, he had rung to change arrangements for the weekend again. Same old, same old, she thought. Now he couldn't attend to his duty because of a bloody audition. An audition, for God's sake! Whatever next? His work she could excuse, but this. Whatever next? And he hadn't even bothered to mention the letter. Had he got it?

Oh dear, now she would have to phone the school. Get the girls into supervised homework on Saturday morning again and inform the school that Andy would pick them up at lunchtime. How could he disappoint his children like that? Still, she had spent the bank holiday with them, enjoyed the simple pleasure of days out. Had got the temporary lapse of judgement out of the way. How could she have missed him so much, the selfish bastard?

Despite all this, she realised she had to look to herself a little as well. After all, her work had intruded on this occasion as well. She had to present her thesis to the University and Saturday was the only available time. She would stay in her flat rather than come back to Shropshire. Still, she reassured herself, work had to be attended to; at least she wasn't singing, for God's sake.

Andy's knees were jiggling as he sat outside the concert hall. This was altogether more nerve-racking than he had thought. And the choirmaster was late. He glanced at his watch. He needed to be away by 12:30 pm, in order to pick the girls up from school. Although the aria only lasted about four minutes, there were all the introductions to be done, the formalities. Where the hell was he?

11:45 am. The door to the hall crashed open and in walked the recalcitrant music master, dishevelled as always, scores clutched under his arm and followed by his pianist.

'Ah, morning Andy! Sorry, I'm late. Got caught up with the chapel choir. How are you? Come on in.'

He led Andy into the main concert hall and walked towards the stage, happily chuntering away as he went.

'Right, Andy. That's great. If you wait there, I'll sort the music out and get you to sing from there. OK?'

This came as a shock; he had anticipated standing informally by the piano, just him and the conductor, running through his piece. It was, after all, just for the choir for heaven's sake. He wasn't planning on being a soloist, standing, exposed, at the back of this cavernous room. And on the stage.

'Well, Andy. What have you prepared for us today?'

'An aria from *The Creation*, John,' Andy answered.

'What? Speak up!' A laugh. 'Let's hear what you've got.'

Andy repeated himself, shouted almost.

'Now Heaven in fullest Glory Shone. Haydn. The Creation'

'Yes, yes! I know what it's from. Wonderful. Off you go then!'

The piano started the introduction and Andy, shakily at first, started to sing. Somehow the sound of his own voice, now more focused and controlled, resonating in this great hall, filled him with confidence and he stood, feet planted, chin up. Not too far. Chest out and concentrating on the sound from his diaphragm. He found himself actually enjoying the experience. He even allowed himself a little decorative trill on the final phrase,' with heart and voice,' leading to the top D as he finished, revelling in this new feeling of accomplishment.

'Ha! Well done.' John came up the aisle, hands outstretched to shake Andy warmly by the hand. 'Yes, indeed. Well done,' he repeated.' Tricky aria that. I've heard pros sing it with less, how shall I say? Gusto!' He laughed again. 'Well, look. You've certainly done enough to join the basses. Might even give you a little solo now and again. How's that?' He planted a companionable hand on Andy's shoulder and led him back up the hall to introduce him to the pianist.

'Yes, very well sung. Great diction,' asserted the accompanist.

So involved had he been in all this, he glanced at his watch as he left the building and cursed.

'Shit! 12:45 pm. I'm late!'

He jumped into the car and speeded across town to the school. He parked and bounded through the open gates, took the stone steps two at a time and entered the hallway. No one was there.

'Hello! Hi,' he called.

No answer.

He went round to the headmistress's office at the end of the corridor. Knocked.

'Come in. Ah, Mr Saunders.' She stood and greeted him. 'What can I do for you?'

'I'm picking up Imogen and Lucy—as arranged.'

'Surely, they're with you. I sent them out to the front when I heard your nanny call. They left, what, 20 minutes ago.'

'My nanny? 20 minutes ago? What can you mean? We don't have a nanny anymore and I've only just arrived. I was held up—'

'Oh dear, dear. Well, they must have gone with their mother—'

'Their mother?' Andy repeated, panic now rising like bile in his chest. 'She—Isabel—is in Birmingham. How on earth? How could you not have checked?'

He turned and ran down the corridor towards the front of the building, this time shouting out the girls' names.

'Lucy, Imogen! Where are you?'

Now frantic, he turned back to the headmistress's office; she now standing, mouth ajar, behind her desk.

'Well, don't just stand there. Where the hell are they? How in heaven's name could you just let them go?'

The headmistress could only stammer that Lucy had come out of the study, saying she had seen a car pull up outside the school. She seemed excited, said her nanny had come back. She just said thanks and goodbye. Polite as always.'

'Polite-polite! What can you mean? What are you talking about? How on earth could you just let two girls wander out of the school unattended? What were you thinking?'

He ran out to the car park and rang Isabel. Perhaps she had arranged for one of the friend's parents to pick them up.

'No, Andy. I thought you were—What are you telling me, Andy? What the fuck have you done now? Where are the girls? Andy, Andy. Are you there—?'

Andy had put the phone down and run back into the school. Think, think. Could Bernie have had them picked up? Yes, that must be it. Got Bernie muddled up with Heidi. He called her.

'Ach, nein, Andy. I am still in the practice. What on earth?'

He slammed the phone down again. Think Andy, think. He called Lucy's best friend.

'Katie. Hi, it's Mr Saunders here, Lucy's dad. Don't suppose you've got your parents to pick the girls up from school, have you?'

'No, Mr Saunders. Haven't seen Lucy since Wednesday.'

'Ah, thanks.' A pause. 'Can you think of anywhere they might go—any other friends, for instance?'

'No, I'm sorry. Shall I get mum to call you?'

'No, no. That's OK. Thanks, Katie.'

He put the phone down again. The police. Yes, we must phone the police. He headed back to the office where the headmistress was now sitting, head in hands, clearly distressed.

'Oh, Mr Saunders. I don't know what to say.'

'Don't say anything. Just call the police. Get them here, now!'

The patrol car pulled up outside the school.

'Let's get some details, shall we?' Confronted by a whey-faced young man, no older than his SHO, pen in hand, Andy's impatience boiled over.

'Now, Mr Saunders, isn't it? Yes, I know you're distressed. But in my experience, there's usually a simple answer to these things.'

'Your experience. What experience? You're hardly old enough to be in long trousers—'

'Ahem. Yes, ha ha. But let's be civil, shall we? As I say, let's get some details and we'll register the incident at the station.'

'Register the incident? For God's sake, my girls have gone missing. Can't you just put out a search. An APB, whatever you call it.'

'Well, sir. We don't usually register an incident as a missing person's enquiry until 24 hours have elapsed.'

'24 hours—24 bloody hours,' Andy spluttered. 'What's the good of that?'

'Well again, Sir, ahem, in my experience—if you'll let me explain. These sorts of things sort themselves out very quickly. They'd have gone off with a friend—be found happily drinking tea at a relative's or something like that, Sir.'

Exasperated by now, Andy gave the officer his details, left the policeman interviewing the headmistress and sped back to town. There he found Bernie, standing in the hall, pale-faced.

'Andy, I can't believe it. I came back to the flat, the phone rang and it was Heidi. After all this time.'

'Heidi? What the hell?'

Andy stood, thought, put two and two together. 'So it was Heidi who picked the girls up from the school.'

'Ya, Andy. I know. Heidi has the girls.'

'What? Heidi has the girls. What on earth?'

'She says they are safe, Andy. They know and trust her, of course. No harm will come to them, Andy.'

'Where are they?'

'She wouldn't say, Andy. She just kept repeating that they were safe. But—'

'But—' Andy now really wanted a drink.

'That they were safe but hidden.'

'Hidden?' Andy couldn't stop repeating everything he was hearing.

'Yah. They—'

'They—?'

'Andy, please stop interrupting. I know you're upset. But remember the girls are safe.'

Andy placed his hands on Bernie's shoulder and tried to control his emotions.

'Bernie. Please, just tell me what has happened to my two little girls.'

'Heidi told me that the children would be released as soon as they have some information—'

'You keep saying they; who are 'they'?'

'Two men and Heidi. Somewhere in Shropshire, it must be. Heidi said that Lucy and Imogen would be returned in exchange for information.'

'Information. What information?' Andy parroted.

'They want the password to Isabel's computer—they want to get access to her work at the University.'

'So Christ! This is blackmail. Extortion, for God's sake. Look, Bernie, I'm going to call the police.'

'No, Andy. Please. There is one more thing. Heidi said that her accomplices were not to be messed about with. If the information that they require is not forthcoming, perhaps the girl's safety cannot be guaranteed—And, yes, we mustn't get the police involved.'

'I can scarcely believe what I am hearing. Your bloody stepsister is threatening my girls?'

'Oh, Andy. Please, not that again. You know how I feel about this. I am so, so sorry—'

'Bernie. You honestly expect me to believe that you didn't know about Heidi and what she was up to. It's too much of a coincidence that she knew where to find the girls. What's going on?'

'Oh, Andy, Andy. If you really believe that of me, then there can be no future for us. You understand that I have nothing to do with my stepsister. Why can't you believe that?'

Andy held onto her if only to stop his shaking, the sobs racking through him. The pair stood in the little flat, held together, their world, once again, shifting on its axis.

Like Andy, Isabel's first reaction had been to call the police.

'No, Izzy. Please. I've already spoken to them. They didn't seem too interested if truth be known. We've been warned to keep the police out of it.'

'Who are these people, Andy? What can we do? How can we get the girls back? Oh, Andy—'

Once again, the turmoil stirred in Andy's stomach. His girlfriend's sister had kidnapped his daughters, for God's sake. And now his former wife was distraught, crying down the phone. He tried to reassure her, tried to instil some confidence into his voice.

'Izzy. The girls know Heidi. They are with her. She won't harm them, whatever else she's done.'

'But how can we get them back, Andy?'

'Well, it might be obvious, but can't we just give them the bloody password?'

'Oh Andy, if only it was that simple. It's not just *my* work. I've downloaded files from the University. Details of all research carried out over the last 10 years.'

'Izzy. Is that really so important in the grand scheme of things—does it matter? Surely, we must do whatever we can to get the girls back.'

'Yes, Andy, of course. Of course—but, this will put all chances of my professorship to bed.'

'I can't believe I'm hearing this,' Andy shouted down the phone.

'Andy, please don't be angry. I'm only thinking aloud. Of course, there's no question. They can have the bloody password. Shall I come up there?'

'No, Izzy. You stay safe in your flat—you're too upset. We don't want another accident. Just send the password to my mobile. OK? I'll let you know as soon as I hear anything. Try not to worry, OK? I'll call soon.'

Andy's mobile buzzed. There it was—Andyandme123. Oh, God. All this trouble and heartache, pain and loss all summed up in that simple logarithm—Andyandme123. The irony of it. Andy and me. The phrase buzzed around his brain. He leaned against the wall, his head throbbing. Right. He went into the kitchen where Bernie had opened a bottle of wine.

'Here, Liebling—please. This will calm you. One glass will not hurt.' They drank. The familiar warmth flooded his body as he tasted the blessed liquor once again. He had been kidding himself. There was no way he could live without this. Who cared anyway? The welfare of his two children dominated.

'Right, let's think. You've got Heidi's number, yes? Let me ring and I'll give her the password—'

'But Andy. How can we know they will do as they say?'

'Yep. True. Look, let me speak to her, anyway. Is that OK?'

A mobile buzzed and Heidi picked up.

'Ah, Mr Saunders. I knew I could trust you—'

'More than I can bloody well trust you, that's for sure. Where are you? Where are the girls? Are they OK?'

'Of course, they are OK; for the moment, at least. The password, Mr Saunders. Do you have the password?'

'Do you honestly believe that I'm going to stand here and give you the bloody password, just like that?'

'What else can you do?' Heidi replied.

'I want to know how you intend to return my daughters to me. How do I know that if I give you the password, you won't harm the girls?'

'Why would I harm the girls, Mr Saunders? I know them—they trust me at least. Now, danke. The passwort please.'

At this moment, a sound alerted Andy. A recognisable sound. Bizarrely, a comforting sound in this crazy situation. A—Could that be? A homely sound. There it was again. Yes, a chime. The unmistakable chime of their old grandfather clock in the hallway of the old house. The clock inherited from Izzy's parents. He loved that clock. The comforting sound of the repeating chimes. The sound of home. He thought quickly.

'Look, there's no way I'm giving you the password over the phone. Let's meet in a public space and I will hand it over. I want to see evidence of the girls—a book, anything. I want a reassurance that as soon as you have the password, then the girls will be handed over, OK?'

189

Silence.

'Look. You have no choice. If you want the bloody password, agree to my terms, OK? Is that clear?'

'I will need to talk to my—my accompliz. I will ring you back.'

The line went silent.

Back in the kitchen, more wine, more confidence, more certainty.

'I can't believe it, Bernie—the girls are at the Old House; in Church Stretton.'

'How do you know?'

'The clock, Bernie. I heard it chiming. Absolutely unmistakable. Lucy and Imogen are being held at our old house. That must be why they went in the car. With Heidi. They trusted her.'

'In that case, let us call the police, now!'

'No, Bernie. No. If the ruddy police go blundering in, sirens going, blue lights flashing, who knows what they might do. No, the police are not the answer. Let me think.'

With that, he emptied the bottle. For Bernie, the bitter aftertaste of Andy's distrust failed to be washed away by the wine.

Chapter 27

'Gareth. Hi. It's Andy.'

Not only was Gareth his oldest mate, but he was also an ex-rugby player. A prop, to be exact. Played in the front row for Pontypridd in his glory days. He still had a considerable bulk, kept himself fit and possessed that old Welsh Celtic devil that gave him such wit. Andy outlined his plan.

'Bloody 'ell mate. That's pushing it a bit, isn't it? Two professional men, at our age as well!'

Andy then guessed the identity of Heidi's so-called accomplices; they were, of course, none other than the two thugs who had attacked him in Frankfurt. Herr Gunter's henchmen. He now had two scores to settle. He outlined his plan to his old friend.

'Surprise, Gareth. That's all it takes. I know the layout of the house by instinct. They won't know what hit them.'

Andy felt the little dent at the bottom of his ribcage. He winced at the memory. Yep, he certainly had a score to settle and Gareth only needed a gentle push in the right direction.

'OK, mate. You've convinced me. Where shall we meet?'

Andy arranged to pick Gareth up at 9 pm, just as dusk began to fall. Once on the A-49, Andy played Bach again, attempting to steady his thumping heart. Once in Church Stretton, he parked the car just below the gravel drive that led up to the familiar old Georgian pad. He had deliberately forsaken the safety net of weapons; after all, surprise, knowledge were the keys.

The two skirted the drive, treading silently on the grass verge, up towards the rear of the house. All the main windows remained black, only a glow emerging from the annexe at the rear of the building—Heidi's old digs. So that's where they were. As arranged, Andy messaged Bernie to get Heidi to the phone. Use the main line in the house's hall. Get her away from the men. Persuade her to bring the girls to the 'phone on some pretext.

They waited, crouched in the shrubbery. After about five minutes, a light flicked on in the hallway. Andy crept closer. Close enough to hear Lucy talking to Bernie on the 'phone. Good. They were now safe and out of the way. The pair advanced toward the annexe. Andy shuffled up to the door. He knew the lock was fragile. He listened. He heard two German voices muttering within. Andy raised his head to peer through the net curtains. The two men were standing in front of the raised bar—clearly discussing tactics, a bottle of beer in each of their hands. A target. He crept around to Gareth and whispered.

'Right. You ready, old mate? OK. Remember your technique; low and hard. Then one blow to the windpipe, OK? Follow me. Good luck. He grinned back towards the reassuring bulk of his friend. He found himself actually enjoying this. The girls were safe—out of the way and he had unfinished business. He stood, took a deep breath and rushed.

The door, as predicted, collapsed with the first kick and time suddenly slowed: the two Germans, shaven-headed, tattooed, turned slowly, it seemed, shocked by the sudden implosion of a shattered door and two large men approaching at speed. Rugby Special would have replayed the two textbook tackles as the men's legs buckled under them. Andy and Gareth timed their knee-high impacts perfectly. The two Germans hit the deck.

'Meine Gott?'

'What the fuck—'

A forearm smashed into the face of the shortest of the men, whilst Gareth knuckled his fist and plunged at the second man's throat.

'Take that, you bastard.' Andy struck again; the German too stunned to respond. 'See how you like it!' Another blow. Gareth's opponent reacted, aiming a punch at his head. Gareth merely leapt on him, smothering him with his dense bulk. Another blow to the trachea. The man stilled. The two thugs amazingly, thrillingly subdued. Now the police could come.

Bernie had alerted the police and now the flashing blue came, the sirens' noise bringing Heidi and girls to the drive to see what all the noise was about.

Two, three patrol cars arrived. Armed police approached the annexe to find two dishevelled, panting but smiling local clinicians sitting on the floor; behind them, two, apparently unconscious, figures lying in a pool of beer.

******

'Well, well, well, Mr Saunders. I certainly didn't expect to be meeting you again and certainly not in these circumstances, I have to say.'

The police had taken Heidi, the two Germans into custody, leaving Andy and Gareth on a warning to attend Shrewsbury police station in 48 hours where they would be questioned. They had only escaped arrest themselves because Heidi and her accomplices had clearly been intruders into Mr Saunder's property. The two girls, in a considerable state of confusion, had been returned to their mother, now back in Shropshire and determined to re-inhabit the family home.

Officer Luke Arnold, clearly relieved to be on an official premises this time, pressed his advantage.

'It would appear that you cannot seem to confine yourself to your clinical duties. Yet again, Mr Saunders, it would appear that you have taken matters into your own hands.'

'It was merely self-defence,' Andy argued.

'Self-defence? You and your friends were the aggressors in this case—'

'Aggressors? They were kidnapping my children for heaven's sake.'

'Indeed, Mr Saunders. And why didn't you think to contact the authorities when you first heard of this occurrence?'

'I heard the clock in the hall—I knew where my girls were—I didn't want to alert these men. I knew they would harm Lucy and Imogen if a load of police vehicles came charging in.'

'Leaving aside the fact that the police have well-established methods of dealing with such matters without 'charging in' as you put it, that you were clearly dealing with known criminals, albeit on your premises, certainly doesn't give you the right to smash a door in and attack whomsoever you may find in said premises.' Officer Arnold had clearly been revising from his 'pompous questioning' manual.

'Look, I'm sorry, but I will not apologise for any actions that resulted in the safe return of my two daughters to their mother.'

'Mr Saunders; whatever your reasons, this was clearly a matter of pre-meditated assault—and let me remind you that that is a criminal offence.'

Andy could see he needed this man on his side.

'Officer. I understand. I can only say that I had my daughters' best interests uppermost in my mind. I realise I may have acted a little, how can I put it, unprofessionally.'

'I think the term un-professional, Mr Saunders, is probably the very best connotation one could apply in this case. I will certainly be informing your employers of this latest, ahem, escapade.'

'Yes, but. Once again, you have bigger fish to fry, I'm sure. You now have even more evidence of a continuing, co-coordinated attack on the integrity of our universities and the people who work within those institutions.'

This line of reasoning gave officer Arnold pause for thought.

'Well, we'll leave it at that for the time being, Mr Saunders. I'm sure you have more pressing matters to deal with. You are, for the time being, free to go.'

A relieved Andy left the police station, dying, it has to be said, for a drink. And he did indeed have more pressing matters on his mind. The 'free-flap' patient had attended out-patients, apparently unhappy with aspects of the grafting procedure. San had seen him and reassured the patient that the graft had settled in nicely and that the donor site was also healing very well.

'Yes, but—' the young man mumbled. 'I expected problems with speech and eating, but I did not expect a hairy palate.'

'A hairy palate?' San repeated.

'Yes. Look.'

San did indeed look and saw that the pink skin lining half of the palate had indeed started to sprout hair. The graft had been taken from the small of the back of the admittedly hirsute young man. Sam explained that this would account for the continued growth of hair from the skin lining the graft and which now formed the roof of this man's mouth.

'I am certain there are things we can do to help you with this, but I feel I must remind you that you have lost a potentially fatal tumour. You are actually doing very well.'

'That's as maybe,' lisped the patient, 'but I wasn't warned of this. I find it distressing, nauseating—embarrassing.'

Sam quickly realised that this was one for his boss and suggested a suitable appointment.

'I don't want an appointment. I want to know what you intend to do about it.'

'Yes, OK. I will have to speak to Mr Saunders—'

'So, you don't know what to do about it?'

'As I say, let me get back to you as soon as I've spoken to Mr Saunders.'

'Fine. I'll let you know what I intend to do about it!'

It took a while for San to reassemble the muffled jumble of sounds that made up this sentence, but he quickly realised that a complaint would surely follow. 'What an ungrateful bastard,' was his immediate response. Back in his flat, Andy and Bernie attempted to assimilate the events of the last few days.

'I just cannot believe Heidi would become involved in such—such criminality—I knew she was unorthodox, but this; kidnapping. Meine Gott. I cannot believe it.'

'It would seem that your stepfather has more influence than even you thought possible.'

'And Andy—I might even have stopped her. I had a feeling that I was being followed just a few days ago. Something seemed familiar. Of course, it must have been her.'

'Why didn't you tell me?'

'It was just a feeling. I forgot about it. But this makes me feel even more responsible—That my stepsister would betray your trust in such a way. Would put Lucy and Imogen in such danger.'

'Well, Bernie, we've discussed all this before and there's nothing more we can do. And of course, there's nothing more Heidi can do. The SIS has all the facts now and Heidi will almost certainly join her father in custody.'

'But all this just for a password. Isabel's password to her computer. Why go to such lengths, Andy?'

'I can only imagine they were hoping to get into the university database; to utilise all the research available—not just Isabel's.'

'But I thought Cell-Procure had been dealt with; prosecuted.'

'Perhaps Gerhardt has other matters on his mind. Revenge for losing his leg. Who knows? What I have to do though now darling is meet up with Isabel to discuss ways forward. Clearly, this will all affect Isabel's attitude towards her work. Perhaps even the girl's schooling. She will now be hyper-protective towards our daughters. I have to talk to her Bernie. I hope you don't mind.'

'Nein. Of course not, Andy. You must do what is right for Lucy and Imogen.'

'Thanks, Bernie. I knew you would understand. This must all be awful for you as well. After all, she is your stepsister.'

'Andy, you mean more to me than my stepsister or stepfather together. You know that—'

She gave a kiss on Andy's lips and, for the time being, at least, he forgot his troubles in her sweet embrace. If he harboured any doubts about Bertie's true involvement in all of this, sexual longing expunged them.

Chapter 28

Andy drove up the gravel driveway to the familiar old house. He sat for a while, engine turned off and reminisced. Realised that he missed the grandeur; the crunch of the gravel as he said his farewell to the girls as he departed for work. The spring Sunday mornings spent mowing the lawn. The sweet smell of newly cut grass. His walks through the woods. The thought slid into his mind that perhaps there was more to life than sex. He thought back to his present cramped living quarters and understood that the only reason he tolerated being there was solely to do with his apparent love for Bernadine. Did this pulsing, all-consuming passion compensate for what he had lost? These thoughts quickly dispersed as Lucy and Imogen shouted their delight as they ran to greet him.

'Daddy, daddy!' They jumped into his arms, clearly having forgotten their recent escapade.

Once in the house, the two girls explained how the teacher had let them leave the school only because Heidi had been recognised as a known carer. It had been the presence of the two men in the car that had alerted them. But by then, the car had left and arrived back here, to their home.

Even then, their young innocence protected them from the full horror of what had happened. They had been roughly bundled into Heidi's old quarters and had listened in fear as the three muttered away in German. Even Heidi now spoke to them in short, sharp sentences; giving them orders. Where to sleep. What to eat. All her concerned friendliness seemingly evaporated. On the night 'daddy came to rescue them,' (they blushed with pride at this retelling of the story) they had been bundled into the main house while they listened to Heidi on the 'phone.

As they recounted their experience, Isabel sat quietly, watching them intensely and observing her former husband. She resisted the urge to run to his embrace. She longed to show her gratitude for his heroic intervention, but let the girls do that for her.

'I suppose we need to talk about the future now,' she started the conversation.

'What's changed?' Andy asked.

'What's changed? Everything, Andy. That's what changed. I can't continue living in Birmingham now. I'll—we'll—have to sell this place for a start. I can't manage it on my own.'

'What about your work?'

'My work, Andy, is what led to this awful mess. I—we—took our eye off the ball and the girls have suffered dreadfully.'

'They seem happy enough to me—' Appeasement was not the best tactic, it seemed. Inwardly, he berated himself. He had expected this, after all.

'Happy enough? What the hell, Andy. They've been kidnapped for God's sake. Lost their parents. Can't you see that it's only because you are here, with me in our house, that is making them happy—for the time being at least.' God, this man could be so infuriating. Frustration replaced her earlier benevolence.

'Well, us sitting here arguing certainly isn't going to help.' He tried another approach. 'Well, I must say, you look very good Isabel.'

She ignored this remark. He went on, 'I must say that I feel very responsible for all that went on, Isabel. After your accident, I saw you as a patient, not as my wife. We lost touch. I drank too much. Whenever I saw you, I saw the scars, assessed your physical healing. But didn't regard you as anything other than a patient to be advised; looked after. I couldn't look beyond that. I didn't take care of you as my wife. I did, as you say, take my eye off the ball.'

Isabel remained silent, apparently absorbing this news.

'And now, look at you. Your eye is better. I love your hair. You are very beautiful, Isabel. I'm proud of you.' Isabel went on regarding him, perhaps a touch cynically now.

'Perhaps, Andy. Thank you. But not as beautiful as your Bernie, eh?'

'Izzy—Let's not talk about her now. We're here with the girls. Let's enjoy it, yes?'

Isabel went on to tell Andy how that her research had stalled a little, that the bloody password that had led to all of this couldn't help the conspirators much.

'What we are seeing at the clinical stage I trials is that the target tumour cells mutate at such a rate that a vaccine is impractical in the longer term. We have to redevelop the vaccine every two or three weeks and that just isn't workable. We had fantastic results initially and then we found that the tumour reappeared elsewhere in the rats and even more virulent. We were creating a more malignant tumour.'

'Bloody hell, Izzy. Does that mean all your work goes down the pan?'

'No, not at all. We found that we can weaponize the body's immune system against cancer cells, but not preventively, as in a vaccine. We've learned loads about possible new drugs we may be able to develop.'

'Does that mean you will take your research in a different direction?'

'Well, no, not really. There are others much better placed to follow that line. I will carry on, but at a slower pace. What this has taught me, Andy, is that I got my priorities wrong. After all that's gone on, I intend to put the children first now. Reduce my time at the lab. But immunology will continue to be my interest. Oh, yes and also I intend to campaign against the 'winner takes all mentality' which has driven this assault on our lives. I believe that our research should be shared. Open to all, to benefit mankind.'

'What about the professorship?'

'More important things to think about, Andy. My place is here now, with the girls. Possibly in a smaller house.'

'So, are you telling me, that even had they got the password, it wouldn't have been of any use?'

'No, of course not. There is loads of valuable info on there. Just not the answer to the 'magic bullet' they were seeking. The Holy Grail that pushed them to such limits. But they haven't got it now, have they?'

A sudden smile illuminated her still unfamiliar, but none the less, beautiful features. Her black bob framed her head and Andy was reminded of why he had fallen for this woman in the first place. Her last comments reminded him of her passion, her intelligence. There was more to beauty, after all. They talked about family; her sister Alice and how Bob had been so upset about their separation. 'Another drinking buddy down the tubes' had been his initial response. They talked about the girls' schooling. How Isabel might move closer to her sister in Sussex. Andy surprised himself by his alarm at this prospect.

'Don't worry, dear. We'll make sure you have regular access. I just want to see the girls in a regular day school now. Weekly boarding didn't work for them, I don't think.'

'But what about your work at the uni?' Andy wanted to know.

'Look. I'm only thinking aloud at the moment. Sifting through options. Don't worry, Andy, I won't do anything unless I discuss it with you first. Would you like a drink?' Izzy had said this before she realised what a stupid question, irresponsible even, she had asked.

Andy paused. Would have loved to share a glass of wine with Isabel at this particular moment but realised that he'd better not. They chatted on, revelling in the evident pleasure the girls derived from seeing their parents happily talking together; not arguing for once. After bed-time, Andy left, placing a kiss on Isabel's cheek and returning to Shrewsbury, two hours later than he had planned. Isabel shocked herself at the realisation of how sad she was to see him leave.

On the other hand, the reception Andy received once back at the flat was perhaps not exactly what he had been expecting;

'What is this? Where have you been? Our supper was ready two hours ago!'

'I'm sorry, darling. There was a lot to talk about; the house, the girls. Isabel was upset as you can well imagine.' A loud crash greeted this admittedly Anglo-Saxon attempt at placating his girlfriend, as the aforementioned supper hit the kitchen floor, scattering porcelain and spaghetti widely.

'Blodsinn,' shrieked Bernardine. Andy had not witnessed this new, alarming facet to his lover's personality before. She was red-faced, arms akimbo, frightening even.

'Das ist mir Scheissegal,' she carried on.

'Look, Bernie. I don't understand what you are saying—my German is not that good—' Further Germanic expletives met his attempt at a smile, this latter not really requiring translation.

'Fich dich.'

Andy tried another approach.

'Bernie, you must admit that Izzy—'

'Izzy, Izzy—Who is this 'Izzy'—don't you mean Isabel. Your ex-wife—'

'Well, she's not really my ex yet, is she, darling?'

'Don't call me darling-Verpiss dich!'

'Please stop swearing, Bernie. All I'm trying to say is that it was, after all, your stepsister involved in all of this.'

'Yes. Do you not think I know that, Andy? That I have not suffered enough because of her—explained to you—apologised to you. I just cannot believe that you spent so much time away—I was worried—I didn't know what to think—' She broke down, sobbing.

'Look, why have you got so upset? You know I have to deal with my family—Lucy and Imogen were traumatised by what went on.' Andy crossed the small kitchen to embrace Bernardine, desperate to reverse this sudden transformation from beatific lover to verbal assailant. Bernardine allowed herself to succumb to his approach.

'Oh, Andy—it's just that I feel so unsure about us. You still own that house; you are still married—I don't know where I am. I was scared to lose you.'

'Dear, dear, dear—I'm sorry, love. Please accept my apologies—you know I love you—' he trailed off, pulled away. 'Let's get this mess sorted out, shall we and try to resurrect what's left of the evening—OK?'

An only partly reassured Bernardine bent to the floor to clean up what remained of the spaghetti Bolognese.

Chapter 29

Stuart and Andy sipped coffee as they discussed the 'hairy-palate' issue.

'Yep, Stu. I examined him this morning. There are tufts of dark hair along the underside of the graft. But what I don't understand is why he is making such a deal. We removed a potentially fatal tumour, for God's sake.'

'Yeah, I know. Bloody ungrateful, to say the least. But it appears he has made an official complaint; claims he wasn't warned.'

'Wasn't warned? We saved his bloody life. He signed the consent form for heaven's sake. We explained everything that could go wrong—graft failure and the rest. Warned him of potentially catastrophic blood loss. What's that compared with a few bloody hairs in his mouth? Jeez Stu, he could be sitting there with a hole in the middle of his face and all he can do is go on about these hairs. Bloody hell!'

'Yes, I know all that, Andy. And we are new to all of this. And to be fair, I suppose it must be pretty uncomfortable to feel hairs growing inside your mouth—'

'Yes. And it would feel even more bloody uncomfortable if he had a hole in his mouth instead!'

'Andy, I know. I sympathise. But this is exactly the sort of thing that gets us a bad press. The plastic guys can't wait to see us getting egg on our face.'

'What do you suggest we do?'

'We could offer some electro-cautery to remove the hair roots. Why don't we offer to meet him again, in a joint clinic?'

'Yep. OK. Good idea. Just hope this doesn't go to the bloody administrators again, that's all.'

'We'll try to head it off at the pass—' Stuart chuckled. 'How is everything otherwise? Dare I ask about domestic arrangements?'

'Well, Isabel is easing off the research stuff for a while—wants to concentrate on the girls for a bit. We've got to decide what to do about the house; whether or not to downsize, now that we are separating.'

'So you're determined to press on with this German girl, Andy? Are you sure you've thought it through?'

'We went through so much, Stuart. I'm not sure we could recover what we have lost. And the other issues—you know—the breakdown and all that. It didn't go down well with Isabel at all. She lost respect for me I think. And Bernardine is so much more understanding, helpful in a way—'

'Yeah, I'm sure, Andy. But don't you think she's putting it on a bit? After all, you're still a catch, Andy—perhaps things will change when you've lived together for a while.' Andy chuckled at the compliment, couldn't help recall the events of last evening as he drained his cup.

******

'Hi, Andy. John here—from the school.'

'Oh, hi, John. What can I do for you?'

'Well, following your audition last week I was so impressed I had a word with my friend—the head of vocal studies at the Birmingham Conservatoire. He was telling me that they had set up a one year post-grad Dip Perf diploma course for mature singers. You know, with an idea to introducing potential candidates to the world of opera and solo performance.'

'Sounds fun, John. But what's this got to do with me?'

'Proper basses, of which you are one, are in short supply in the opera world and I happened to mention you. I hope you don't mind.'

'No, of course not. I'm flattered. But I still don't understand—'

'Let's put it like this. I think it might be fun for us both to work up three arias, just for the hell of it, to a good enough standard to at least sing for Danny. You've got nothing to lose. And who knows where it might lead?'

'Are you seriously saying I should consider giving up my job so that I can sing opera?'

'Ha ha. Sounds bonkers I know. But, as I say, you've got nothing to lose and it'll be fun working with you. If even that works out, I can get you to sing some of the Bass roles for the choir. What d'yu think?'

'John, thanks a lot for your confidence in me. Can you give me a few days to think about it?'

'Of course. You know where to find me.'

******

When Bernie arrived back at the flat after her implant clinic, she was surprised and it must be said, thrilled, to hear Andy's voice booming out over the soundtrack of Verdi's *Nabucco*. Score in hand, he was attempting to emulate Sir Jon Tomlinson's rendition of the priest's prayer, as he steps over the sleeping bodies that made up the chorus of Hebrew slaves.

'Wow. Meine Liebling. How wonderful. I've never heard you sing like this before.' She stood back, giving Andy time to complete the aria. He turned towards Bernie, flushed but beaming as he recalled the conversation he had just had with the Master of Music at Shrewsbury School. Once again, music created its own harmony with the couple.

Over the next few weeks, Andy became thrilled at his vocal progress. John had arranged vocal tuition at the school and his progress was remarkable. However, he was less pleased with the news that, yet again, he had been summoned to a meeting at the hospital. On this occasion, he found arranged before him the usual panel in the now familiar boardroom, this time minus the drug-control executive. Andy did not glean a great deal of satisfaction from this. His replacement by another suited individual of a more severe countenance did nothing to allay his fears. As before, Grey Bob began proceedings.

'I think that it is fair to say, Mr Saunders, that it is a matter of great regret we find ourselves yet again in a situation in which we have cause to consider your conduct at this hospital.'

'Could you please be a little more concise?' is all Andy could muster by way of a reply.

'Yes, indeed. An official complaint has been raised against you, Mr Saunders.'

'I am aware of this and—'

'Please excuse me for interrupting, Mr Saunders, but I have not yet finished. Not only has a complaint been made regarding your treatment of a patient in your care, but, I regret to say, we have also received a—(she turned to a colleague)—notification, if I can put it like that, from the police.'

'The police?'

'Yes, indeed. Apparently, you were in involved in what can only be termed as a fracas—an actual physical assault.'

'I was, for your information, defending my property and protecting the welfare of my children.'

'It is my understanding that your actions were, in fact, pre-meditated.'

'They were only pre-meditated in the sense that I was aware that my children were being held under some duress in my property. I would go so far as to say that it was my duty, as a father, to intervene in the manner in which I did.'

'That's as maybe, Mr Saunders, but what about your more pressing responsibilities as a consultant surgeon?'

'More pressing? What can possibly be more pressing than the welfare of my children?'

Stuart had clearly had enough of this escalating exchange. Turning to the chair, he had this to say.

'With all due respect, ma'am, do you think we could concentrate on the central issue here? The nature of the complaint against my colleague.'

'Yes, of course. But we cannot ignore behaviour that has led to the police becoming involved with the activities of one of our senior staff.'

'I think Andy—Mr Saunders—has given a perfectly proper explanation of his defence of his home and family and I have no doubt that the police will continue their enquiries in that regard—'

'Very well. Let us return then to the matter of the complaint. As I understand it the complaint is less to do with the procedure itself but rather more with the nature of the consent.' At this juncture, the formerly passive new-suited panel member gave a little cough.

'Indeed. If I can introduce myself to you, Mr Saunders. My name is Mr Bebby and I am the medico-legal representative acting on behalf of the hospital's trust.' Andy realised that this interview was becoming increasingly confrontational.

'Am I to believe that this is now a legal matter?' he asked.

'Mr Bebby is here in an advisory capacity,' commented Grey Bob.

'In which case should I not bring an end to this witch-hunt and seek my own counsel. Consult my indemnifiers?'

'Of course, Mr Saunders, you will have every opportunity to defend yourself.'

'Defend myself? For God's sake, what the hell am I supposed to be defendir myself against?'

'Let me return to the matter of the complaint—'

'Complaint—complaint? I've done everything in my power to help this young man recover from a potentially life-threatening malignancy. A few years ago he would now be walking around with a lump of pink plastic filling his face!'

'That's as maybe. Let us return to the matter of consent. In fact, let me be more precise, Mr Saunders; the issue here is one of *informed* consent.' Stuart looked at his colleague; expressionless. Andy continued.

'We took this young man through the entirety of what he might expect from this procedure; risks and benefits. The fact that the graft itself may fail.'

'Yes, but—his main grievance is with the matter of the, ahem, hairs growing in his mouth. The gentleman is most concerned about this development.'

'Yes and I'm certain he would be even more concerned if he had a tumour eating away at his jaw.'

'That, again, is as maybe. But did you warn the patient specifically regarding the risks associated with taking a hair-growing skin graft and transferring this into his mouth?'

'Well, no. Not specifically. The procedure was very complex and surely this growth of hair is relatively insignificant—'

'Insignificant to you, perhaps Mr Saunders, but certainly not to the patient.'

'Look, this is frankly ridiculous. I can't see any point carrying on with this interview.'

'This gentleman has made a formal complaint, Mr Saunders and it is this board's recommendation that you advise your indemnifiers as soon as possible.'

'You can't be serious. Are you telling me I am being sued?'

'That would indeed appear to be the case, Mr Saunders.' Then again, this time from Grey Bob. 'This complaint, placed alongside the matter of the police investigation, places this hospital in a very difficult situation, Mr Saunders.'

'So this *is* a witch-hunt. You're intending to suspend me again, aren't you? Is that the reason you've called me in here? Haven't you lot got better things to be dealing with rather than hassling your clinical staff? I feel I must remind you that this is a hospital. We are here to treat the sick and the suffering. All you're concerned with is money, legality, corporate bloody responsibility. Absolutely nothing to do with helping people, encouraging your clinicians. You're all a bloody disgrace—'

'Andy, there's no point in losing your temper.' This from Stuart.

'No point? No point? I'll tell you what's no bloody point. This effing hospital and you poxy administrators and solicitors.' Andy stood to his feet and pushed the chair back. 'The next you will hear from me is to offer my resignation. I've had it with you lot, this hospital and this bloody job!' With that, he turned and left the room, once again the air reverberating with the sound of the door slamming behind him.

******

'Andy, meine Liebling—you can't possibly resign your post. Your career, your calling—'

'I can and I intend to. I've had enough of the stress, the demands, the sheer nonsense we have to face every single day.'

'But what about your income, your children?'

'I have a decent pension and there will be some profit from the sale of the house—'

'What will you do, Andy? You can't just give up a career. What will you do? What will *we* do?'

'I might take up that offer of a post-grad course in music at the conservatoire.'

'You can't be serious—'

'Why not? Other people have made a success of a career change at my age.'

'But your security—your—'

Andy interrupted. 'I thought you, of all people, would understand. All we've talked about has been the release from stress, responsibility—the wonderful release that music can bring—'

'Yes. I know we love music. But that's just a pastime. I didn't think that you would resign from your job as a surgeon. Meine Gott!'

'So you're really the same as everyone else. Really just concerned about appearances, money—'

'Andy, how can you say that? We are different, our love makes us different—'

'Does it really, Bernie? When push comes to shove, all you're really concerned about is my income, my reputation. What about my sanity, my health. What's more important, Bernie?'

'Oh, Andy. You must take time to think about this. Perhaps you should talk to Isabel.'

'Oh, that's great. Talk to my ex-wife now. It's fine to talk to her now, is it? What has happened to you, Bernie?'

'Nothing has happened to me. I just think that this is a big mistake—'

'A mistake? I thought you cared for me Bernie—for *me*—not my bloody job. I thought you would support me, help me through all this.' Bernadine went towards Andy, perhaps to comfort him, to find a way back to how they were. Instead, he pushed her away, turned and left the flat, once again slamming the door as he left. The seeds of doubt now well and truly planted.

******

He sped down the A49 back towards Church Stretton, his mind reeling. He needed a drink, that is one thing of which he was certain. Back on the familiar gravel drive, he knocked on the front door and found himself looking at his former wife. She stared for a moment before inviting him in.

'What on earth is the matter, Andy?'

'I've resigned.'

'Resigned?'

'Yes. I've finally had enough, Izzy. They've beaten me down at last.'

'For heaven's sake. Come in, Andy.' To his surprise, he found that Isabel was far more attuned to his predicament than Bernie had been. Perhaps she too, he thought, had been reassessing her life, her priorities.

'Sit down, Andy. Let me open a bottle of wine and let's talk about it.'

This offer of a drink had a remarkable effect. He realised that he was not an alcoholic. He realised that his admittedly high intake of alcohol had merely been a lubricant in order to enable the increasingly complex cogs of his life to keep turning. He understood that if he could shed at least some of his burden, he could enjoy wine. Relish the enhancement of mood. Become a much missed accompaniment to food and conversation.

He saw his wife in a different light. Found the muddled mist enveloping his conscious thought, lifting. Could see light at the end of a long, long tunnel. In this enlightened mood, he resisted the temptation to swig the full glass in one gulp but sat in the familiar surroundings and outlined the events of the last few months: the graft patient, the complaint, the police investigation, even his increasing aversion to the smell of the blood.

'Well, I can help you there,' Isabel said. 'The SIS officer—Mr Arnold—came to see me yesterday and explained that Heidi and the two accomplices have now been returned to Frankfurt and will undergo trial along with her father. Apparently, Heidi claimed Bernadine knew all about what was going on.'

'No, I can't believe that. I know what you think of her, perhaps quite rightly. But she has been horrified by all of this—'

'Perhaps she has. But I think you have to accept, Andy, that she may not have been as innocent as you let on—'

'I can't have been so stupid. No, Izzy—I won't believe it.' Even now, Andy still struggled to disentangle the mess of intertwined emotions. He took another gulp of wine.

'Well, perhaps the truth—the full story—will emerge during the investigation. In the meantime what are you going to do?' Andy tried to explain his ambition to become a singer, immediately felt foolish, but again found that Izzy responded in a way he hadn't expected.

'Andy, I've had a lot of time to think, to reassess. I now realise that I didn't fully understand the depth of your feelings of loss over Seb. I became too involved with my work. Took my eye off the ball. Perhaps if we had talked more we may have avoided all this. When you went off the rails, my reaction was poor; I didn't support you, didn't understand. We both let our careers get the better of us. Perhaps you could pursue this new idea. I don't know enough about it to be honest. But look, come here—' Isabel held out her hands and Andy allowed himself to be embraced.

'Oh, Andy. I've missed you—I've missed our life together—missed you being around the girls. I meant everything I wrote in that letter.' They held each other for a while and it was this scene that met Lucy and Imogen as they ran into the kitchen.

'Mummy, daddy—how lovely! Is daddy coming back home?' Isabel pushed Andy gently away.

'Well, I'm not sure about that, honey. You'll have to ask your father.'

In that moment, Andy realised how much work needed to be done, how much healing, how much planning if they were to become a family again. How much forgiveness. He looked again at Isabel and saw, once more, that Galway girl. Looked into those hazel eyes and absorbed once more the old, familiar smile.

The future could wait awhile. For now, all he could say was 'Yes, darlings. Yes. Daddy is coming home.'

Epilogue

Andy sat on top of the moor. He gazed around at those blue-remembered hills. Absorbed the warm scent of peat and allowed the sun's rays to wash over him. His thoughts turned towards Bernadine and he wondered if she might, even at this moment, be beaming those blue eyes at another man; perhaps in Germany now—her blonde hair cascading over another lover's pillow. He misses her. He has to admit that much. He smiles, a wry smile, as he stands and swings his rucksack onto his back. He turns towards the valley that would lead him home to his resurrected family. For that, at least, he is grateful.

The End

Glossary

SR: Senior registrar. The penultimate training grade before achieving a post as a consultant.

SHO: Senior house officer. Post-qualification the first training grade is house officer. This is primarily a clerking grade. The first rung on the training ladder. Usually after six months a trainee will become a senior house officer.

ENT: The specialty concerning the treatment of ear, nose and throat.

RTA: Road traffic accident.

IMF: Inter-maxillary fixation. In order to immobilise a fracture of either the upper or lower jaw the teeth are wired together for a period of approximately six weeks.

CXR: Chest x-ray.

PhD: Doctor of Philosophy. This is an academic qualification. Some regard this as the only entitlement to the term Dr.

Medical and latterly dental, practitioners, use this as a purely courtesy title.

Bio-Oss: Artificial bone, usually made of silica and delivered in granular form rather like sea salt. It is used as a biological spacer which acts as a scaffold for new bone growth.

Zygomatic Arch: Also sometimes referred to as the malar bone. The cheekbone. This is linked to the skull via a bony strut which forms the arch. This is commonly fractured following facial trauma.

Retro-bulbar: The space behind the eyeball. In facial trauma this space may become filled with blood which pushes the eye forward and can even lead to full avulsion of the eye.

Venflon: A tube-like device inserted into a vein usually in the arm or back of hand that enables the delivery of saline or other blood products and medications.

Trachy: Tracheostomy. If the airway is compromised, the anaesthetist or surgeon will puncture a hole directly into the windpipe and pass a tube through thus enabling the patient to breathe.

CSF: Cerebro-spinal fluid. This substance surrounds the brain and the spinal cord. It cushions these vital structures and can aid nutrition.

Osteotomy: Literally bone cutting. In maxillofacial surgery, this can sometimes involve deliberately fracturing either the upper or lower jaw in order to reposition them. Often used in cases of facial deformity.

Ectropion: A cosmetic and functional defect whereby the lower eyelid is everted so that the moist, inner surface is exposed. Control of tears is compromised. Following trauma or surgery.

Crepitus: The feel and sound, of crackling, under the skin, signifying broken bone fragments and sometimes air itself.

Le Fort fracture: A classification of fractures of the middle third or upper jaw, of the facial skeleton. Le Fort 1-1V, increasing in severity.

Compound: Describes a fracture that penetrates the skin.

Canthal (ligament): The attachment of soft tissue tendon joining the corner of the eye to the nasal bone.

Comminuted: Fragmented.

CEO: Chief executive officer.

BKA: The federal criminal police office of Germany.

SIS: U.K. secret intelligence service, also known as MI6.

CBT: Cognitive behavioural therapy.

EMDR: Eye movement desensitisation and reprocessing.

CAT: Cognitive analytic therapy.

AUG: Acute ulcerative gingivitis. An unpleasant oral infection usually infecting the gums and caused by fusiform bacteria. Symptomatic of poor oral hygiene and general debilitation. Characterised by a foetid mouth odour.

Ablative: The destructive removal of tissue in order to eradicate a cancerous growth.

Fach: A German term. A person has found an area of expertise that suits their ability and temperament.

Ingram Content Group UK Ltd.
Milton Keynes UK
UKHW020612070423
419773UK00007B/658

9 781035 807116